ST. BRODAG'S ISLE

Thanks for all
the support.

Andy

ST. BRODAG'S ISLE

Andrew Walsh

IndyPublish

ST. BRODAG'S ISLE

Published in the United States
by IndyPublish.com
1487 Chain Bridge Road
Suite 304
McLean, VA 22101

ISBN: 1-58827-020-3 Paperback
ISBN: 1-58827-021-1 Rocket eBook

Printed & bound by Antony Rowe Ltd, Eastbourne

Dedication

To Angela, Jamie, Caitlin and Ethan for being there, to Kath for reading it and laughing, to Bolton Wanderers despite everything and to all the people I've ever met who live on islands.

Contents

A Day At The Office

'Only the gulls know where the sea is' - St Brodag

In an office, deep in the inner corridors of Whitehall, a thin man and a fat man were nearing the end of a long and involved conversation. The Thin Man was in his early forties with small, dark eyes and a hooked nose. The Fat Man was in his sixties and wobbled when he laughed. They both wore dark suits and sat on leather armchairs.

The office, itself, was a grand affair, dominated by a huge oil painting of someone who used to be very important but who was now long forgotten. A vast oak desk sat underneath the painting. The desktop was perfectly clear, as though any clutter would diminish the pomposity of it all. A row of bookshelves ran along one wall, populated by ancient volumes detailing the ins and outs of government.

"So you see, Philip," continued the Fat Man " it's a great opportunity for you. A Governor's position before fifty - well done". The Fat man took a slurp of strong milky tea.

The Thin Man, Philip, shifted awkwardly in his seat.

" I was rather hoping for somewhere...well....warmer".

The Fat Man sighed.

"Warmer?"

"Well, the Caribbean or sub-tropical Africa".

The Fat Man looked out of the window.

"Have you ever been to the Caribbean, Philip?"

"No".

"Bloody awful place. You don't want to go there".

"What about Africa?" asked Philip.

"I'm afraid all the warm places are gone. Independent. Don't need looking after any more. That's why they get themselves into such a bloody mess. Look at the Commonwealth conferences. Populated by bloody idiots, the lot of them. Claim they want to rule themselves? Couldn't organise a piss-up in a brewery, most of them. Shame, really. Had some great times out there when I was younger. You could really let your hair down. Never had so many women in my life. It's the heat you know. Does strange things to an English Rose".

As he said these words, the Fat Man looked out of the window and smiled to himself. The Thin Man looked down at his shoes.

The Fat Man had been a mover and shaker in the Foreign Office, a man with real power. He had spent most of the 60s and 70s in Africa, overseeing independence for half a dozen different countries. Sometimes he got it right and a duly elected democratic government took over. Sometimes, he got it wrong, and a nasty little dictator found himself living in the old governor's residence, drinking the old governor's port and generally living a life of luxury while his countrymen wondered at the marvels of self-rule. Now, although his actual power was much less, he still wielded an awful lot of influence.

"Cheer up" the Fat Man continued. "You never know, this could be the making of you".

"It might be the death of me. Do I have a choice?"

"Yes of course you do".

"What's the alternative?"

"Unemployment!"

"Oh".

The Fat Man stopped wobbling and looked at Philip.

"You see, Philip, we are coming under increasing pressure to make....reforms".

"You mean cuts".

"Well, partly. The Government are very keen to be seen as wise and prudent with the nation's finances. It seems that we just can't have all the people around here that we used to".

"Oh".

"You see, the present administration have discovered our little secret".

Philip frowned.

"What's that?" he asked.

"We don't have an empire anymore. We've been trying to keep it under wraps ever since the last war but I suppose it had to come out eventually. We really have very little influence in the world. Our place has been taken over by hamburger companies and fizzy drink enterprises. Damn shame but there we have it. We've got to make cuts so you either take this job or you're off".

Philip sighed. In the distance, Big Ben chimed eleven.

"Then, I will have to accept".

"Good, good" said the Fat Man climbing to his feet and reaching over to shake his hand. The Fat Man coughed. "I've arranged for some papers to be delivered to your flat. You know the sort of thing. Profile of the government, exports, imports, who's shagging who".

"Good. I don't know anything about the place".

"Not much to learn really. Play it by ear, that's my advice".

The Fat Man pressed a button on an intercom unit. Somewhere in the distance Philip could hear a soft buzzing.

"Hope you don't mind. A few of your colleagues would like to say congratulations to you. Come in, chaps". From a door in the far wall, three equally besuited gentlemen entered the musty interior of the office. They crossed the carpeted floor and stood around Philip.

"Well done, Philip" said a tall man by the name of Grozzlethwaite. He had the appearance of a weasel that had recently come across a dead chicken and licked his thin lips often with a wippety tongue.

"Good show" said another, a rugby player type. All muscles and broken nose and the intellect of a frog. His name was Wyatt, though many called him Thicko behind his back.

"Wish you well," said a small man with large glasses and a moist handshake called Mr Grim.

The Fat Man stood back and looked at Philip.

"Well, there's no need to delay further. Off you go, Philip. See my secretary on the way out. She has all the details. You know, sailings, accommodation. I'll be on the blower soon. Cheerio".

Philip turned and moved towards the door when he heard the Fat Man clear his throat behind him.

"Oh and Philip!"

Philip turned around.

"Don't bugger it up, will you, there's a good chap".

Philip, unsure of what to do, gave a little wave and left. As he pulled the door to, he could hear the sound of champagne corks popping. He lingered by the door just long enough to hear the sound of laughter and the beginnings of a party.

Philip decided to walk home that night. Sometimes he took the tube but tonight he needed time to think. A thin, stale breeze blew along the well-lit streets disturbing the litter and causing it to drift across the pavement. Philip didn't notice the litter. He didn't notice the many shop windows newly decorated with their Christmas displays. He didn't notice the government buildings that he passed on his way home. He was more involved in his own internal debates. He passed the delicatessen, the small boutique and the local Sainsburys. He didn't once look up at them. Then he came to a pub - the Blue Dragon - and stopped. The thick scent of spilt beer assaulted him and from within he heard the Siren's call.

'*Come in, come in*' he heard it cry. He stepped forward to look in at the window. The pub was full. The people inside were happy. They were shouting, laughing and dancing. Slade were on the jukebox. It was a warm and jolly place.

He was disturbed from his daydreams by an old man who came rattling out of the door and launched himself across the pavement. The old man raised his fist to some unseen person inside.

"Bastard" he cried, steadying himself against a refuse bin. "Bastard Christmas".

He turned around, tottering on uneasy legs, until he faced Philip. Philip met his eyes and held them. The old man looked back at him, eyes focusing then re-focusing.

"Bollocks" cried the drunk and staggered off.

"How profound!" said Philip to no one in particular. He half-turned around and saw the old man fall into a shop doorway. He thought about going over to see him to make sure that he was fine. But then he remembered that he was in London so he looked away. He took one last look at the pub then walked on and kept his eyes looking down at the pavement.

Philip turned down a side street near Westminster Cathedral. He stepped into the road and was nearly hit by a taxi that accelerated off with a cloud of fumes that choked him, an appropriate hand gesture and a cry of 'wanker!'.

Philip sighed, checked both ways, then crossed the road. He wandered down the pavement deep in his thoughts. He passed the nurses' home, the post box, the basement flat that had the strange hangings in the window. He passed the apartments where, it was rumoured, a minister of state 'kept' a woman. How do you keep a woman, thought Philip. Must be like keeping a hamster.

As he came to the main door of his apartment block, his mind was a whirl. He took his key out and let himself in, the door closing gently behind him.

In the plush lobby, he looked up at the video camera (as he always did) and smiled. He didn't know who was on the other end of it but he thought that a quick smile would not go amiss. He pressed the button to call the lift and waited.

The lift door slid smoothly to one side and Philip walked forward into the mirrored interior. He pressed another button and watched the lobby disappear from right to left. He looked at himself in the mirrors and noted how gaunt he was looking. There was panic in his eyes as well.

It was one thing to be offered a Governorship; it was another thing to receive approval from Patricia, his wife.

The lift reached his floor and opened up so that he could exit. Philip paused, wanting to delay the moment for a little while longer. He reached out a finger and pressed the button to take him back down to the ground floor again.

Philip hurried back to the pub and ordered a double whiskey with a splash of water. He downed it in one and returned home.

As he turned the key to let himself into his flat, his heart was in his mouth.

"St Brodag's Isle! Sounds nice".

Philip Digby-Fischer had just broken the news of his appointment to his wife, Patricia. They were standing in the lounge of their London flat. It was a large flat, bright and airy, decorated in plain but tasteful hues. The lounge has a plain carpet and was filled with comfy sofas.

"Governor! Daddy will be proud".

Patricia put her arms around his neck and hugged him in a rare display of affection. The Digby-Fischers were not renowned for their emotional outbursts.

Patricia Digby-Fischer was a fine looking woman in her mid-forties. She had an elegance about her that betrayed her roots in aristocracy. It was said that one of her ancestors had been a mistress of Charles II, a rival to Nell Gwynne. Apparently, the family were pleased that they could trace their family line back to a whore which was a much more acceptable occupation to the aristocracy than a merchant or politician (and, of course, they did have a point).

"Where is it?" asked Patricia.

Philip shuffled.

"It has a nature reserve and plenty of history".

"The Caribbean? No? Not the South Pacific! Gosh, that would be wonderful. Happy talky, talky, happy talk". Patricia performed an inelegant jig that embarrassed both herself and her husband.

Philip coughed. He was finding this uncomfortable.

"It's not in the South Pacific," he said quietly.

"No. Well, I can't think of anywhere else. Where is it, Philip, please put me out of my misery".

"About fifty miles off the north-east coast".

Patricia grew suddenly stern.

"Where?"

"In the middle of the North Sea".

Patricia's face drained of all colour. She reached out to steady herself then sat down on one of the sofas.

"Our North Sea?"

"There's only one. It's not that bad. There's a ferry link every other day with Hull and in summer, there's a Sea Cat service to Newcastle".

"Newcastle!" whispered Patricia with some distaste.

"There's a Marks and Spencer".

"There's a Marks and Spencer in Sarajevo!" said Patricia crossly.

"Yes but.....is there?" asked Philip, suddenly taken aback.

"Oh, I don't know. It's not important".

Patricia clambered to her feet.

"I'm going for a lie down".

"OK, dear. Not feeling too well, eh? Probably the shock".

Patricia disappeared into their bedroom.

"Well, that went better than expected" he said to the wall.

Philip went into his study, sat down at his desk and switched on the computer. He then spent the next few minutes searching the Internet for references to St Brodag's Isle. He found three: the official St Brodag's Government site, a mention on the 'Dullest Places in Europe' page and an extensive manifesto written by a group called the St Brodag's Liberation Front. It was not the most promising introduction to the island.

> *St Brodag's Isle lies off the Northumbrian coast and can be reached by a three-hour ferry ride from Hull. It is home to a population of 25,000 people, most of who live in and around Port Victoria, the island's capital and main harbour.*

It was discovered by the Celtic Saint Brodag after leaving the religious centre of Lindisfarne in 897AD.

The island is mainly rocky, with several headlands framing long, sweeping beaches. It stretches fifteen miles from North to South and ten miles, at its widest point, from East to West. The inner region of the island is boggy and flat

The main industries are fishing and farming. The island is too far south to be able to benefit from the North Sea Oilfields. An attempt to establish a financial centre on the island failed in the mid-nineties, although several high-tech office blocks were built to accommodate the expected influx of banks and financial houses.

The island is famed for the St Brodag's Kittiwake, a rare species of sea bird that can only be found on the headlands of the island.

During World War Two, the island was abandoned by the British Government and went about its own business. It was invaded once by a U-Boat crew who spent less than an hour on the island before deciding that there was nothing worth staying for.

Today, the island is much as it was thirty years ago: a cold, damp, inhospitable place with few natural resources and a dearth of development opportunities.

"Doesn't seem so bad" muttered Philip to himself as he printed himself a hardcopy of the information. He then disappeared into the kitchen to make himself a nice hot cup of cocoa. When he returned, he opened an old atlas that he kept next to his desk.

It was a very, very old atlas. On the general map just inside the cover, half the world was coloured red and marked 'British Empire'. Philip chuckled to himself and flicked the pages looking for the maps of the British Isles. He located St Brodag's Isle, or at least the tiny pinprick that passed for it, on the map.

He leaned back and took a swig of the cocoa.

Later that night, Philip listened in at the bedroom door and heard his wife sobbing. He decided to act sensibly and made up the bed in the spare room. Then, he fell asleep.

A Place Far From Home

'I heard a gull cry in the night' - St Brodag

In the second week of January, Philip found himself on board a glorified tugboat on his way to the island. His dark blue Range Rover had been secured to the ships deck by several large hemp ropes. A group of goats stood in a pen nearby and seemed to be taking the prospect of a watery death in their stride.

The last few weeks had been difficult for Philip.

Firstly, Patricia had decided not to accompany him. She reckoned that she would be a hindrance to him during his first few weeks in his new job. Philip was not so sure and was coming around to the opinion that Patricia wasn't too keen on his new position.

Secondly, the information on St Brodag's Isle arrived in twenty-four sealed boxes, filling the guest bedroom, and turned out to be next to useless. Most of the papers referred to events that had happened years before and were filled with tedious details. Philip read through the papers in one box and then gave up. He had left these papers behind at the flat.

Finally, the flat had been burgled, an event that had sent Patricia wailing back to their Hertfordshire country home. The thieves took the television and video and several items of jewellery that had belonged to Patricia's family for generations. She was not best pleased ("By this time tomorrow some cheap slut in a council flat will be wearing my rubies!").

The thieves, had, unfortunately, left the boxes of papers concerning St Brodag's Isle untouched.

The Digby-Fischers had celebrated Christmas at Patricia's parents' house and New Year at a party in the Cotswolds. Philip had felt miserable at Christmas and worse at New Year.

"What is there to celebrate?" he would ask anyone who was unfortunate to listen to him. "Another year older, another year of bodily functions slowing down, another year closer to worm food". At this point, most people would look at him, smile and hurry off.

Patricia had enjoyed herself but not with him. At midnight, Philip had wandered around trying to find her and couldn't. She turned up again a little later all flushed and excited and gave him a peck on the cheek. Philip got well and truly drunk.

He had spent his last few days between their two homes packing his personal belongings. He had said goodbye over the phone to Patricia (she had previously planned a shopping trip with a friend) and had driven all the way to

Hull by himself with an overnight stop at a small hotel just off the A1. The proprietor of the establishment was a mixture of Bruce Forsyth and Uriah Heep. Philip woke early the next morning, had a large breakfast and continued on his way.

And now, he was on a boat bound for St Brodag's Isle.

Philip looked out of the little cabin at the mountainous grey seas around him. A huge wave crashed against the boat, washing the windows of the cabin.

The boat was called *Margie's Dream*. Philip wondered who Margie had been and had a little boat like this been her dream. Somehow, he doubted it.

The ferry crossing should have taken three hours on a good day. Today was quite obviously not a good day. They had been on board for seven hours already.

Captain Ahmed, a jovial middle-eastern gentleman, leaned over to Philip.

"It's a bit on the bumpy side today, eh?"

"Yes, rather choppy".

"Ha, ha, ha" laughed the Captain. "You British!" and wandered off to the far side of the cabin where he flicked a couple of switches. Nothing happened, so he flicked them back again.

Philip marvelled at the Captain's relaxed demeanour. He seemed to be unflappable and never seemed to lose his sense of humour. He was always pleasant and smiling, except when he addressed the members of his crew, who were, in the main, from Portugal.

The boat rolled. Philip grabbed hold of a nearby table. Across the cabin, Captain Ahmed kept perfectly upright by performing a dance as the floor fell away from his feet then raced up to meet him again. He caught Philip's eye and performed a little bow.

"How far are we from land?" shouted Philip.

The Captain checked his watch, then seemed to be counting on his fingers. He looked out of the cabin at the sea beyond, then back to Philip. He closed one eye as he made his mental calculations.

"About another hour".

"Oh. When will the normal ferry be running again?"

The Captain smiled, a beam appearing from ear to ear.

"When the weather's better".

"When will that be?"

"June" he laughed.

It appeared that the St Brodag's Line Ltd., who ran the service, were having problems with their new ferry, the *Spirit of St Brodag*. There had been some mistake made when ordering the ship and instead of receiving a brand new roll-on-roll-off ferry, an aircraft carrier, complete with ten Harrier jump jets, had been delivered. Apparently, they had very similar reference codes in the catalogue and it was a mistake anyone could have made. The boat had been refitted (unfortunately, the ship builders had wanted the Harriers back) but in anything more than a gentle swell, the boat became unstable due to insufficient ballast.

Captain Ahmed barked something unintelligible to one of the crew, a man hairier than a goat and twice as ugly. He rasped something back in reply which made Captain Ahmed dissolve into fits of laughter.

The tiny boat lurched and Philip lurched with it. He had already lost the contents of his stomach several times over and felt the worst for it.   He shook his head and steadied himself against the tiny cabin wall.

Philip wondered where his wife was now.

Philip found his thoughts drifting back to the time when he had first met Patricia. It was at a Navy ball in Portsmouth. She had looked so beautiful on that night with her auburn curls falling in great swathes onto her bare shoulders. Her ball gown was immaculate, plain and elegant. They danced all night, cheek-to-cheek, and left together at midnight to catch some air.

Philip only realised some months later that Patricia's father was an admiral. What he would have thought if he had seen them later that night under the walls of Old Portsmouth, Philip did not like to consider.

By chance, after meeting Patricia, his career then progressed with indecent haste, soon captaining his own frigate.

After eighteen months of courtship, Patricia and Philip were married in the chapel on Patricia's family estate. It had been a grand affair, attended by the rich and wealthy. They had even featured in the gossip columns of the papers during the week of the wedding: the Admiral's daughter and the handsome Captain. A honeymoon in Florence followed. Great things were being prepared for Philip.

Then, it all went sour. Philip's command, H.M.S. Shelly, collided with the harbour entrance at Portsmouth. Thankfully, it happened at midnight on New Years Eve so nobody knew about it. Philip resigned from the navy and joined the civil service, which was really a blessing as Philip had never really found his sea legs and was usually quite ill on any journey.

From then on, Patricia always seemed to be so disappointed with him. Not that she tried to disguise. The civil service was an honourable profession but is just wasn't the navy. She had run home to Daddy on so many occasions that Philip had lost count.

Their relationship ran hot and cold, with the average being lukewarm. Patricia started to do her own things while Philip stayed at home, reading and playing with his computer.

Philip reckoned that she had been unfaithful to him. He just couldn't decide how many dozen times she had done it. Their own sex life had faded away years before, after a night when Patricia had poured abuse on Philip's sexual technique. By this time, though, it was just another way in which Philip had failed his wife.

Never mind, he thought. This was an opportunity to prove her wrong and to show her and her family what he was made of. He had always been intimidated by her father who always seemed to refer to Philip as 'that man' even when Philip was in the room.

He was woken from his daydream by a nearby cry.

"Land ahoy" shouted the Captain.

"Thought you said it would be an hour away," said Philip accusingly.

"I guessed" came the reply with a smile.

Looming out of the foaming surf, Philip could see an island, quite close now. By the shore, he could see street lights blinking through the spray. Philip reckoned that the lights they were heading for must be Port Victoria.

"That's Port Victoria," said Captain Ahmed.

"That's what I reckoned," said Philip.

As they entered Port Victoria Bay, the wind died down and the waves lost their intensity. Philip could see the harbour ahead and the twin lights on either side of the harbour entrance where two piers reached out into the swell to guide the boats home. A broad promenade hugged close to the coastline, backed by long rows of hotels and guesthouses.

Margie's Dream pulled alongside the quay near a couple of trawlers. The crew busied themselves on deck. By means of a series of planks, hard pulling on the ropes and a good, differential gear box, the Range Rover was manoeuvred off the boat and onto the quay itself. Captain Ahmed waved to Philip. Philip waved back then grabbed hold of a metal ladder and pulled himself upwards. Then, he stood up, on dry land for the first time in eight hours. His coat was caked in vomit and ruined. He was wet through and totally miserable.

"Attention" barked a voice.

Philip turned slowly around, his eyes widening as he looked at the scene before him.

On the quay, close by and oblivious to the rain, was a welcoming party. Twenty members of the St Brodag's Guard were lined up before him in their colourful uniform of blue bearskins, white tunics and navy kilts. A bagpipe started to whine into life.

Philip clicked to attention, trying hard to forget the drips of water channelling down his back and diving between his buttocks like a miniature Niagara. He took the salute as the guard marched past.

A man in thick yellow oilskins approached him.

"Good afternoon, Sir " came a heavily muffled voice. "Welcome to St Brodag's Isle".

Welcome To St Brodag's Isle

'If a man is stupid, I call him a fool' - St Brodag

"Is it always this wet?" asked Philip.

"No" said the man in the oilskins "sometimes it really chucks it down".

Philip looked at him incredulously.

"Only joking," the man continued, "though it's pretty typical, I'm afraid. It's the horizontal rain that you'll have to get used to".

The man stuck out an enormous hairy hand.

"Henry Geruish, Prime Minister of St Brodag".

"Hello, Philip Digby-Fischer".

"I've got a few people to introduce you to. If you'll just follow me over there".

Geruish put his head down and led Philip over to a bus shelter that stood at the other side of a small square beneath the imposing presence of the St Brodag's Line Building, a dark monstrosity with an ugly entrance. Inside the shelter, there was a group of four individuals all dressed in a similar fashion to the Prime Minister, thickly covered against the elements.

Geruish pushed his hood back to reveal a fine, hairy head.

"This is John, our Finance Minister".

John shook Philip's hand and muttered something that Philip missed in the wind.

"This is Peter who's in charge of Agriculture and Fishing".

A tall man, who looked rather like a large trout, nodded and hung onto Philip's arm.

"Nice to have you here" he shouted.

"Nice to be here...I think" screamed Philip.

A large wave hit the harbour wall, spraying the outside of the bus shelter.

"This is Sandra who looks after Home Affairs.

A small woman, dwarfed by her waterproofs, ambushed Philip's hand with a firm squeeze.

"And this is Nigel, in charge of Tourism. He's going to be your assistant, too".

Philip shook the hand of a young chap in his early twenties who gave him a broad, beaming smile.

Geruish stood to one side and looked at Philip. Philip looked at Geruish. Geruish made a gesture with his hand. Philip understood. A speech was expected.

Another wave hit the harbour side. A wash of water ran over the ground to a depth of an inch, further wetting everyone's feet.

"Well. Er. Good Afternoon. I'm here, at last. I'm looking forward to getting to know you better over the next few weeks. Thank you for turning out to see me on such a day like this. I hope that, during my time here, I can have a positive contribution to the life of this island. Once again, thank you".

There was a ripple of polite applause, then Geruish stepped forward again.

"Look, I've got a car waiting over there, why don't you hand over the keys of your Range Rover and I'll get Nigel to follow us".

Philip passed the keys to Geruish who flicked them in the direction of Nigel, who fumbled them and nearly lost them down a grid. He gave Philip a sheepish smile. Philip turned and followed the Prime Minister over to where an old stretch Bentley was waiting.

Nigel caught him up.

"What's the engine size?" he asked.

"Four litre" said Philip, hesitantly.

"Cool" said Nigel who bounded off to the car.

Philip clambered into the Bentley first, followed by Henry. Once in the car, Henry started to get rid of his oilskins.

They passed through customs with a wave of Henry's hand, the officer looking relieved that he could stay in his hut.

A few hardy souls had turned out to greet the new arrival. They stood there, waving their union flags and St Brodag flag. This depicted two, pink hills on a background of blue, and was supposed to be a pictorial representation of the island. From a distance, it just looked like an arse to Philip. They raised a half-hearted cheer as the Bentley whizzed passed them. Then they all went home for tea.

In the car, Philip surveyed the Prime Minister. Here was a man that he would have to work with over the next few years. It was important, reckoned Philip, to get the measure of him as soon as possible.

Henry Geruish was a giant of a man in every sense. Standing over six feet and five inches tall, he carried his twenty stones well. He had a dark, bushy beard, flecked with grey, and thick curly hair to match. His eyes were blue and twinkled. He had hands the size of a bear's paws and, indeed, the first impression that someone formed when meeting Henry Geruish was just how bear-like he was. His voice was deep and gravelly and when he laughed he could make large inanimate objects rock.

"Of course, it's particularly bleak here at the moment with the winter storms. The North Sea can be a rough old place when the wind gets up".

"You don't need to tell me. I think that I've experienced that at first hand".

The Bentley left the quayside and made its stately way up the promenade, passing the lifeboat station on the way.

"Where is the residence?" asked Philip.

"Just on top of the headland over there" said Geruish, pointing with his big, hairy paw.

Philip peered out of the window and could just about make out a long finger of land reaching out into the sea.

"Oh super. I bet the views are fantastic from there".

"When you can see more than a few feet, yes, they are".

Philip decided to try to find out a little bit more about what was in store for him.

"So, what happened to the last Governor?"

The big man let out a deep chuckle.

"Didn't they tell you?"

Philip shook his head, feeling that this was obviously an important piece of information that had been left out of his briefing. He wondered why it had never occurred to him to ask before.

"Well, basically, he went mad. He really wasn't our sort at all, you know. Home Counties type. Liked his tennis. Can you imagine playing tennis here? Well, he began to become a little withdrawn. Stayed up at the residence all day, never came out at all. The only people who had contact with him were the cook and the gardener. He used to have whiskey delivered by the caseload. Eventually, I went up there to see what was going on. Found him in his bedroom wearing a frock, completely drunk and reciting Chaucer to a couple of dead pigeons. Still, shows what the island can do to you, if you're not fully prepared".

"Poor man" said Philip. "How long had he been on the island for?"

"About two months".

Philip felt a sense of nausea creeping over him. He was not having a good day by anyone's estimation. He looked out of the window. The wind had picked up again and gigantic waves were crashing onto the beach, sending sheets of spray and shingle across the promenade.

"Better get off here" Geruish said to the driver. "Turn left at the next junction. We'll take the back way up to the headland".

The Bentley turned and began to head uphill. In the distance, Philip thought he saw a brilliant green sign that said 'Marks and Spencers'. Philip drew a little assurance from a familiar sight.

"The one before him lasted longer" continued Geruish. He was here for nearly a year. Couldn't settle. The one before him couldn't keep his pants on at all. Seemed he though he was on some sort of divine mission to bring new genes to the island's bloodstock. In two years, he got six young lasses pregnant, dirty bastard. The one before him died in a mysterious boating incident".

"Sounds like the job's cursed".

Geruish looked at him, his big eyes all wide and twinkling.

"Aye, some have said that".

Philip gulped.

Soon, they had left the houses of Port Victoria behind and were heading along a country lane, bordered on both sides by stunted and leaning trees. From this point, Philip could see across the width of the island and to the dark and boiling sea that lay to the east. He felt very small and very alone which was peculiar since he was sitting in the back of an enormous car with a huge giant of a man beside him.

Just then, they turned off the main road and drove down a single-track lane though a small wood. When they emerged on the other side, Philip could see the grim magnificence of the Governor's Residence, desperately clinging to the rocky headland like some primeval lungfish that had changed its mind mid crawl.

They swung through a pair of large gates. A sign written in black on a white background was stuck on the wall at the side of the gate: 'Ash-Na-Garoo', The Official Residence of the Governor.

"What does Ash-Na-Garoo mean?" asked Philip.

"Well, it's a Brodagan name that means the House of My Tomorrows".

"And why is it called that?"

"Don't know" came the reply. "It just sounds nice".

The Bentley came to a stop on the gravel outside the main entrance. Philip opened the door and clambered out if the car.

There was a guttural roar of an engine and the Range Rover appeared. It came to a sudden stop in a shower of gravel. Out jumped Nigel with an idiot grin on his face.

"Think I chipped your paintwork there" he said.

Philip stared at him then took a few steps backwards and surveyed his new home.

The style of Ash-Na-Garoo could be described as eclectic. The older part of the house looked like a small peasant's cottage. Built onto this was the main part of the present residence, a Georgian affair, with a splendid entrance. A large, ugly Victorian Gothic tower had been added from which a concrete extension been built in the 1960s. Behind him, Philip could see steeply terraced gardens plunging down into the sea below.

"They threw away the plans when they made this place" shouted Geruish.

"Thank goodness" said Philip to himself.

"Impressed?" asked Geruish.

"I've seen more homely dwellings," Philip admitted.

"Ah, yes, but anything as dramatic".

Philip gulped and responded that he had not.

They made their way forward to the front door. Geruish felt in his pocket for the key. It turned with a click and he pushed the door open. He stood back and waved Philip forward. Gingerly, he stepped into the darkness.

Compared to outside, it was very still in the house. Still and very dark.

"It's very dark," whispered Philip.

He heard another click behind him and was momentarily dazzled when the lights came on.

Philip blinked then blinked again.

A huge and very impressive entrance hall was revealed. The light came mainly from a chandelier that hung down from the ceiling like a frozen waterfall. A broad staircase ran up to the first floor. Large mirrors, many in gold frames, reflected the light in all directions. On the left hand side, an old and ornate Grandfather clock stood. The floor was made of marble, polished and shining.

"It's beautiful," said Philip.

"Not bad for a crappy bit of rock that no one really gives a shit about, eh?" The bear man gave out a gruff chuckle.

"Where did all this come from?"

Geruish smiled.

"It's what we've built up over the years. Grants, hand-me-downs from the British Government. We even got a chunk of money out of the EU a few years ago".

Nigel busied past them carrying some of Philip's things.

"Be careful of those bags," shouted Philip.

Nigel just grinned at him.

"Come on," said Geruish laying a hand on Philip's shoulder "let me show you the rest of the place".

It was the same throughout the house. Each room was tastefully decorated with the finest furniture, delicate antiques and valuable paintings. There was even a small cinema.

"We've got satellite television beamed through into here. For the football. Had fifty people in here the night Man United won the Champions League. Bloody marvellous".

"Who looks after the house?" asked Philip as they made their way back into the entrance hall.

"Well, Mrs. Kinloss is the cook and cleaner, but she's away and not back until Monday. Then, there's Jim. He's the gardener and handyman. He'll do whatever you need him too. Salt of the earth. Jim lives in a cottage just off the estate".

"What about other staff? Administrative and secretarial?"

"Yes, you have a secretary, Mary. She'll be in first thing Monday to sort you out. Then, there's Nigel who you met earlier. He will act as your assistant".

"Good".

"Nigel will stay in the West Wing tonight" said Geruish, nodding in the direction of the driver. "Just to make sure that you settle in fine. Any problems then give him a call".

When they arrived back at the entrance, Geruish pointed Philip in the direction of the stairs. At the top, they turned right and made their way down a red-carpeted corridor to the Governor's suite of rooms.

"This is your bedroom," said Geruish, flinging open a door to reveal a massive room panelled in oak with a large four-poster bed in the middle of it.

"Through the left hand door is your bathroom and the other door leads onto your office. That's worth a look".

They moved forward and through the right hand door. Philip found that his office was jammed to the ceiling with books. A large picture window looked out over the foaming bay to Port Victoria. A set of french windows opened out onto a sheltered terrace.

"Perfect" said Philip.

"We try and do our best. Through there" he said, motioning with his head "are the rest of the offices".

Philip looked around and rubbed his hands together, feeling rather pleased with the way that things were beginning to pan out.

They made their way back to the entrance hall.

"Now I'm not prepared to leave you by yourself this evening, not on a Saturday night with you just come to the island. I insist that you come round to our place for a meal. Nothing fancy, mind, just the family. How does that sound?"

"Very nice, thank you. I'll be delighted".

"Good. I'll send someone round for you at seven-thirty".

"Seven-thirty. Good".

"Now, I've left an itinerary for your induction week on your desk. Have a read through it. If you have any security issues, ring nine from any phone. That'll get you through to the Police Station just down the road. Apart from that....I can't think of anything else. Have you got anything that's pressing?"

"No" said Philip. "It's just that... well, I'm really looking forward to working here. I'm committed to this job, I want you to know that".

Geruish smiled and turned away.

"See you later" he shouted over his shoulder. Then he closed the door and Philip was alone.

"Hi, Patricia, hi, how are you doing?"

Philip could hear the sound of a party on the other end of the phone. He had resisted calling his wife for approximately three minutes after Geruish had left.

"Who's that?" came the familiar voice.

"Philip, darling".

"Who?"

"PHILIP".

"Oh, hello, darling. Did you make it?"

"No, I'm actually phoning from the bottom of the North Sea".

"Don't try and be funny, Philip, it's not you".

"Sorry".

Silence between them. Lots of music and laughter in the background at Patricia's parents house.

"Having a party?" asked Philip, not knowing quite what else to say.

"Oh, just some chums round. Listen, darling, it's a bit inconvenient at the moment. Can you ring back tomorrow - no make it the day after".

"I suppose so. Did you..."

"Goodbye then". CLICK. The line went dead.

"Goodbye" said Philip sadly.

Philip threw the phone down on the bed. He looked around his bedroom. There were a couple of seascapes hanging on the walls. Yachts were seen dipping in and out of the surf, their spinnakers' cutting a dash of colour across the canvas. Philip half expected to see *Margie's Dream* bobbing up and down on the waves.

Philip could hear the storm continuing outside and began to feel very alone. He decided to soak himself in a hot bath before being picked up.

A Family Meal

'Charity begins in someone else's purse' - St Brodag

Philip was standing in the entrance hall when he heard a car rolling over the gravel outside. He put on his coat and opened the door. The handle was ripped from his hand and the door flew open. Above him, the chandelier began to swing crazily, casting peculiar shadows across the floor. Philip struggled to pull it shut behind him, then locked it with a key. Then, he sprinted over to where the small BMW Roadster sat. He yanked open the door and jumped inside.

"You must be our new Governor then" purred a voice.

Philip looked across at the driver. She was a woman in her late twenties with dark, curling shoulder-length hair. Even in the darkness inside the car, her eyes were sharp and bright.

"Philip Digby-Fischer". Philip reached out a hand. The girl took it and gave it a good shake.

"Amanda Geruish. I'm Henry's daughter. The middle one".

"You have other brothers and sisters?"

"Two of each".

"Wow".

Philip fell silent.

"Buckle up, Mr Digby-Fischer. We're off".

And without allowing Philip the time to ensure that the seat belt was in place, Amanda was off, screeching down the lane. She managed to keep up a good level of conversation as she drove. Philip, on the other hand, was more concerned with reading the speedometer.

"Do you always drive this fast?" asked Philip unashamedly, pushing his backside deeper and deeper into the leather seats.

"No. Most of the time I'm quite a sensible driver. It's just that...well...I'm a bit tense at the moment. It's a woman's thing".

"Oh" said Philip, closing his eyes and not wishing to pursue the matter.

Within a few minutes, they were streaking down the coast to the other side of the island. There were no street lights to be seen anywhere outside of Port Victoria. The moon was hidden. Only a strange sheen could be detected coming off the sea.

"What's that?" asked Philip, sitting up suddenly.

"What's what?"

"The sea. It's.....glowing".

Amanda laughed.

"That'll be St Brodag's Haze that you're looking at," said Amanda. "A phenomenon in these parts. If you go down to the beach at night, you can read a book by the light that comes off the sea".

"What causes it?" asked Philip.

"Nobody seems to know. Strange, isn't it".

"It's beautiful".

Amanda smiled.

"Yes, I suppose it is. Never thought about it much before".

The car screeched around corner after corner. Philip took to looking out of the side windows to calm his nerves, though it didn't seem to really help very much.

"Is it far, now?" asked Philip hesitantly.

"Are you worried that we won't make it?" asked Amanda.

"No, no. It's just that...".

"Well, we're here," said Amanda.

The car turned through a wide opening to the right and came to a halt outside a large house perched above a small cove.

"Here we are - home" said Amanda.

"Philip. How are you? Do come in".

Henry Geruish stood in the hallway and welcomed Philip into his house.

"Can I take your coat, man?" he asked.

Philip took off his coat and handed it over.

"This way" and he pushed Philip forward towards a door.

Philip pushed the door open and walked through. To his surprise, there must have been thirty people in the large lounge beyond. They all turned to look at him.

"Philip Digby-Fischer" announced Geruish "our new Governor".

Hale and hearty welcome's followed. Philip noticed that nearly everyone that he had met so far was in attendance. He looked round and wandered back over to Henry who was opening a bottle of champagne.

"I thought that you said that this was going to be a family meal".

"Big family" came the reply.

"But don't a lot of these people work for you in the Government?"

"Yes. We're a committed and caring family too".

POP went the cork followed by cries of 'glasses, glasses!'

Philip thought to himself, sucking his teeth as he did it.

"Come on, Philip" said Geruish. "Have a glass of bubbly".

Geruish put a big bear-like arm around Philip and gave him a flute of champagne.

To be truthful, although Philip was a little concerned at the amount of potential nepotism that he felt he was witnessing, he was rather enjoying himself. He soon fell into conversation with two of Henry's cousins: the Chief of Police, Brian; and the Head of the Fire Brigade, Tony.

Suddenly, their conversation was disturbed by a loud cry.

"Dinner is served!"

Philip followed the others through another door on the far wall and into the dining room.

The meal itself was a delight. They all sat around on benches alongside two large tables. Philip found himself between Amanda who, despite her womanly problems and her own admitted tenseness, was extremely chatty and pleasant company. On his other side sat Lewis, one of Geruish's sons, who seemed to be in a world of his own, though occasionally returned to reality to demand more bread, or more wine.

The first dish to be served was a hearty ham and vegetable broth, with warm crusty bread as an accompaniment. Philip cut himself some thick slabs of butter, which he dropped onto the bread and watched it melt.

Next came a warm salad of seaweed and whelks, served in a creamy sauce. Henry Geruish passed round bottles of a light Riesling from Alsace that perfectly matched the dish.

"Bread" roared Lewis. Amanda apologised for her brother and mumbled something about the missing link. She smiled at Philip. He returned the smile.

The main course comprised of thick slices of roasted Brodagan Lamb served with steaming vegetables: potatoes, both mashed and roasted; pureed swede; spinach tossed in olive oil, with pine kernels and garlic; a plate of wild mushrooms gathered that morning; and broccoli spears simply cooked and oozing with butter. All this washed down with a dark Chateauneuf-de-Pape that warmed the soul as it slid down the throat.

Philip looked down the table to where Henry and his wife, May, sat. Henry was deep in conversation, sometimes whispering conspiratorially, at other times bellowing like a beast. His wife just sat there, a calm smile on her face, delighted with the way that her hard work was being received by their guests.

The puddings, themselves, were a real treat: thick toffee pudding sitting in a sea of home-made custard; pecan pie cut into wide slabs; apple tart, sweet and light; and a trifle of dangerously alcoholic proportions.

Philip tried every pudding that was on offer - twice.

"So, how long were you in London for?" asked Amanda.

"Ten years in total" mumbled Philip, trying hard to swallow a piece of pecan pie.

"Did you like it?"

Philip paused. He was about to say yes when he realised that he had not even given the question a moment's thought. Did he like it or not? Well, London was London, wasn't it? Big, busy, bustling. But had he enjoyed it?

"To be really honest, Amanda, no, I didn't. It just felt that I had to be there. Like the whole world revolved around the tube and getting to work. There's no real consideration of anything beyond London. It acts like it is the centre of the universe. Which, of course, is absolute.....absolute.....".

"Absolute bollocks, Philip".

Philip laughed.

"Yes, you're right. I was going to say 'absolute balderdash' but I think that your selection of word was better. People say London's a great place to live because of the museums, the art galleries and the theatres. I have never been to an art gallery and the only time I went to the theatre was to watch *Evita*. Most people in London can't afford to go to places like that. People just live there because they believe the myth. Why live somewhere you don't like because you feel you have to? It's so wrong".

"Tell me about it!" said Amanda with a wry smile.

Philip was about to question Amanda on this when Lewis screeched out 'Cheese' and spoiled the moment.

Then, the table was cleared and huge platters appeared, full of fresh fruit. Cheese boards were also placed on the table, the highlight of which was a huge Stilton that seemed to melt and ooze before their very eyes.

The port was passed, then other liquors were offered.

Philip confessed to himself that he was feeling woozy. He had enjoyed himself and had branded Henry Geruish a capital fellow.

"So do you think you'll stay?" asked Amanda.

"I hope so," replied Philip. "I'd like to make a real go of this job. It's the first time I've felt excited about work since leaving the navy".

"Well, I look forward to seeing you make an impact, then" said Amanda.

They continued to chat with Philip trying his best to control his voice so that he didn't sound well and truly pissed. He looked around and saw a sea of glazed eyes and idiotic grins. What a night!

"It can be a difficult place," said Amanda.

Philip laughed. "So everyone keeps telling me".

"Ah, yes, but you can believe me" she laughed.

The call of nature began to make its voice heard. Philip rose, a little unsteadily, and excused himself.

He wandered back into the hallway and found that the downstairs toilet was being used. So, being of sound mind and quite capable of a coherent decision, he staggered up the stairs in a quest for the toilet.

He tried two or three doors which all led into bedrooms or cupboards. Then he tried a fourth. He was in luck. Beyond a darkened bedroom, an ensuite bathroom could be seen. Someone had left a light on.

Philip staggered towards the light like a butterfly that had overdosed on nectar. He fell into the bathroom, closing the door behind him, and lay on the thick carpet for a while. Ahead of him lay a shower cubicle, a bath, a toilet and a bidet. He shook his head and re-focused on the toilet. Behind him, there seemed to be a dressing area.

The bathroom was thickly scented in a rich perfume and this had an adverse affect on Philip. He stomach began to lurch and roll, twisting and turning into knots. He hurriedly crawled over to the toilet, lifted up the lid, and let fly with a fulsome roar, ending with an ensemble of retch and after-spit. He pulled a handful of toilet tissue from the wall and dabbed at his mouth. He then lobbed the ball into the bowl and reached a hand up to pull the handle. The water level in the toilet rose and rose, then drained away with a deep growl.

Philip felt better almost immediately. He managed, somehow, to stand up and pull down his flies. His head began to spin, so he decided to try the sit-down approach. He unbuckled his belt, let his trousers fall to the ground, pulled down his boxers and landed, rather heavily, on the toilet seat.

Philip's satisfaction and relief was short lived. Somehow, a jet of urine had found its way between bowl and seat and had dumped half the contents of his bladder onto the crumpled pile of trouser and shorts around his ankles.

"Bugger" said Philip, suddenly sobering up.

Another handful of toilet roll was grabbed as he tried, in vain, to mop up his mess. Three handfuls later and they were still wet through. He pulled his feet out of the clothes and looked around. A hair-dryer was attached to the wall at the rear of the bathroom in the dressing area. An idea came into his head. He crossed the floor and soon was busy applying the jet of warm air onto his clothes.

He had just finished drying his boxers when he heard the door of the bedroom open and shut again. He immediately turned off the hair dryer and listened. His heart began to beat very loudly and a pulse in his head seemed to be hammering at his brain. He looked down at his naked bottom half and then at the clothes in his hands. He began to look around for a hiding place.

The door to the bathroom opened and Philip threw himself to the ground. Luckily, a wicker clothes basket lay close by and he crawled behind it, hoping that it would give him plenty of cover.

The other person started to run a bath.

Curiosity got the better of Philip and he peered over the top of the clothes basket. It was Amanda. Not only was it Amanda, it was a naked Amanda.

Tabloid headlines raced through Philip's mind as he listened to her padding around the bathroom. How the hell did he get into this mess? How the hell was he going to get out of the mess? He began to wish that he would die - right there in the bathroom. Of course, the press would have a field day and Patricia would be mad but at least he would have got himself out of this tight corner. Philip held his breath, half hoping that it would bring on a heart attack or a stroke or something.

Then, reason got the better of him and he returned to his senses.

Come on, Philip, he said to himself. Think. How do we get out of this? Right. Option one: stand up and confess. Bad move. Option two: stay there all night and make a dawn escape. Not much better. Option three: get the hell out of there as soon as possible. The only option. Good. So, a bath is being run. Therefore, a bath will be taken. That might just allow for an escape.

Just then, Philip heard a splash. He peered around the basket again. Amanda had disappeared into the bath, submerging herself, for an instant, under the steaming water. This was his chance. Grabbing his boxers and trousers, he slithered across the carpet and made his escape. He paused in the bedroom, briefly, to pull on his damp clothes. Then, he crept out onto the landing and slid downstairs.

As he burst into the room, he realised, at once, that the party was over. Most people were pulling their coats on and shouting farewells to the glorious host and hostess.

Henry Geruish saw Philip and bellowed out to him.

"Got a taxi on order for you, Governor. Courtesy of the people of St Brodag's Isle". Philip grinned sheepishly.

The taxi arrived promptly and, with a heart still thudding away, Philip was on his way home. (Home!? - unusual context).

As he sat on his bed, the room spinning around his head, he thought about his near disastrous encounter.

Don't bugger it up. He hadn't been on the island for more than eight hours and he had just come through a crisis whereby he could easily have been accused of exposing himself to the Prime Minister's daughter.

Philip reached across for his mobile phone. He picked it up and selected Patricia's number. He let it ring...once...twice. Then he ended the call.

Philip dropped the phone and, fully dressed, fell into a deep slumber.

A Case For Twiglets

'I call the puffin my brother. Is not the squid my sister?' - St Brodag

Philip woke with a heavy head and a craving for twiglets. He often woke in the morning with a craving for twiglets. It all started when he was forty. He didn't know why or how. He had blamed it on some industrial strength Cabernet Sauvignon that some friends of his had picked up on a booze trip to France and now it was just a fact of life.

He showered and dressed quickly, his mind beginning to clear from the numbness of the night before. Today was his first day on the island and, although, until his investiture, he was not, officially, the Governor, he thought that he had better make a good show of it. He dressed in relaxed, country fashion: a good shirt, tweed jacket, sensible shoes. He looked at himself in the mirror.

"Philip, old boy" he said out loud, "you don't look bad for forty-two".

He left his suite of rooms and made his way to the kitchen. He was beginning to realise that, although the residence gave the impression of being large and rambling, it was actually quite a modest affair. It had just grown in an awkward fashion.

In the kitchen, he found a tub of twiglets. He buttered some bread and made a twiglet sandwich. Sheer ecstasy. He then found the coffee machine, which was soon dribbling away to itself. He picked up the coffee tin and breathed deeply.

Funny how the smell of ground coffee is better then the taste, he thought.

Philip looked out of the window. The sea was calm. The sky was clear. The wind seemed to have dropped to a breeze.

He poured himself a large mug of coffee, dropped a spoon and a half of sugar into it, stirred the mixture around for a few seconds, then sat down on a stool and took stock of his life.

In the last twenty-four hours, he had nearly been drowned, he had got himself completely rat-arsed at a dinner party given by the island's Prime Minister and had done his best to expose himself to the said Prime Minister's rather attractive daughter.

This will not appear in my memoirs, he thought to himself.

Philip looked around at the immaculate kitchen that Mrs Kinloss kept. It was well laid out with the finest oak units you could ask for. A huge, green range dominated one end of the kitchen. The whole area looked tidy and efficient.

Stainless steel containers sat in perfect rows on low shelves. There was not a single item that was out of place or not kept immaculately clean.

Well, thought Philip, here I am.

His mind raced over all the facts that he had so recently accumulated about the place; it's people and customs. It was all new to him but he knew that he had to do a good job. This was a great opportunity, the Fat Man had been right. Granted, it was a small piece of rock stuck out in the North Sea but a power base is a power base. No matter how small or insignificant it might be. He was going to show Patricia and her family that he could make something of himself, that there was a life outside the navy. He was going to be the best Governor that St Brodag's had ever had. In years to come, they would erect a big, bronze statue to him on the sea front. He felt sure of this.

Then, he remembered the Fat Man's parting words to him on the phone the other day: *don't bugger it up, whatever you do.* Some of his doubts returned. What if....what if he did bugger it up. This was going to be his last chance with Patricia. Make a mess of this, my son, and you can forget her.

In an effort to get himself going again, he decided to go for a walk. He found a door at the back of the kitchen and, locking it behind him, he strode out into the bright Sunday morning.

A path seemed to snake away from the gardens around the headland. He decided to take this and to see where it would lead him to. He kept up a brisk pace and soon the house had disappeared behind him. Out at sea, several fishing boats were making their way back to port after a busy night's work. In the distance, Philip thought that he could make out the Northumbrian coastline.

The air was cold and stung Philip's face as he marched onwards. His spirits began to rise again. He started to whistle to himself. This was fine, he thought. Better than London. The air had never seemed so clear, so bright, so fresh there. Nothing but city smells and people. Always people. Everywhere you turned.

After half an hour, he found that the path came to an abrupt end. A fence had been built across the way, preventing anyone from making further progress. On the other side of the fence, a small wood of pine trees ran across the cliff top.

Philip marched up to the fence and inspected it. It had only recently been erected. He could tell by the cleanliness of the concrete at the base of each support.

Feeling adventurous, Philip clambered over the fence and plunged into the wood. The aromatic pine scent was rich and powerful. He breathed deeply, filling his lungs with the smell and savouring the moment. It reminded him of Christmas. He bent down and collected some cones, which he placed in his pockets.

As he did, he heard a noise, close by in the wood. It sounded like the spluttering of a generator being cranked into being. He stood up and looked around; trying to work out from which direction the sound came. He edged forward.

Suddenly, a new scent attacked his nose. It was the smell of petrol and came wafting through the woods in an invisible cloud. Then, the generator fell silent and the scent dissipated into the air.

He continued to wander further into the wood when suddenly an eerie feeling began to overtake him. He stopped in his tracks and turned around. Nothing. He could see nothing, he could feel nothing, yet he could sense that he was being watched.

Suddenly, a shot rang out and Philip dived to the ground.

"COME OUT, YOU BASTARD" shouted a deep, throaty voice.

Sensibly, Philip turned down the invitation. Instead he began to crawl backwards, back in the direction of the fence.

"COME ON. OUT YOU COME.".

BOOM . Another shot blasted into the trees above where Philip crawled, sending a shower of twigs and pine cones cascading down on top of him. Philip's crawl began to speed up. He felt involuntary sphincter movements begin in his pants.

BOOM. This time, the shot was directed further away from him. Philip decided to chance it. He jumped up and sprinted like a madman for the fence, which he cleared in one bound like Red Rum in his prime. He managed another two or three strides before his legs gave way and he landed in a heap on the ground.

As he rose from the ground he heard someone behind him.

Philip slowly turned around.

There, looking at him over the fence was a man that could only be described as a man-pig. He had a big, pink face, a little snouty nose and tiny little eyes. He snorted once or twice, which Philip took for laughter.

"Bet you shit your pants didn't you?" asked the Pig-Man.

Philip drew himself up.

"What the hell was all that about? You nearly killed me".

"You were trespassing on my land. Law says I can shoot you, didn't you know that?"

"No I didn't".

"Never mind, good bit of sport, though. Thought you looked like Linford Christie when you dashed off. Made me chuckle, that did".

"Do you know who I am?" said Philip indignantly.

"No, and I don't care. You were trespassing. Be thankful that I doesn't shoot you now".

"What's your name?"

The Pig-Man snorted.

"That's for me to know and you to find out".

"I'll report you".

"Scared!" said Pig-man unconvincingly. "Anyways," he continued. "Best be on my way. Can't stand here chatting all day. Cheerio, now".

Then, he disappeared back into the wood.

Philip breathed deeply and let out a long sigh. He checked that the pig-man had disappeared then turned to retrace his steps down the path.

When Philip got back to the house, Henry Geruish was waiting for him outside with Norman.

"Morning" he cried, as Philip marched up to him. "Been for a walk?"

"Yes. I took the path up around the headland. Do you know it?"

Geruish grunted.

"I was nearly killed up there by a mad man with a gun" said Philip, his voice rising with indignation.

"That'll be Old Ted having a laugh with you".

"Having a laugh! I nearly had a heart attack".

"Great sense of humour, Old Ted" continued Geruish.

Seeing that he was getting nowhere with Geruish, Philip decided to drop the matter for the moment.

.   "What are you doing here?"

"Making sure that you're all right. You did seem to take in a bit of ale last night".

Philip nodded.

"You could say that again. Splendid evening, though. Compliments to Mrs Geruish".

Geruish grunted.

"She's a fair cook is May. Loves to entertain. Your head OK?"

"It is now. Listen, Henry, do we just let madmen with guns shoot at anyone around here?"

"No, not normally. But Ted's Ted, I'm afraid, a law unto himself. He normally aims to miss, so I wouldn't worry. He's just a bit protective of his land".

Philip was not convinced. It was bad enough nearly being drowned, never mind being shot at.

"Anyway" continued Geruish. "I thought that you might like to take a trip around the island, just so that you can get your bearings".

Philip accepted cautiously.

"I just need ten minutes to clean up," said Philip.

Eleven minutes later, they both clambered into Geruish's Jaguar and off they went.

St Brodag's Isle is roughly shaped like a five-pointed star. The coastline is mainly formed of rocky headlands with wide, sweeping beaches in-between. The hinterland is mainly damp and boggy. The highest point is Mount Elizabeth, a mere 640 feet high. There are no rivers and no valleys to speak of.

Most of the islands population lives in and around Port Victoria. The only other sizeable town is to the north-west and is called Cragmuir. A road runs around the island, keeping close to the coastline. In one spot, near Port Victoria, this road becomes a dual carriageway, a fact that all the islanders are proud of.

To the newcomer, the island's scenery was bleak and uninviting and reminded most people of pictures of the Falklands that they had seen. This was unfortunate and gave people a more upbeat image of what they were about to encounter.

Henry Geruish gave Philip a quick ride around the coastal road. He pointed out the beach where the Grey Seal colony lay.

"Of course, we're an ornithologists paradise" he continued. "Birds stop here on their migratory journeys. Every spring and autumn we have a rush of bird watchers. They come here in their tens". Geruish snorted.

They passed the island's airport, which was little more than a flat field. The small terminal building seemed run down and decaying and the windsock danced merrily on a pole. The last commercial flights had ceased in the early 1970s, though a small charter service called Weasel Airlines ran from a converted barn on the far side of the strip.

"Some real old characters there" declared Geruish.

They stopped off for lunch at a small pub just north of Port Victoria. Philip was able to sample the excellent local brew, Craddles, which was a yeasty golden brew with a fine head. Over a lunch of Mussels in Wine (served with crusty toast), Geruish filled Philip in a little further on the duties of the Governor. In particular, he mentioned that the government could do with a little help with tourism.

"I'd be delighted to help out. Who's currently in charge?"

"Oh, my nephew, Nigel. You'll see him tomorrow, anyway. Just mention it to him".

"Great".

Philip tore off a piece of the bread and began to spread butter on it.

"What about industry?" he asked.

Geruish grunted.

"There a couple of factories on the island. There's the brewery, of course, just outside Cragmuir. Then there's the fishing fleet - herring, cod and scallops. And agriculture. We're pretty self-sufficient for the basics".

"So what's the future looking like?"

Geruish sat back and downed his pint.

"Now that's a very good question," he said slowly, lowering the glass to the tabletop. "Let's just say that, at this moment in time, the future's looking pretty rosy for the island".

"Good" said Philip. "Anything you can tell me about?"

Geruish chuckled.

"Not yet, Philip. Not yet".

Geruish stood up and went across to the bar to order more drinks.

Philip sat on his chair, eating his bread and wondering what on earth Geruish was talking about.

Philip returned to his residence later that evening after listening to Geruish for hours on the ins and outs of island life. Some of the gaps in his knowledge were being gradually filled in.

He went to the TV room and watched *Ballykissangel* in full Dolby Digital. Then, he made himself a small supper, poured himself a large scotch and went to bed.

That night, alone in the house, Philip's dreams were all about men who turned into pigs and pigs who turned into men. Then, a man who looked like a bear laughed at him.

He woke in a sweat feeling miserable.

Hello, Hello, Hello Again

'Need is a word born of necessity' - St Brodag

On the Monday morning, Philip woke early. He showered and pulled on a smart navy blue suit with a light blue shirt and a sober tie. He skipped downstairs and pushed open the door to the kitchen.

"Out," shouted a voice.

Philip stopped in his tracks.

"Hello?"

"Get out of my kitchen". The voice belonged to a large, grey-haired lady with a fierce countenance. She wore an immaculate pinafore, starched and ironed.

Philip stalled.

"NOW". Philip shot back through the doors.

There was a short pause as he waited in the corridor outside.

"Now knock".

Philip obliged.

"Enter" came the voice now changed to a lighter tone.

Philip pushed the door open slowly and went through. He stood on the other side of the door and waited.

"I am Mrs Kinloss and you are, I believe, the new Governor. In this kitchen, you will always knock before entering. You will not take food from the larder without permission and you will not, as happened over the weekend, leave dirty cups in the sink. This kitchen will not tolerate such behaviour. This kitchen is determined to remain tidy and hygienic. Do I make myself clear?"

Philip nodded meekly.

"It's a pleasure to make your acquaintance, Mrs Kinloss. Please call me Philip".

There was a grunt from the cook.

"I will refer to you as Governor. You will address me as Mrs Kinloss at all times. This kitchen will still be here when you are long gone. I will still be here when you are long gone. Under these circumstances, familiarity is to be avoided if not abhorred. Do I make myself clear?"

"Of course. Now...breakfast....."

"In this kitchen, breakfast is available between the hours of seven-thirty and eight-thirty. Other arrangements can be made if I am consulted forty-eight hours in advance. Breakfast is served in the morning room adjoining this kitchen. This kitchen provides the choice of a cooked breakfast or, for those of a weak disposition, a *continental* type breakfast". She could not have held more contempt than that with which she said the word continental.

"Oh, great. What does the cooked breakfast consist of?"

"In this kitchen" announced Mrs Kinloss" the cooked breakfast commences with a bowl of porridge, salted not sugared. This is then followed by sausages, bacon, black pudding, eggs - scrambled, fried or boiled - mushrooms, tomatoes, potato wedges and fried bread. Kedgeree or kippers are also available at 48 hours notice. Orange juice and tea will also be served with the cooked breakfast. In this kitchen, we do not partake of coffee before 11 o'clock in the morning".

"Cooked breakfast will be fine. I'll just go and wait....next door...in the morning room".

Philip escaped and sat down at a table in the window of the room next door. A neat white cloth lay on top of the table. A place had been set for him.

The sun glistened on the bay outside and just beyond the window a man whistled noisily. Philip reckoned that the whistle belonged to the gardener as. From time to time, the scrape of a spade could also be heard.

The door opened and Mrs Kinloss entered carrying a tray.

Philip sat down.

"Thank you, Mrs Kinloss. It looks lovely".

"Humph" was the only reply.

After breakfast, Philip decided to make a swift exit to avoid having to hear what else this kitchen did or did not approve of. He made his way upstairs and entered his office through his bedroom.

It felt a little strange sitting at the huge oak desk and looking out at the sea. He reached down for his briefcase, put it on the desk and opened it. He pulled out a few personal items: a pen; a calculator; a picture of Patricia. Then he arranged these items on the desktop. He looked at Patricia and smiled. Then he frowned. Then he looked away.

He closed the case and placed it on the floor next to his desk.

Philip picked up a leather folder and pulled out a piece of paper from inside. This had written on it his itinerary for the next few days. He checked and re-checked the list, noting a few items down in a diary he kept in the inside pocket of his jacket.

ITINERARY - 1st Week

Monday	am:	At the office
	pm:	Ditto
Tuesday	am:	Medical - the Hospital
	pm:	Prime Minister (at Parliament)
Wednesday	am:	Tourism Summit
	pm:	Ditto
Thursday	am:	Radio Interview

               pm: At the office
Friday   am: Trade Meeting
               pm: At the office

Should be an easy enough introduction, thought Philip. Nothing much can go wrong with that.

Philip heard voices from beyond the door that connected his office with the others. He stood up and fiddled with his tie. Then he crossed the floor and opened the door.

In the other office sat a young girl and Nigel. The young girl wore a smart suit with a white blouse underneath. Nigel was wearing a crumpled jacket that had seen better days and trousers that did not match.

"You must be Mary," he said addressing the girl. "Hello and good morning".

The girl shot bolt upright.

"Good morning, Governor" she said politely, if a little nervously also.

"Relax, relax. I won't bite". He turned to Nigel. "Good morning, Nigel. How are you this morning?"

"Fine, fine, Governor". Nigel was smiling. He was always smiling, as though he was remembering the punch line to some blue joke that he had heard once.

"Good. Oh, please call me Philip, both of you. We're going to all have to work together so we might as well start off being friendly".

Mary visibly relaxed. She was small and thin, about twenty years old, and had a wide and engaging smile. Philip warmed to her immediately.

Nigel didn't seem to be at his best. He looked tired and a bit dishevelled. Not the way to look on your first day at work with a new employer, thought Philip. Never mind, I know that he is willing.

"Just give me five minutes, then come through," said Philip. "I'd just like to spend a few minutes talking with you about my way of working and how we are going to sort things out over the next few weeks".

Both Mary and Nigel smiled and nodded.

Philip turned back to the office. Then, he stopped and addressed Mary.

"Has my paper arrived this morning yet?" he asked.

"No. They don't normally arrive until much later".

"When exactly?"

"About ten o'clock tonight".

"What!"

"Sorry. It's the boat sailings, I'm afraid. We are a little out of the way here".

Philip sniffed.

"Just one of those things that I'm going to have to get used to, I suppose".

He walked back into his office.

"So if you'll keep the official diary for me, Mary, I'll transfer the important dates into my pocket diary".

Mary and Nigel sat in front of Philip who was pacing backwards and forwards behind his desk. Mary had a pad on her lap and was noting down every word. Nigel was looking out of the window, a blank expression on his face.

"Very good, Philip. I'll make sure that happens".

"Good, excellent. Now. Telephones".

There was a knock at the door.

"Come in" called Philip.

In bustled Mrs Kinloss with a pot of coffee and a plate of chocolate digestives.

"Ah, good. What a good idea. Coffee".

Mrs Kinloss fixed her eyes upon the Governor.

"In this kitchen" she started "we do not drink coffee before 11 o'clock but we do partake of coffee and a small biscuit at 11.15 am. If you wish to change this arrangement then please give me 48 hours notice so that I can ensure that the supply of digestives is suitably restricted".

Philip swallowed.

"Coffee at 11.15 am is fine by me, Mrs Kinloss".

She snorted at him and retired.

Philip sat down while Nigel poured the coffee.

"Is Mrs Kinloss...." he started.

"A capital woman. Yes, she is" said Mary.

"No" said Philip. "What I mean is she always so......".

"Kind and understanding. Every time".

"No. Please, Mary, let me finish. What I mean to say is she..."

"Listening at the door!" whispered Mary, leaning forward.

Philip looked at Mary who nodded back at him and pointed to the door.

"Oh" said Philip. He stood up and crept across to the door. He yanked at the handle, pulling the door quickly open. Mrs Kinloss tumbled into the room, glass in hand.

"Let me help you up there" said Philip.

"Looking for spiders" cried the old woman. "There's a lot of them about".

"Of course" said Philip. "Nasty things. We don't like spiders in this kitchen do we, Mrs Kinloss?"

Mrs Kinloss fixed him with a withering stare.

"I shall be away back to my work. Lunch will be served at 12.30 precisely. In this kitchen, we like to be prompt".

Then she turned and left.

Philip closed the door and skipped back to his desk.

"Thank you, Mary".

"No problem" she said with a smile.

Nigel sat there tittering for a while, recovering a little from his stupor of earlier.

"Now, telephones. I noticed that I have two on my desk. A black one and a red one. Now, I have used the black one and know that it is a normal telephone. Can someone please tell me what the red one is for?"

Silence.

"Any ideas?"

"I've got one in my office too" said Nigel.

"Have you ever used it?"

"No".

"Why not?"

"Because it's red!"

"So no one here knows what the red telephone is for?"

"I'm afraid not," said Mary. "I certainly have never used it. The last Governor didn't use it either".

Philip rubbed his chin.

"I wonder what it does then? It says on here 'DIAL 1234'".

He hesitated then reached out and picked up the receiver.

"What can you hear?" asked Mary.

"A dialling tone".

Philip reached out a finger and tapped in the numbers into the keypad.

"What's happening?" asked Nigel.

"It's just beeping at me. Can't be anything that important, then".

Philip put the receiver back down and they continued on with their meeting.

As Philip waved goodbye to the fire engine as it rattled its way back towards Port Victoria, he mused on the fact that the telephone did, indeed, do something.

The police had arrived first, including the Special Unit carrying semi-automatic weapons. Then, the fire brigade arrived and then the ambulance. By the time Henry Geruish turned up, followed by two members of the local press, it was all over and Philip was waving them off.

Geruish wound down the window on his Jaguar.

"You used the red phone, didn't you?"

"I'm afraid I did".

"Well don't" and with that he accelerated off in the direction from whence he came.

Once the false alarm was over, and Mrs Kinloss had returned to making the lunch ('In this kitchen, we view false alarms with a severe nature as they may lead to the burning of buns or the catching of a deep fat fryer'), Nigel, Mary and Philip continued to make good progress.

Mary was to be in charge of the post and was free to open any item of mail apart from those marked 'Private and Confidential'. She was also to screen all telephone calls.

Nigel was to help Philip with all items relating to Brodagan issues, composing briefs and reports on all the main topics relating to Philip's position as Governor.

"We need to set this Tourism summit up," said Philip. "Where do you think we ought to hold it?"

"Erm, I think....well, I'll phone around. I suggest a room at Government House. There's plenty of space there".

"Government House?" said Philip. "I've not heard of that".

"It's where all the offices are," said Nigel. "It was built with EU money to house all the offshore investment people that were supposed to come here. It was never used because they all buggered off to Jersey or the Isle of Man instead".

"Oh. Sounds excellent".

"I'll go and do that now then".

Later that afternoon, Philip had a phone call from Henry Geruish.

"We've set up the day of your investiture," he growled down the phone line. "Two weeks on Thursday. Might be a bit cold but you'll be used to that by then. That OK with you?"

"Fine" said Philip.

"Good".

As Philip settled down to his evening meal, he reflected on a day that he thought had gone particularly well. Mary seemed very good and Nigel, despite all his obvious failings, seemed to know what was going on. He was so happy that he began to whistle.

A head appeared around the dining room door.

"In this kitchen, we do not allow whistling in the dining room".

Mrs Kinloss disappeared and Philip pulled a face in her direction.

Being Stuffed

'A mile is longer than a yard' - St Brodag

Philip's first duty on Tuesday was to attend the hospital in Port Victoria for a health check. He had undergone a medical quite recently and expected there to be no problems.

Philip turned up at nine o'clock sharp for his appointment.

The hospital was located half a mile inland on the edge of the town. The building had the appearance of a colonial bungalow, with timber clad walls and a low roof. It was set back from the road with long lawns stretching down to the pavement.

Philip checked in at the reception where a pleasant, round-faced lady gave him a card and asked him to wait. He found a chair to sit on and began to browse through some old copies of the *Reader's Digest*. He was particularly drawn to a story entitled 'I am John's Spleen' and another that told the story of a family who were marooned on top of a roller coaster for two weeks one Christmas holiday.

"Mr Digby-Fischer. Room 25, please".

Philip put the magazines down and set off down a short corridor, stopping outside a bright yellow door with a number '25' painted on it.

Philip knocked on the door. A female voice called out from within and Philip entered.

"Take a seat," said a voice from behind a curtain. Philip obeyed.

"Now tell me," the voice continued. "How have you been feeling, Mr Digby-Fischer?"

At that point the doctor appeared from behind the curtain. It was Amanda Geruish.

"Amanda!" cried Philip with a start.

"Hello, Philip" she chuckled. "I'm afraid you've got me for the old MOT. I'll find out if you're fighting fit or not". She smiled at him. Philip smiled back.

"Can you fill this in for me, please" she said, handing him a form on a clipboard. "Just a few questions of a personal and intrusive nature".

Amanda threw him a pen and settled down at the desk. She busied herself preparing her equipment as Philip scribbled away answering the questions.

"Great night on Saturday night" said Philip.

"Hmmm" responded Amanda.

"Lovely meal".

Amanda grunted as she polished her stethoscope.

Eventually, Philip had answered all the questions.

"Finished" he said triumphantly.

"Good" said Amanda, standing up.

She took the board off him and checked all the answers that he had written.

"First things first" she said. "Can you roll your sleeve up so that I can take your blood pressure?"

Philip did as he was told.

"You didn't tell me you were a doctor".

"You didn't ask".

"Oh" said Philip.

Amanda laughed. "It's all right, though. I can do medicals, you know".

Philip laughed.

"Good" said Amanda. "That's all in order. Eye sight next. Just stand on that line over there".

Philip stood up and crossed to the line. Amanda put some charts up on the far wall and asked Philip to read them, line by line.

"Excellent. Nothing wrong there at all. Right. Sorry about this but can you take your clothes off. Just down to your underwear".

Philip complied, folding his clothes neatly and leaving them on a chair.

"I just want to listen to your chest".

The icy cold stethoscope caused him to take a sharp intake of breath as she placed it on both his chest and his back

"Sorry. Just try and breathe naturally. Breathe in.........and out...........in ....and out. Good. Everything's fine there. Any back problems?"

"No".

"Good. Can you touch your toes?"

"I can try".

As Philip bent down and stretched his arms to the floor.

Quite suddenly, Amanda plunged her hand down the back of his shorts and grabbed hold of his testicles, clamping them between her fingers and applying enough pressure for Philip to begin to pray. She leaned close to his ear.

"It was you in my bedroom the other night, wasn't it?" she whispered venomously.

Philip stuttered to get the words out from his difficult position, his voice becoming high and strangulated.

"Er..........yes" he whispered.

Amanda sighed and gave a small tug causing Philip to gulp.

"I don't like strangers in my room, especially if they puke all over the carpet".

"Sorry....I'm really........sorry".

"Good. Then you won't do it again?"

"I didn't mean to do it in the first place....I got ......lost".

Amanda let go and Philip keeled over. He lay on the floor gasping for a while. "Did...you...have to...do...that?" he panted.

"No. But it was fun".

Amanda turned away and sat down at her desk. She started flicking through some papers.

Philip clambered to his feet and pointed at her with a quivering arm.

"You are mad. You are a mad woman! I mean, what the....I don't know what to say".

Amanda looked up from her desk and smiled.

Philip pulled on his clothes quickly though he fumbled when he came to securing his belt in place. He was both embarrassed and annoyed.

"You're not upset, are you, Philip?" asked Amanda innocently.

"What do you think? I could have you for assault".

Amanda giggled.

"After what you did the other night? I don't think so".

"Well, you could have asked me for an explanation first or something".

"What! And miss out on putting my hand down your pants - never!" She paused and smiled to herself. "By the way, Philip. Nice dick!"

Philip looked at her. He knotted his tie.

"Please leave my genitals out of this".

He turned to leave.

"Excellent dick, in fact" she called after him.

And when the Governor of St Brodag's Isle left that room, he had a broad grin on his face.

"Hello, Philip?"

It was Amanda on the phone. Philip was sitting at his desk.

"Yes?".

"Look about earlier. I'm sorry. As I said the other night, I'm a bit moody at the moment. I was just a bit pissed off. It wasn't a nice thing to do and I'm sorry".

"You're right, it wasn't a nice thing to do at all".

"Yeah, well. As an apology can I buy you a drink tonight. Down at the Ship Inn on the quay".

Philip paused.

"No grabbing my balls?"

"Not unless you want me to".

Philip laughed.

"OK. What time?"

"Eightish?".

"See you then".

Philip replaced the receiver.

What am I doing here? he asked himself. I'm a married man and this is quite obviously some sort of mad woman who, only recently, had my privates in her fist.

"Oh shit" he whispered to himself.

The Ship Inn was a large, friendly looking establishment that stood on the quayside at Port Victoria. It was run by a Geordie called George. After an afternoon of going through papers with Henry Geruish, Philip was looking forward to a drink and spending some time with the Prime Minister's daughter, even if she was a lunatic.

"A pint, is it?" asked George as Philip walked into the bar.

"Please".

"You'll be the new Governor, then" said George.

"Er, yes".

"Nice to meet you. It's nice to get a better class of customer in here. Too many sailor types. I'm opening up a wine bar in a back room here soon".

"Really" said Philip. "That's a bit cultured for the island".

"I know. I've really splashed out on it, you know. I've got a couple of crates of Blue Nun in and a few of them boxes of red wine. Can't stand the stuff, myself though. Rots me guts but I know a lot of you sophisticated types like it. Can't beat a good pint, if you ask me. Anyway, I'm decorating the back room. Got a job lot of pink paint from my mate Baz who works over the road in a warehouse. It'll look brilliant when its finished".

George handed Philip his pint. Philip felt in his pocket for some change and handed it over. He took a sip of his beer.

"That looks good," said a voice at his side.

There was Amanda dressed in a dark jacket, purple silk blouse, jeans and boots.

"Drink?" asked Philip.

"Great. Yes. Pint please, George".

"You drink pints?" asked Philip incredulously.

"I _was_ a medical student," said Amanda. "And, anyway, it's cheaper than drinking halves".

"You're looking right sexy tonight, love" shouted George as he pulled the pint.

"You silver tongued charmer!" said Amanda. "I bet you say that to all the girls".

"I do, you're right. Always like to treat a lady nice, like. Bit of a compliment before you go down the pub with her. Something like 'Ah, that perfume's right lovely' or 'I like the way that skirt shows off them lovely long legs of yours'. Works a treat with the ladies. Love it, they do. Love it".

Philip paid for Amanda's drink then she gestured towards a table in the corner of the pub by a window.

"It takes all sorts," said Philip.

"Yes it does. Most of them seem to live on this piece of forsaken rock".

"You don't seem all that enamoured to be here," said Philip.

Amanda smiled. "Ah, you noticed".

"What's the problem?"

"Well" said Amanda. "Put yourself in my shoes. I've spent the first eighteen years of my life here. Fine. Great. No real crime on the island so I can wander where I want to without any danger. That's fine when you're ten. But I'm not. I've grown up and been away. I spent seven years in Birmingham training to be a doctor. My life doesn't revolve around here anymore".

"So why did you come back?"

Amanda sighed and looked at the ceiling.

"Family pressure. My father can be, well, very persuasive. There was a job here and it was well paid".

"But you're not happy".

"It's too small. Everyone knows everyone else's business. It's unhealthy. I can't even go out on a date with anyone. I'm related to half the island!"

Philip took a sip of his beer.

"Just because you feel you should be here, it doesn't mean it's right. We talked about this the other night. You don't have to be somewhere that you don't enjoy. That's just...."

"Absolute bollocks, if I remember correctly".

They laughed.

"No, I know you're right. It's just...Oh, I don't know".

"What about your brothers and sisters?"

"They've mostly escaped. Apart from Lewis, of course. We don't let him out much".

She threw her arms in the air.

"Anyway that's enough about me," she continued. "I could carry on depressing you all evening if you wanted".

"It wouldn't be that bad" said Philip.

"Oh, it would. Now, tell me. Why isn't your wife with you?"

"Patricia? Not her scene, this" he said with a wave of his hand. "Far too 'home counties' is Patricia. She either needs a hot sun or a decent range of shops to keep her happy".

"She'd be buggered, then, coming here".

"I reckon so. She's happy where she is - with her family and her friends".

"They're not your friends then" asked Amanda perceptively.

Philip pulled a face.

"No, not really. I mean, I've known most of them for ages. I even trained with some of them in the Navy. It's just....I suppose that they're just not my type of people. They are so concerned with themselves and their circle of friends that they don't give a stuff about anyone else. They're loud, arrogant and dismissive".

"They sound charming".

"Hmmm. Patricia feels so at home with them. It's her scene, definitely".

"But not yours?"

"No. To be honest, I'm much happier by myself. If I could disappear off into a corner somewhere with a book I'd be happy. Hunting and balls and drinks at Peggy Leggy-Weggy's just isn't for me".

"What about your family? Are your parents still alive?" asked Amanda.

Philip shook his head slowly.

"Both died when I was a teenager. I was an only child as well. I've got a mad uncle who lives in Barbados and a spinster aunt who lives in Tonbridge Wells and writes letters to the newspapers".

"That sounds like a very sad existence".

"Certainly is. She thinks that Hitler was a bit of a wimp and could have done better. She's never had a single letter published as far as I can remember. They don't put that sort of bile in print, not even in the tabloids".

He sighed.

"So, all I've really got in the world is Patricia".

Amanda shifted in her seat.

"Tell me if I'm over stepping the marker here but it sounds to me that you are not too happy with your relationship".

"I'm not. It's going down the pan - quickly, too. I'm sure that she's seeing someone at the moment. I've just got this feeling. I know that she's done it in the past, quite a number of times".

Philip fell silent. Amanda raised her glass.

"Here's to misery".

Philip responded gloomily. "Misery".

At that moment, George sidled over and sat down next to Philip.

"Look here, Governor. My mate Bob has just offered me a couple of crates of Romanian Champagne - Romagne it's called. Now, I don't know much about wine but I reckon I could be on a winner with this one. What do you think?"

Philip looked at Amanda who looked back at him.

"Do you know, George" said Philip, putting an arm around the landlord "I think you're right. Get as much of it as you can. Sounds great".

George started beaming.

"Oh, that's great. That's fantastic. I knew I was on to something good. I'll let you have a bottle for free. Cheers".

George jumped up and bounded back to the bar. Amanda and Philip both started laughing.

"I don't believe you did that," said Amanda.

"Why should we be the only miserable ones around here? Another one?" he asked, motioning towards the empty pint glasses.

"Yeah" said Amanda. "Why not!"

Sacred Summits

'A warm welcome is like a drink of clear water' - St Brodag

The centre of Port Victoria was dominated by the old Parliament Building (the Assembly) and Government House, a modern office complex. They were both built on a slightly raised area, a couple of hundred feet back from the sea front. A broad tree-line avenue ran past them both and down the hill to the promenade.

The Assembly Building had been built in Victorian Gothic style, complete with life-sized gargoyles and a bell tower. The very centre of the building was the Round Chamber and this was where the Assembly sat, rubber-stamping the decisions that had previously been made next door in Government House by Henry Geruish and his Executive Committee.

Government House had been partly financed by the EU in an effort to attract business to the island. When no business came, Henry moved the various Government Departments into it. Henry had a suite of plush offices on the top floor of the building. It was said that from his office, he could see everything that was going on in the island.

Philip entered Government House and crossed the large, imposing entrance hall to the security station. He handed his ID card to the security guard who sat at a small desk. The guard had a large cup of tea on the desk in front of him, next to a copy of *The Sun*.

"Good morning, Governor" said the guard in a loud voice.

"Good morning" responded Philip with a quick smile.

"Navy man, aren't you?"

"Yes".

"I served in Her Majesty's Royal Navy also. I was a mechanic on HMS Deliverance, you know, nuclear sub - hush, hush". He winked at Philip who stood there patiently.

"Took a certain sort of man to work on a sub like that. Self contained. Not the sort of job for a man who needs a lot of space. Sent quite a few people completely barmy".

"Really" said Philip. "My card?"

"One day we saw this blip on the screen. It seemed to be following us all over the ocean. When we moved, it moved. When we stopped, it stopped. Thought it were one of them Russian hunter-seeker subs. We had to go on silent running for three days. At the end of that, we surfaced and low and behold if it weren't a bloody whale following us".

"Thanks" said Philip grabbing his card.

"Nice to have a chat" shouted the guard who returned to his seat and opened a small bag on his desk that contained a large, cream doughnut. He smiled and put the cake away.

Philip crossed to a suite of lifts and jumped inside the first one to open. When the door opened on the fourth floor, he skipped out and made his way down a long corridor. He took a left, then a right, followed by another left. Then he saw a sign saying 'Conference Rooms' and he knew he was close.

Philip found his way to conference room 4. There were a few people there already. Nigel was standing talking to a group of three men and a couple of women in the far corner. When he saw Philip enter, he walked over to him.

"Found us, then?" he asked.

"Yes. Not too bad really".

"It is a bit of a rabbit warren, isn't it? Grab a coffee and I'll introduce you to a few people.

Philip placed his case on the floor by a chair and went over to a table that ran along the edge of the room. On the table sat several large stainless steel vacuum flasks. Philip picked up a cup and poured himself a coffee. He took a sip and grimaced. It had a distinctive metallic taste to it, with an after taste of oil. He popped three spoonfuls of sugar into it to see if any improvement could be made. He also grabbed a handful of bourbon biscuits.

Philip wandered over to the group where Nigel was. Nigel did the introductions. There was Pete Brody, who used to be Tourism Minister before Nigel; Hank Geruish, Henry's younger brother and in charge of the Hoteliers Association; Jenny Lowther, who ran various children's groups on the Island; Nigel's brother, Paul; and three or four other people who, for one reason or another, had a vested interest in bringing more people to the island including a number of representatives from the St Brodag's Line.

Nigel had made a series of badges with everyone's name on them so he handed these out. Then, everyone sat in a big semi-circle around Philip and a whiteboard.

After a short introduction and a quick talk on the reasons for calling such a meeting, Philip took off his jacket, rolled up his sleeves and got down to work

"So" said Philip enthusiastically. "Let's try and be creative today. Let's, firstly, try and answer the most important question of all. What do we have on this island to offer visitors?"

"Bugger all," whispered Pete Brody.

"Come on. Don't be negative. Why should people come and visit us?"

Silence.

"There must be something".

"There's the kittiwake," offered Nigel. "No one else has got a St Brodag's Kittiwake, have they?"

"Good, good" effused Philip, writing the word kittiwake on the whiteboard with a bright orange dry marker. "What else have we got to offer?"

"I think the kittiwake's got it wrapped up when it comes to 'What have we got to offer visitors' on this island" said Nigel.

There was much murmuring and agreement from the group.

Philip sighed.

"OK. Let's leave it there for the moment. What have we set up, then, to make the most of having the kittiwake here?"

"Not much" said Pete Brody. "Can't stand them, myself. Always shitting on your car. I think we should invest in tiny little bungs to shove up their arses so they don't shit on people's cars".

"One of them killed all my goldfish," said Jenny Lowther from the back of the room.

"How do you know it was a kittiwake?" asked Nigel.

"What else could it have been?"

"One of your cats".

Jenny gave him a withering look.

"He's right about them shitting on cars though" said an older man. "Just after you've washed it too".

"You're bloody right," said Pete turning around. "All over the windscreen and the roof, the dirty little buggers".

"Well, I like them," said a man in his twenties at the back.

Everyone turned and looked at him.

"Mind you, I couldn't eat a whole one".

The place dissolved into laughter leaving Philip at the front getting more and more annoyed.

"Come on, you lot. Be serious. We've got to attract more people here. How can we make it easier for people to see the kittiwake?"

"We could build an observation point near the headland," suggested Nigel.

"Great. Good thinking". The words 'observation' and 'point' made it onto the whiteboard.

"We could make a path so that people could get there easier," shouted the older man.

'Path' was written on the whiteboard.

"We could build a cafe or restaurant at the foot of the path, near a car park. We could have a play area for the kids and a museum there, dedicated to the kittiwake".

Philip busied himself scribbling away on the board.

"We could have one of those interactive displays," said Pete Brody. "You know, the full kittiwake experience. Indoor cliffs, the sound of the sea and a series of robotic birds that fly down and shit on your car".

Philip glowered at Pete who shut up.

"I think we've got some great ideas there. What do you think, Nigel?"

Nigel nodded his head. "Aye. I have to say that I'm surprised. I'm sure we'll clear the money through the treasury department. We could start planning it today".

"Good" said Philip. "What else have we got to offer?"

"We've got St Brodag himself," suggested Jenny Lowther.

"He's dead," said the older man.

"I know he's dead," said Jenny turning around to him. "I don't mean him himself. I mean, well. All the things around here that are attributed to him like St Brodag's cave".

"And what's there?" asked Philip.

"Nothing" said Jenny. "It's just a cave".

"Good. I like the general idea" said Philip writing down 'St Brodag'. "Anything else?"

"There's the grey seals," said Pete Brody. "I like them. They don't shit on your car".

"Look" exploded Philip. "Will you stop going on about shitting, please, on people's cars".

Pete pulled a face.

"You've obviously not experienced them crapping on your car".

Philip began to turn purple with rage.

"We're trying to brainstorm here. We're trying to come up with ideas. We don't want to hear about shitting on cars. That's the last I want to hear about it. OK?"

"Fine" said Pete sulkily.

Philip stared at him for a while, then turned back to the rest of the group

"Right. Let's split into small working parties and see what we can come up with".

Nigel hurried around organising people into their respective groups and attaching different coloured stickers to everyone's name badges. Pete Brody objected to the colour of his and he and Nigel squared up to each other. Philip had to intervene.

Fisticuffs apart, the small groups went surprisingly well and they re-assembled just before lunch to see what they had all come up with.

One group decided that it might be a good idea to hire someone to dress up as St Brodag and welcome people to the island when they got off the ferry.

"He could dress up as a monk," said Jenny "in a brown cloak and sandals".

"That'll put people off," said Pete. "Some old git with a disgusting habit". He snorted as he laughed.

"We thought that it was a good idea, actually" said Jenny haughtily.

Philip turned to Pete Brody.

"Well what has your group come up with, then, Pete?" asked Philip.

Pete cleared his throat.

"Well, we thought that we'd go back to a few ideas that were knocking around back in 1995 when I launched the 'Brodag 95' initiative".

"What?" said Nigel. "Do you mean the initiative that caused fewer people than ever to visit the island?"

"The weather was bad that year," said Pete, slowly and deliberately. "We had everything set up. Strippers, lap dancers the lot".

"You're disgusting," said Jenny Lowther.

"It's not really the sort of thing I was thinking about, Pete," said Philip.

"Well, we had a Film Festival too".

"Hardly" scoffed Nigel. "I don't think that re-showing *Kramer versus Kramer* counts as a film festival!"

"It was a retrospective. If everyone hadn't walked out we'd have shown *Tootsie* too. It was all a tribute to Dustin Hoffman".

"A film festival's not a bad idea, though, Pete," said Philip. "We could show some of the latest European films. Maybe get a premiere".

"I'm not watching any of that shite," said Pete. "At least *Kramer versus Kramer* has got a decent plot. And it's in English. I can't understand half them foreign films. Mind you, there's always plenty of shagging in them".

"Anyway" said Philip with a sigh. "I think that the film festival could work. Let's think about it over lunch and we'll talk about it some more later".

At the prospect of lunch, the proceedings came to a halt and they all disappeared to find the restaurant. Philip took some messages that had been phoned through from Mary and made some calls himself. Then, he joined the rest of the group to eat his lunch.

During the afternoon session, they all decided to concentrate on the kittiwake as the first big project.

"Bloody waste of time" said Pete Brody, picking at his teeth with a pen top.

Philip ignored him.

"I think we should set up a sub-committee who will look after the project," said Philip. "I suggest that Nigel should chair it".

"That'll be effective, then" said Pete slyly.

Nigel jumped up and dashed at him, grabbing his lapels and pushing Pete backwards.

Philip tried to pull him back while a couple of others tried to separate them.

"You're just jealous," shouted Nigel. "Just cause you were sacked".

"I resigned!" said Pete glowering at Nigel.

"You had no choice," cried Nigel.

Philip had had enough.

"Will you two stop it! Come on. Behave like adults not like little kids".

"He started it," whispered Nigel.

"I don't care," shouted Philip. "Do you behave like this at home? Do you?"

"No" the two of them said in unison.

"Well, don't do it here then. Now both back to your seats".

Pete brushed himself down rather too over dramatically. Nigel went back to his chair and glowered.

"Right. Good" said Philip. "Now let's get back to what we should be talking about. The kittiwake. Now, I suggest Nigel should chair it. I'd like to sit on the committee myself, if that's possible, to see how things work on the island. Any other volunteers?"

Two more people put their hands up. Philip took their names.

"Once the restaurant and museum are up and running, we'll invite the RSPB to open it" suggested Philip.

"That would be great," said Nigel. "They have a special committee dedicated to preserving rare sea birds".

"Good. I really think we're on to something here," said Philip with a smile. "Now, has anyone got anything further to say?"

Silence.

"Good. Thanks for coming".

And that was the end of the summit.

Later that day, Philip heard from Nigel that a gang of men would start cutting the path at the beginning of the following week. It was hoped to have all the work done within a matter of two or three months.

"Apparently, there's quite a lot of catering equipment sitting in a warehouse by the quay" said Nigel. "Brand new".

Philip poured them a cup of tea and declared the tourism summit to have been a major success.

The Spirit of Radio

'I heard a voice and it was good' - St Brodag

Philip met Amanda in a corridor as he was making his way to his radio interview.

"It's my very first time," confessed Philip.

"Ah, virgin radio" laughed Amanda.

"Sorry?" said Philip.

"It doesn't matter. I'm sure you'll be all right. Just be yourself".

"That's what I'm afraid of".

The previous day, Philip had phoned Henry Geruish for some advice and some background information on Charlie Bright who would be interviewing him.

"Our Charlie!" said Geruish when questioned. "Life and soul of any party, that man. Never seen without a smile on his face. Do you know he used to work for Radio Caroline? Apparently, he was just about to go on and do his first show when the bloody boat sank. Missed out on the launch of Radio One, too. Had a bad time with piles back then. Laid him low for a few months, they reckon. Still, he's not bitter. I mean, you know, don't bring it up in conversation or anything. You'll be all right, I'm sure. Nice bloke, our Charlie".

Philip pulled up outside a pre-fabricated building just behind the harbour. Philip looked at the building through the windscreen of his Range Rover. A sign scrawled in red on a white piece of cardboard said 'BRODAG FM'.

Must be the place, thought Philip.

Philip chuckled to himself as he jumped out of the car and ran into the radio station, the wind taking his breath away as he sprinted for cover. This was going to be an easy introduction to his broadcasting career. Philip's confidence began to grow.

Inside, the station was rather tidier than Philip had anticipated. A smart reception area lay before him. Awards in wooden frames adorned the walls. There were massive pictures of the three broadcasters. Across a carpeted floor, there lay a desk and behind the desk, a receptionist.

Philip crossed the carpet and announced himself.

The receptionist nodded and then disappeared, returning with Charlie Bright who was, most probably, the jolliest looking person that Philip had ever seen.

"Governor, Governor, welcome, welcome". He pumped Philip's hand as a beamy smile spread across his jolly face.

"Please, I like to keep things informal. Call me Philip".

"Philip, excellent. Charlie Bright - 'Spread a little Brightness' as I tell my listeners". At this, Charlie launched into a deep, throaty chuckle that was both pleasant and off-putting at the same time.

"Do come through" beckoned Charlie when his composure had recovered. Philip moved down a corridor to a rear room that was divided in two by a glass wall. On one side was the studio proper and on the other, a couple of technicians sat at a series of dense looking control units.

"Of course, one of our main functions as a station is to bring everyone up to date on the weather. Lots of fishermen listen in".

"Do you get requests from them, at all?"

"What, like anything by the Average Whiting Band?" chuckled Charlie.

"Or Cod Stewart?"

"Or New Years Ray by U2?"

"Or Stair Ray to Heaven by Led Zeppelin".

They both dissolved into laughter.

"Very good, Philip. I once worked as a gag writer for Jimmy Tarbuck, you know. Great man, Jimmy. Marvellous wit about him".

Charlie nodded in the direction of the two technicians.

"This is Dave and Dave. The little guy at the back is Big Dave. This monster here is Little Dave".

"Hi" they said in unison.

"They're the back room boys. Without them there would be no show would there?".

"No, Charlie" they piped back.

"This is number one studio. Number two is just a little way back down the corridor. I don't use that place. Nasty little cupboard".

He coughed.

"Listen" he said continuing," there are a few minutes before the show, how do you fancy a quick drink in my office".

"That would be lovely," said Philip.

Here, though Philip, was a genuine man, a man after his own heart.

They made their way back down the corridor a little and entered a side office. Charlie beckoned Philip to take a seat and closed the door behind them. Charlie sat down behind his desk and pulled out a small flask.

"Just the thing to calm a few nerves" he said with childish delight.

Charlie pulled out two glasses and poured equal amounts into each one. He nudged the glass forward in Philip's direction. Taking the hint, Philip raised the glass to his nose. Scotch. He took a sip and relished the warming fluid tumbling down his throat.

"Excellent!" he concluded.

Charlie gave him a big beaming smile, his face becoming that of a naughty schoolboy in the process of doing something that is so wrong, yet is such good fun.

They merrily chatted on for a few minutes: Charlie recounting tales of his radio days and Philip countering with slightly exaggerated stories of his time in the Navy.

Presently, there was a knock on the door, which opened to reveal Little Dave filling the whole void.

"Five minutes, Charlie" he said, slowly, as if he had trouble with words.

"Ah, our audience awaits. Come, come, we must not disappoint them".

Philip was feeling great. Charlie had relaxed him entirely. He was now looking forward to an interesting experience.

They arrived in the studio. Charlie beckoned Philip to a chair and asked him to put on the headphones. Charlie sat on the other side of a desk and did the same. Big Dave mouthed the countdown from the other side of the glass. Charlie gave Philip a cheery thumbs up sign.

Suddenly, a red light flicked on overhead and a heavenly choir sang 'Brodag FM'.

"Good Morning and welcome to Brodag FM. This is Charlie Bright and I'll be with you through until eleven o'clock".

"Charlie BRIGHT-IGHT-IGHT-IGHT-IGHT" went the jingle.

"I have for you, today, a very special guest, our new Governor - Philip Digby-Fischer. Governor, good morning".

"Good morning, Charlie, and please call me Philip".

"Great. So, Philip, how are you settling in?"

"Fine, Charlie. I came across at the weekend and, although its early days yet, I must admit that I'm enjoying it".

"And who wouldn't, given the privileges that you will enjoy as Governor".

"Quite" said Philip. "I know that I've got a lot of hard work to do over the coming months and years. I'm looking forward to the challenge".

"But don't you think that the concept of Governor is a bit outdated, a bit antiquarian in this modern day world in which we live in?"

"Well, I don't think......".

"Don't you consider it to be a hang-up from Britain's colonial past, when a gunboat up the Zambezi was enough to quell a local uprising?"

"Well, I'm sure that....".

"Keep the natives in their place. Don't let them think that they are capable of governing themselves. Kill all free thinking and enslave the masses".

"Well, Charlie....".

Philip looked across at Charlie who was looking down reading his script. This was not turning out how it was supposed to.

"And let's turn back to these privileges of yours, Governor. Is it true that the island is being levied by the British Government to finance your appointment".

"I'm....I'm not sure...".

"Come on, Governor, the people of St Brodag's want to know. Are we being levied to pay for your appointment?"

Philip began to sweat profusely. Drips began to trickle down from his forehead. He looked back across at Charlie who still had his nose in his script.

"This really isn't a matter for....".

"Answer the question, Governor. Are we paying for you?"

"I've really no...".

"I won't go away, Governor. Are we paying a levy to finance you being here?"

"I DON'T KNOW," screamed Philip. He looked up. Both Big and Little Dave were looking at him through the glass, their mouths wide open. Charlie continued to read his script.

"Thank you for your honesty. So what else 'don't you know'? Can you confirm that the British Government will release funds frozen in the last round of finance talks at the EC?"

"I don't know the answer to that particular question but...."

"Can you confirm that the British Government is committed to maintaining the island's special status within the umbrella of the EC?"

"No, I'm afraid that...."

"Can you confirm that the people of St Brodag's will not be sacrificed in the next high level discussions on fishing policy within the remit of the European Union Fisheries Policy review?"

"I cannot categorically say at this point - but what I will say...."

"It seems to me, Governor, that the sole purpose of your appointment is to prepare the people of St Brodag's to be sacrificial lambs on the altar of Britain's determined integration within the European Union. You haven't said anything today to make me, or the listeners, think anything else".

Philip sat back, barely controlling his anger. This had turned so.... paxmanesque. Should he walk out? No, that would play into that miserable bastard's hands. He needed to fight.

Just then, when it really wasn't needed, the voice of the Fat Man popped into his head. *Don't bugger it up.* He determined to fight.

"Well, I don't think that the listeners have heard my voice at all today. I'm afraid that all they have heard is your voice. Now, may I please say something?"

There was a pause. Dead time. It seemed to last for a century.

"Of course" said Charlie.

"Good. Well, what I really want to say is........"

Then, a slow, creeping dread began to take over Philip, like a big blanket to smother him.

His mind went completely blank.

Silence. Dead air.

Philip began to shuffle in his chair. He tried to speak on several occasions but no words emerged.

Finally, he sat back and hung his head.

Looking up from his script for the very first time, Charlie said "Thank you, Governor, for sharing those thoughts with us".

Philip caught his eye and Charlie looked away.

"That was Philip Digby-Fischer, our new Governor".

'BRODAG FM' sang the chirpy jingle.

Philip's sense of shame and embarrassment now gave way to rage. He took his headphones off and threw them across the table. Then, he jumped to his feet, waving his arms about wildly.

"What the hell was that all about? Eh? What the hell were you trying to do to me?"

No reply.

"Oh yes, butter me up first, why don't you. Make me feel at ease. Let me drop my defences then...BOOM. Just what the hell were you playing at. It's not that this is anywhere special, is it? This isn't Broadcasting House. This is a shitty little radio station in a shitty little building on a shitty little island. What were you trying to do?"

Still no reply.

"It's not like I wanted to come here. I had no choice. It was either here or lose my job. Do you have any idea about how that makes me feel?"

The silence continued.

"I wanted somewhere bigger, hotter, more prestigious, not this pile of turd in the North Sea populated by people who think that a cousin is a distant relative. I've never seen a more inbred bunch of idiots. But, oh, get a decent guest on your radio show and its 'lets get the knives out'. You ask me what the British Government want to do with this place? Well, shall I tell you? They don't give a shit about what happens to you or this crummy piece of rock. They don't care, they just don't care".

Philip looked at Charlie who was staring back at him, open-mouthed. Outside, the two Daves looked aghast. Then Philip followed the direction their eyes were pointing in and saw the red light still flickering above them.

"And now, 'Wichita Line Man' by Glen Campbell" whispered Charlie.

When Philip turned up in Henry Geruish's office at Government House, he was beside himself with both anger and embarrassment.

"You have got yourself into a bit of a pickle" said Geruish, a deep chuckle emanating from deep within his chest.

"I didn't know the microphones were still on, did I? I mean. What the hell was all that? All those questions. It was like being grilled by the KGB. I don't know why he didn't just connect a set of electrodes to my testicles and let rip".

"You should have asked him for a list of questions beforehand. Then you would have known what was coming".

"Now you tell me. What a little shit! What a little shit!"

Geruish waited patiently as Philip's tirade continued.

"What am I going to do, Henry? What can I do?"

Geruish smiled.

"I think that we're going to have to put a bit of spin on this one, aren't we?"

"How?"

Geruish chuckled again.

"I'll use my contacts in the press. We'll put out a story that some madman impersonated you in the radio interview. Charlie was completely hoodwinked. Of course, you'll have to go on air again, repeat the interview".

Philip looked at Geruish strangely.

"Do you think they'll believe that story?"

"Philip" said Geruish with a smile. "This is St Brodag's Isle. They'll believe anything we choose to tell them".

"OK. I find your cynicism disturbing but I'll go along with it".

"Good. Anyway, Philip, I'll ring Charlie and tell him of your displeasure. We'll sort it all out, don't worry".

"Good. I don't want to make an arse of myself in this job. I want to have the people's respect". He checked his watch. "Must go. Mrs Kinloss is cooking broth for lunch and I daren't be late. See you later. I'll phone".

"Bye" said Geruish as Philip rushed out of the office.

He picked up the phone and dialled a number.

"Charlie? Is that you? Good. Thanks for that. I owe you one".

Geruish replaced the receiver and threw his head back, laughing heartily.

Lying Low

'Not all is as it seems to be' - St Brodag

Philip decided that it was wise to lie low after the radio incident. On the Friday, instead of holding the meeting of the Trade Committee, he spent the day not answering the telephone at Ash-Na-Garoo. Mary was good about things and Nigel thought that it was all positively hysterical. Mrs Kinloss did not venture an opinion but for the next few days the standard of food in the house deteriorated markedly.

Amanda called around in the evening. She did her best to raise his spirits. They watched television for a while and ate a bowl of twiglets but Philip's heart really wasn't in it.

"I've made an arse of myself again, haven't I?"

"Well" said Amanda " I can either say 'yes' or 'no'. The honest answer is 'yes' but if 'no' will make you feel better then I can always lie".

"I'd rather you didn't. I really didn't mean half the things I said".

"No, I know that. But it's true, though, you had to come here, didn't you?"

Philip nodded.

Amanda looked at him and decided that he was about to disappear up his own backside in self pity unless she did something.

"Poor old Philip" said Amanda with a frown. "Your life is really shit, isn't it? Marriage down the pan, job you hate, island you loathe - who'd be you?"

Philip looked up at her.

"Are you taking the piss?"

"Excessively!" she admitted. "Come on, it's not the end of the world. My Dad will sort it out for you. By the end of next week, everyone will have forgotten it, I'm sure".

"Hope so".

Philip kept his low profile for the whole of that first full weekend. He phoned Patricia - twice - and spoke to her - once. Apparently, there was a big bash on at Toby Blackford's that weekend and Patricia was going to that.

"He's ordered these ice statues in the shape of Greek gods. Bloody marvellous, that Toby. Thinks of everything".

Philip met up with Nigel for Sunday lunch. They went to a pub near Cragmuir to watch the football. It was a poor game. They emerged at ten o'clock, stumbled into taxis and went home.

The next week passed without incident. The pathway to the observation point for the kittiwakes was ongoing, the workmen battling hard against the elements. The observation hut was half built by the end of the January and a couple of barns at the bottom of the pathway had started to be modernised to house the restaurant and museum.

Philip's only concern was the tender for providing the food at the restaurant. They had only one application and that was from George at the Ship Inn. Philip was not keen but Nigel convinced him that George would be OK.

"He's not poisoned anyone in ages" said Nigel. "He's got some great ideas. He wants to call it the Kittiwake Cafe and have pictures on the walls".

"That confirms my worst fears," said Philip.

However, since no one else had come forward, George won the tender.

Philip's investiture went well. Patricia couldn't make it. She had already promised Imelda that she would accompany her on a day out to Cheltenham that day and, of course, Philip would understand how disappointed she would be if Patricia was to let her down.

"What about me?" asked Philip.

Patricia went silent on the other end of the phone for a moment then tutted.

"Honestly, Philip. You're so selfish at times".

Philip was now officially Governor of the island and that rather pleased him. He had enjoyed the pomp and ceremony immensely.

"Just wait until Assembly Day," said Henry to him after the investiture had finished.

"What's that?" asked Philip.

"Biggest day in the Brogadan calendar. You and me and every other Tom, Dick and Harry get to dress up like a bunch of pansies and mince around like idiots. Still, everyone gets a day off, so I suppose it does some good".

"I'll look forward to it. When is it?"

"Second Thursday in May".

"Great".

On the occasions when Philip went on a trip to check on the progress of the project, he would often find George there before him, hustling and bustling and generally getting in the way. The Ship had become Philip's second home and he would often meet Nigel in their after work. Sometimes, Amanda would join them and Philip would love these evenings best of all. She was witty, bright, funny and attractive. During the nights when Philip was there just with Nigel, he would often turn towards the door on hearing it open, hoping that it was Amanda who was on her way in.

"Aw, I'm well made up" said George on one day, when the roof had just been fitted to the restaurant. "I've racked my brains for this one, Governor, I really have".

"How long did that take?"

"About five min....yer what?"

"Nothing, George. I'm glad to see you've got so much enthusiasm for the project".

"Well, Governor, I have to admit that without you, I wouldn't have had the confidence to go out on a limb for this one. I really admire you, I do".

"Why?"

"On two accounts. Firstly, I think it was disgusting that that Charlie Bright character allowed that man on his show impersonating you. I mean, like, it didn't even sound like you. A lot of people would have been embarrassed and kept their heads down but not you - no way. You're out and about like a trooper".

"And the second thing?" asked Philip wearily.

"I reckon that you're my lucky mascot. You remember that Romanian Champagne I asked you about. Well, I bought as much of it as I could. It's great tasting wine, that is. Mind you, not quite as nice as a bottle of that Spumante stuff, but what do you expect for one pound fifty a bottle? I've sold cases of that stuff, I have. Just so happens a Romanian cargo ship pulled in to the harbour the other day to repair an engine. They wiped me out of the stuff. Bloody brilliant. So, I've decided to make you my unofficial business consultant. It has to be unofficial, like. I wouldn't want the government finding out or anything. We might both get into trouble for that insider dealing. You know, like that Nick Leesom bloke".

"I'll bear it in mind, George. Hush-hush. You don't tell anyone and you can be sure that I won't".

"It's a deal" said George.

"Now I've got to be getting back". He winked at George. "Government business".

"Oh, aye" said George winking back. "Government business".

Nigel wrote to the RSPB suggesting a date in March for a visit by the Special Committee that had responsibility for the kittiwake. Within a few days, one David Brannigan had written back saying that they would be delighted to officially open the new observation hut and associated facilities.

"I've met him" said Nigel.

"What's he like?"

"Tosser!"

Despite this opinion, Philip was ecstatic that at least something he was involved with was working.

In his fifth week on the island, Philip repeated his radio interview. This time, there was no laughter, no drinks and no aggravation. A list of the questions appeared on Philip's desk two days before the interview was to take place. A muted Charlie Bright did not once deviate from the script and the whole episode passed off with no further problems.

One afternoon in the middle of February, just before sunset, Philip drove down to the beach where the seal colony lay. He walked out over the golden sand and soon came to the waters edge. Away, out to sea, a large tanker passed by, its lights already shining out in the half gloom. A little nearer the shore, a family of seals played in the surf.

As the sun dipped below the horizon, Philip breathed the cold air and did not wish to be anywhere else on earth.

The restaurant and the museum were finished in the first week of March, which was good, considering that the RSPB were due the following week.

Philip and Nigel wandered around the site. They took the pathway up to the headland and clambered into the observation hut. They opened the slit-like windows on the far side, nearest the birds, and could see them plainly, nestling on the cliffs or taking to the air and gliding down to the sea.

"Do you know" said Philip turning to Nigel "I feel so good that we're actually contributing to the preservation of this bird".

Nigel nodded. "I know what you mean. It gives me a lot of satisfaction".

"How many of them are left?"

Nigel shrugged his shoulders.

"Forty. Fifty. Something like that".

Philip whistled.

"Not many then".

They left the hut and walked back down the pathway. Halfway down, they met George on his way up.

"Morning, Governor" he called cheerily.

"Hello there, George" responded Philip. "You must be getting excited now".

"Aw, yes. I can hardly keep it in. Next Thursday's the big day, isn't it , Nige?"

"Sure is" said Nigel. "Will you be ready for it?"

"Of course" said George. "I must admit, though. I think I've surpassed myself with my ideas for the lunch when the RSPB arrive. It'll be a right special meal and no mistaking".

"Look forward to it" said Philip with a chuckle. "Must be off".

"See you".

"Bye".

Philip and Nigel continued their descent and came, at last, to the museum and restaurant which they inspected and, finding everything in order, they got in the car and made their way back to the office.

Later that day, Philip, Nigel and Mary were in a meeting to finalise the plans for the RSPB visit.

"So, Nigel, you've sorted out the displays with the various schools?"

"Yes. They all know what they have to do".

"Good. What about the band?"

"They'll be there" confirmed Nigel.

"The platform at the docks?"

"No problem".

Philip looked out the office window at a dull, breezy day.

"Hope the weather's good" he said.

"I'm sure it will be" said Mary. "There's a high coming in from Scandinavia. It should settle over us here over the weekend bringing dry but bitterly cold weather. We should expect frosts and the possibility of fog".

Philip looked at her.

"GMTV?"

"They never get it wrong" affirmed Mary.

Philip smiled.

"Well, I hope they're right. I don't mind the cold as long as it's dry".

"Don't worry. It will be".

Philip turned to Nigel.

"Is there anything that we've forgotten?"

"Don't think so" said Nigel. "Mary's sending out the invitations for lunch tomorrow".

"Have you found out, yet, what George is planning?"

"Won't let me have the menu. Says it will spoil the surprise".

"I should start to panic" said Philip.

"You leave the worrying to me" said Nigel. "It's my baby".

Philip looked at him, a frown spreading across his brow.

"OK. Just keep me informed".

Mary and Nigel got up to leave when Mary remembered something.

"You two are coming out tomorrow night for my birthday, aren't you?"

Both Philip and Nigel nodded.

"Good. It's just a few friends. I've invited Amanda Geruish, Philip. Someone for you to chat too".

Nigel sniggered then left.

Not far from where Philip, Nigel and Mary were talking, Henry Geruish and Old Ted were standing in a field, deep in conversation.

"I tell you, it's broken".

"You're not trying hard enough" said Geruish.

"Don't you dare say that to me. You know that I'm as committed to this as you are".

"Yes, Ted" said Geruish. "But I've got more to lose than you".

They fell silent.

Geruish nodded to a pine plantation on the far side of the field.

"Has Digby-Fischer been up here snooping again?"

"No. I shouldn't think I'll see him again. Scared him half to death, I did. Do you think he'll be a problem elsewhere?"

"No".

"Are you sure?"

"Look" said Geruish angrily. "Leave him to me. I have got connections. Digby-Fischer won't be around for very long to trouble us".

Old Ted laughed.
"You think of everything, you do, you devious bastard".
"I try my best".

A Girl's Night Out

'Celebrate tonight, come on' - St Brodag

Mary's birthday celebration started at the Ship at seven o'clock. This was going to be Philip's first heavy bash on the island and he was unsure of what to expect. He had noticed that Brogadans loved their beer and could drink it in great quantities.

He sat next to Amanda who was on good form.

"Look at her" said Amanda nodding to where Mary sat with a few of her old school friends. "Little Miss Snow White. If she was any more pure she'd be on television advertising soap powder. Little Nanette Newman, that's what she is".

"You're only jealous" countered Philip. "You can feel middle age fast approaching".

"Hark at you, Old Father Time" said Amanda. "When I'm your age I'll worry, thank you very much". She grimaced. "Bet she's not been laid yet".

"Bet she has" said Nigel, butting in.

Amanda and Philip turned to look at him.

"Not you?" asked Philip.

"No, not me" said Nigel wistfully. "It was Barry Larsen. Seems like Mary didn't want to be left out. So, she agreed that Barry could do the dirty deed if, and only if, they did it doggy-fashion so that she didn't have to look at him".

"Bloody hell" said Amanda.

"It isn't the most sophisticated island in the world, is it" said Philip.

"There's hope for the girl yet. What's your favourite position?" asked Amanda of Nigel.

"Bloody anything. I'm just grateful for every scrap I get".

"You're disgusting" said Amanda. "No wonder you don't get anywhere. You've no understanding of what a woman wants".

Nigel looked hurt.

"I tried to get in touch with my feminine side, once" he said.

"Did you?" asked Philip.

"Yeah, but it kept on bollocking me for going out to the pub every night".

They all laughed.

"Time to go to the Bistro" yelled Mary pulling a party popper.

"Great" said Amanda.

The Quayside Bistro was one of the most popular restaurants on the island. It sold good, basic food and good, cheap wine.

Mary's party was shown to a table at the rear of the main dining room. By the time they had all sat down and had enjoyed their first round of drinks, they were all in the mood to party. The starters came and went in a flurry. The main courses were eaten quickly, in between slurps of the house red. Philip poured some of the wine onto the back of his hand to see if he was allergic to it. He wasn't.

Amanda sat next to Philip. Philip felt very relaxed in her presence. She always seemed so calm and unruffled. Every now and then, the very edges of their legs would meet, as they shuffled on their seats. To Philip, the touch felt like electricity.

Puddings and coffee came and went. They settled the bill, found their coats and left, braving the battering winds outside.

"Well, I guess that's it" said Amanda. "I'll be off".

"You can't go yet. We've still got to go to the Fisherman's" said Mary.

Amanda grimaced.

"Not there, surely. It's ages since I've been there. I'd better go home".

"No you shouldn't" said Mary. "Tell her, Philip. She's got to come".

Philip turned to her and held out his arms.

"Apparently, you've got to come".

Amanda looked at him.

"Do you know what you're letting yourself in for? Do you know what the Fisherman's is?"

Philip swayed a little and smiled.

"Not a clue".

Amanda sighed.

"Oh, all right then. Somebody's got to look after you".

She hooked her arm around his and dragged him after the rest of the party. Nigel lagged behind, stumbling along at his own place.

The Fisherman's Bar was situated in the Plough Hotel on the main promenade. The Plough Hotel had seen better days and was known as quite a seedy establishment. To get to the Fisherman's Bar, you had to climb up a long, wide staircase from the hotel lobby. You were then faced by what could only be described as a student-like bar, with a counter down the full length of one side. At the far end was a small, raised area with a dance floor in front of it. To the left of the door was a side room that was invariably inhabited by ex-pat geordies and known as 'Oor Jackie's Snug'. The bar was dark and full and very, very noisy.

"Do you like it?" asked Amanda.

"Sorry?" said Philip.

"DO YOU LIKE IT IN HERE?"

Philip pulled a face.

"It's.........interesting".

Amanda nodded.

Mary and her old school friends had already pushed forward and were now on the dance floor, moving smoothly to a series of 1960's hits.

Philip looked around the place and observed that the clientele was rather older than he had imagined. There was one old lady, in particular, who seemed to be clutching onto a half pint of mild as though it was one of the crown jewels. Philip watched her all evening and at no time did she ever drink from it or renew it. Elsewhere, whole families seemed to be present from young children to great-grandmothers and each one took a turn on the dance floor.

There was a blast of feedback over the sound system. Philip looked up to see a man in his fifties and wearing a scarlet baseball cap at the centre of the stage. He tapped the microphone.

"Is that on, Ted?" he asked of someone to one side.

"Get on with it, you tit" shouted someone from the crowd.

"Who said that?" asked the man at the microphone. "I'll bar you, you bastard".

He regained his composure. Nigel appeared and thrust double whiskies into Amanda and Philip's hands.

"Right" said the man on the stage. "It's time for our main feature, tonight. You know them, you love them. Please give a warm welcome to *Rowdy Scythe*". He left the stage applauding.

Rowdy Scythe took their places. The group comprised of a man in his forties on the synthesiser, a woman who must have been his mother on the accordion, and a man who was obviously a close relative on the electric violin.

"It's like the Adams family" called Amanda.

The keyboard player hit a button and a synthetic beat began.

"I'm Ron" he said.

"I'm Sheila" said the woman.

"And I'm Randy" said the violinist.

"And together" continued Ron on the keyboards, "we're Rowdy Scythe".

The bar erupted into applause, catching Philip off guard with their raw enthusiasm.

"We're Rowdy Scythe and this is Radio Ga Ga".

The band launched into the first few bars of the famous Queen hit. Philip's eyes opened as wide as they could. He pinched himself to make sure that he was awake.

"All we hear is (clap, clap) - Radio Ga-Ga (clap, clap) - Radio Goo-Goo, (clap, clap), Radio Ga-Ga".

"It gets better" shouted Amanda to him, seeing his concern.

And, surprisingly, it did. They rattled off a couple of Slade hits, 'Every Breath you Take' by the Police, and then went into a medley of Beatles' numbers. By the time that Ron was singing "I am the Egg Man" he had the audience eating out of his hands.

They took a short break and then were back.

"There's a special lady in here tonight" announced Ron. "She's called Mary and she's twenty today".

There was a huge amount of cheering at this.

"We dedicate the next one to her. Here goes. This is *Paranoid*".

And off they went into the old Black Sabbath number, the electric violin shirking and howling as Randy gave it his all.

"This is unbelievable" said Philip staring at everything around him.

"It's your worst nightmare" growled Nigel.

Rowdy Scythe stretched the number to twenty minutes after which most of the audience went off to the bar to cool down.

"I'm OK until they play Status Quo" said Amanda.

Philip looked at her strangely.

"It does things to me" she admitted.

"It's lovely to be here tonight, rocking in Port Victoria" announced Ron. "But do you know what? It's even better to be Rocking All Over the World". As he said this, he attacked the keyboard with gusto.

Amanda sighed.

"Oh, bollocks".

She threw her coat down and dragged Philip forward through the crowd onto the empty dance floor. She took up a position right in the middle of the space, leaving Philip hovering on the side. She opened her legs wide, formed a guitar with her arms, and began to play air guitar along with Rowdy Scythe, her long curling hair bouncing from side to side.

Philip looked at her, embarrassed as hell. She looked at him and beckoned him to her.

"I like it, I like it, I like it, I like it, I li-li-li-like it, li-li-li-like it and oh, oh, rocking all over the world" sang Ron.

Philip stepped forward and took a position mirroring Amanda but standing back to back with her. He felt a prat and totally self conscious. Then he looked around. Nigel was there and he gave Philip a thumbs up sign.

Philip stretched out his left arm and began to strum with his right hand.

"Bloody hell" said Amanda half twisting around. "This is the Quo not George Formby. Give it some welly".

Philip obliged.

Amanda swung round and stood at Philip's side. She motioned for him to copy her. She swung her imaginary guitar from the side to the front and back again. Philip did the same. She backed into him and he could feel the curve of her buttocks in his groin. Her hair hit his face from time to time and, as it did, he breathed in the scent of her shampoo.

"Fun, isn't it" she shouted.

You don't know the half of it, he thought.

"Yes, great. I haven't realised just what I've been missing all my life" he said sarcastically.

The music finished and the crowd applauded.

"Time to go" said Philip.

"Not yet" said Amanda pulling him back by the hand.

"Now, I've had the time of my life" crooned Ron, "and I've never felt this way before".

Amanda smiled at him, a mad look in her eyes.

"Stand still. Don't budge" she demanded. Philip obliged.

Amanda slinked away and stood about an arm's length in front of him. Then, she took a step forward, in time to the music, and twisted down to the floor, her head at the same height as Philip's groin. She then slowly twisted back to her feet. She did this three times.

Sheila began to sing the female part in a thin, wavery voice.

"I owe it all to you"

Amanda danced around Philip as a crowd formed a clapping circle around them.

I do not want to be here, thought Philip.

Amanda jinked backwards and forwards, sometimes touching him, sometimes teasing him by backing off at the last minute.

Then, she jigged away to the far side of the dance floor. Philip looked at her.

"Catch me!" she bellowed as she came hurtling towards him.

Oh fuck, thought Philip as Amanda leapt into the air and blackness surrounded him. He threw his hands into the air and, somehow, managed to both catch her and hold onto her as she stretched out her arms above his head. Her breasts hung down into his face and the thought he was going to suffocate until she shouted 'down' and he popped her onto her feet.

Again, the bar exploded into applause. Nigel gave Philip a wink as several people stepped forward to pat Philip on the back.

"Philip and Amanda" screamed Ron. "Our Governor and the Prime Minister's daughter. Give it up for them. Come on".

The next song was YMCA which meant another few minutes on the dance floor for Philip.

She is definitely mad, said Philip to himself as his arms formed a letter 'M' in the air.

The rest of the evening passed in a similar vein. Rowdy Scythe played all the old classics and Amanda wouldn't let Philip slink off to the bar for a refill.

"Now. Let's slow it up for our final number" announced Ron. "Everyone grab a partner".

Philip looked down at Amanda. The hair around her face was damp. She looked back at him. All around the sick, the old and the infirm were pairing off.

"Whiskey" she said slowly. He nodded and they went off towards the bar.

Philip and Amanda shared a taxi on their way home having said goodbye to Mary and her friends inside the Plough. Mary was evidently out of it. She had tried to use her tongue when Philip had kissed her goodbye. When he mentioned this to Amanda she told him not to worry because she had done the same thing to her.

Nigel had disappeared. Philip wasn't too worried. He was used to Nigel by now and knew that he would turn up eventually.

At Ash-Na-Garoo, the taxi stopped.
"Well, this is it" said Philip.
"Yes" said Amanda.
Silence.
"Thank you for.....an evening" he said eventually.
She stole a sly look at him.
"Bye then" he said. He leaned forward and kissed her on the cheek.
"Goodnight, Philip. Sleep well".

That night, Philip dreamed of Amanda and Amanda, to her astonishment, dreamed of Philip. Somewhere, out there, their dreams met and ran wild for a while.

Long Live The Kittiwake

'And when I was lonely, my friend, the kittiwake, talked to me' - St Brodag

The day of the visitation by the Special Committee of the RSPB dawned bright and crisp. The previous night, Philip had looked out of the windows of Ash-Na-Garoo and had seen dark clouds gathering in the West. Nothing, however, came of them and Philip secretly resolved to watch more breakfast television.

Philip was down at the docks in plenty of time ensuring that all was ready. A small platform had been raised in a large space on the quayside. A huge sign saying 'WELCOME RSPB' had been erected above the platform and long lines of bunting were draped between lamp posts. Three grandstands had been erected in front of the platform to form a square. Beyond the grandstands, a group of school children were running riot in and out of a small hut where their teachers were trying their best to maintain some degree of control. The Port Victoria Working Men's Brass Band were sitting on chairs to one side of the platform and were tuning up with great enthusiasm but little skill.

As Philip looked on, a man dressed as St Brodag, in sandals and habit, walked past, braving the cold weather.

"Bloody stupid idea" muttered the holy man as he flip-flapped towards the ferry terminal.

In the cold light of day, Philip probably agreed.

Slowly, the grandstands began to fill.

At ten o'clock, Nigel turned up and started hurrying around shouting at people and handing out hastily photocopied timetables for the celebrations. At ten-thirty, *The Spirit of St Brodag* came into view around the headland and at 11 o'clock precisely, the ferry was safely berthed, bobbing and swaying in its usual alarming way.

Philip watched as the doors opened and the vehicles emerged into the sunlight one by one. In the distance, he could see St Brodag waving cheerily as each car and lorry drove past. Presently, the Volvo Estate of the Special Committee came into view and was waved into a space near to where Philip and the rest of the group stood.

First out of the car was David Brannigan, who exuded enthusiasm and excitement. He rushed over to Philip and Nigel and pumped hands. Behind him, came Colonel Arthur Sproggat, a retired army man and a bluff Yorkshireman. His handshake was firm and strong. Lastly, Lady Anthea Woodrow-Wilson, a frail old lady well into her eighties, pulled herself out of the car. She shook fingers and remarked how frightfully nice is was to be on firm ground again.

"If you would like to follow me" suggested Philip waving the committee forward to the small platform." We have prepared a small welcome".

The three dignitaries plus Philip and Nigel took their seats on the stage. Thick blankets had been provided for them all to wrap around their legs. Philip stood up and moved forward to a microphone.

"Ladies and Gentlemen. As Governor of St Brodag's Isle, it is both my honour and my privilege to welcome the members of the RSPB Special Committee to our shores". (*Muted applause*).

"We are here to celebrate our own St Brodag's Kittiwake, a rare and beautiful species of seabird".

"GET ON WITH IT" cried a voice.

"The history of this island has been intertwined with the fortunes of the kittiwake throughout its history, ever since St Brodag first talked to the birds in 899AD".

"BORING" shouted another voice.

"So" said Philip looking up and smiling, "without any further ado, let the festivities begin".

The band struck up and a group of children, dressed as kittiwakes came forward. They bowed, as instructed, and then began to perform a strange dance which seemed to involve them in running around and flapping their wings to no set pattern or rhythm. At the end of their spectacle, they bowed once more and left the arena to polite applause.

Then, further children came forward and read poems, praising the kittiwake.

As a grand finale, a huge inflatable kittiwake was revealed. The inflatable went soaring into the air, and was barely contained by the dozen men holding onto ropes on the ground below.

Then, David Brannigan stood forward and addressed the crowd.

"Thank you, thank you, for a wonderful welcome. I've been to this island so many times over the years and I have always been received warmly by you good people. We, as the Special Committee of the RSPB would like to thank you for all your efforts in protecting the kittiwake over the years. We look forward to seeing all the work that you have put in over the last few weeks and hope that this can be the beginning of a new chapter in the history of this quite remarkable bird. Thank you once again".

He stood back as the band played the Brogadan national anthem. Then, the committee members returned to their car and followed Nigel and Philip in the Bentley to the headland.

They parked by the restaurant and museum and took the path up the headland to the observation hut.

David Brannigan was very excited.

"You don't know what this means to me, Philip" he said as they climbed the path. "I've been coming here for twenty years, watching these glorious birds. I've been involved in the tagging operation as well. I know each one of the birds like a friend, all twenty breeding pairs. Do you know, there was a time, not all that long ago, when we thought that the bird would become extinct. We were down to only six pairs. That was about eighteen years ago. You can't believe what this day means to me, you really can't".

They came, at last, to the observation hut. It was a majestic setting, situated high on the headland near the cliffs where the birds nested. The hut had been constructed magnificently, with a turfed roof and front wall, ensuring that the kittiwakes could not tell that this was a building for humans.

At the entrance to the hut, a ribbon had been hung. Nigel brought out a pair of ceremonial silver scissors and offered them to Lady Anthea.

"I now declare this observation hut well and truly open". She snipped the ribbon and a ripple of polite applause went around the group.

Inside, the hut was plain but comfortable. Underfloor heating had been installed and this kept the temperature at a reasonable level. Five slit-like windows had been made in the far wall. These were opened and the guests move forward to see what they could.

The view was breathtaking. The cliffs could be seen in all their magnificence, a series of unlikely ledges sitting above a perilous drop. Only one thing was wrong: no kittiwakes.

"Can't see the buggers" murmured the Colonel.

"It is a little unusual" said David. "They must be feeding. If they come across a big shoal out in the bay then they might all disappear at the same time. Still, I would have expected to see one or two of them out here".

"Isn't that one of them" whispered Nigel.

The three special guests turned around to look at him.

"That, young man" said Lady Anthea "is a Common Gull".

The Colonel and David tutted and went back to their observations.

"Extraordinary" said David. "I can see their nests quite clearly. You really would expect to see one. Very friendly birds, the St Brodag Kittiwake".

They stood there for another fifteen minutes without seeing a single specimen.

"Never mind" enthused David. "I'm sure if we come back later we'll see lots of them. I must congratulate you on these facilities. Splendid. Splendid!"

"No bloody birds, though" chunnered the Colonel.

"Shall we go for lunch, then?" suggested Philip.

They all though that this was a capital idea. They left the hut and descended the path to the restaurant below.

While they had been away, a few extra people had turned up including Henry Geruish and Amanda. Philip introduced them to the guests before they all sat down in the restaurant itself. The decor of the main dining room was based around the kittiwake with large colour photographs of the bird adorning every wall.

As they were preparing to eat their first course, George crept out of the kitchen and wandered over to where Philip was sitting.

"Don't you worry about a thing" he whispered. "We've prepared a cracking meal for you". He gave a wink and sidled off back into the kitchen. A slight feeling of panic began to overtake Philip. He didn't know why but he just began to feel a little uneasy.

The first course was a simple egg mayonnaise served on a bed of young spinach leaves. A final dusting of paprika seemed to do the trick, introducing a sharp aftertaste to the dish. Light bread rolls, fresh from the oven, were served too.

"This is excellent" remarked David to Philip. "I've never tasted an egg mayonnaise with such flavour".

Philip nodded and smiled.

Across the table, Henry was busy flirting with Lady Anthea who would, from time to time, throw her arms in the air and dissolve into a high pitched, shrieking laugh.

The Colonel was deep in conversation with Nigel. Apparently, the Colonel knew the key to tuning around the fortunes of English Cricket and was busy letting Nigel in on the secret.

Philip caught Amanda's eye and, instead of smiling straight away, they just looked at each other for a fraction of a second. Then, they smiled, hesitantly though, as if by smiling they were somehow spoiling the moment.

The plates were cleared away.

"You know, Philip" said David " I am so glad that you yourself have taken such a personal interest in the Kittiwake. I have never been convinced that the government here has ever really been serious in preserving the bird. That fellow over there, Geruish, I'm convinced is the biggest rogue I have ever met. But you, Philip, you seem to have a very caring heart".

"Well" said Philip, rather taken aback "I'm just trying my best in my new position. St Brodag need the kittiwake, I must confess. It's not all done simply for the kittiwake's benefit".

"And I understand that Philip. But this is a prize project. Finance, preservation, government, tourism and the ornithologists' needs - all brought together in one project. I have to say, Philip, that I am impressed. Very impressed".

The dishes were being presented for the main course.

As soon as Philip saw what was on his plate, it all began to make sense to him. The reason for his feeling of panic became clear all too soon.

There, on the white porcelain plate, lay a small bird, about the same size as a pheasant.

As the waitresses placed potatoes and other vegetables on his plate, Philip just stared.

Next to him, David was soon tucking in.

"Oh, excellent, Philip. This bird is fantastic. What is it?"

Philip continued to stare at his plate.

Just at that moment, George emerged from the kitchens. David waved him over.

"I must say that this bird is truly remarkable. What is it?"

"Can you not guess?" asked George with a grin.

"Mmmm" said David. "It's too light to be pheasant. Quail?"

"No, man" said George with a self-satisfied smile on his lips.

The others had been listening and now joined in with some enthusiasm.

"Wood pigeon?" shouted the Colonel.

"Nope".

"Grouse?" proffered Lady Anthea.

"Nah".

At this point, Amanda, who was sat down the other end of the table, looked at Philip and it clicked. The colour drained from her face and she slowly slumped backwards in her chair.

"Look" said David "We're not having much luck here. Just tell us what it is, there's a good fellow".

George proudly drew himself up.

"It's Roast Kittiwake".

Silence.

More silence.

Bedlam.

"What the hell..!." started David, climbing to his feet.

"It can't be...." said Lady Anthea.

"You daft buggers" cried out the Colonel.

"Did you know about this?" asked David, turning on Philip.

"No" whispered Philip.

"What's the matter?" asked George nonplussed.

"Don't you realise what you've done?"

George shook his head.

"No. I just thought, you know, 'Kittiwake Cafe' - what can I serve that'll be special and unique. I know, I says to myself, serve up kittiwake. I've got a freezer full of them in there" he said, pointing back towards the kitchens.

David nearly fainted. He steadied himself by placing his hands on the back of his chair.

"How many.....have you......butchered?"

George began to count on his fingers.

"I make it about forty in all".

"Forty" shrieked Lady Anthea.

"Forty" said David, hanging his head.

Philip shifted awkwardly in his seat.

"Forty!" continued David. "The whole colony.....gone! I can't believe this, I really can't believe what I'm hearing. Were there any eggs left? We may be able to save the bird that way".

George winced.

"You just ate them as your starter".

David began to growl and launched himself at George who parried the blows and skipped back. Nigel grabbed hold of David and pulled him away.

"You animal. You animal!" shouted David.

"What's your problem?" asked George.

"I'm bloody upset" shouted David.

"You're upset!" said George. "You're upset! Just think what this does to my Summer trade!"

"You just have no idea of the damage that you have done. Just wait until I get back. I'm going to have you for this. All of you. My kittiwake...gone".

David broke down and began to sob. The Colonel marched over and patted him on the back.

"There, there, David".

He pulled out a large, spotted handkerchief and passed it to David who blew his nose noisily on it. He seemed to regain some of his composure.

"Are you all right?" asked George. "Shall I get you a drink?"

David stared at him.

"Leave me alone. You've done enough damage". He turned around to his fellow committee members.

"Come on, Colonel. Come on , Lady Anthea. We'll stay here no longer. Let's go".

"Don't you want to try my soufflé?" shouted George after them.

David stopped in the doorway of the restaurant and marched back over to where Philip sat. Philip inclined his head a little and raised an eyebrow.

"You should be ashamed of yourself. Call yourself a governor! You couldn't govern a public convenience. You should be shot!"

And with that, the Special Committee of the RSPB were gone.

The other guests also began to leave. George went back into the kitchen wandering what all the fuss was. Philip just sat there, looking at his feet.

He felt a hand on his shoulder.

"I'm sure it's not all that bad" whispered Amanda in his ear.

"I want to die" hissed Philip.

Amanda kissed him on the cheek, patted him on the shoulder and left. Her perfume lingered a while after she had gone. Philip breathed deeply, savouring the scent.

Geruish wandered over to him and began to chuckle.

"I have to give it to you, Philip. When you fuck up, you fuck up big time".

Philip looked at him.

"I didn't know, Henry. I didn't see the menu beforehand. What can I do?"

Geruish looked puzzled for a moment.

"This time, Philip, I'm not sure. We might just have to sit this one out. You never know, it might just blow over".

When Philip made it back to his office that night, the phone had not stopped ringing all afternoon. Apparently, there being no news at that moment in time, television crews were expected on the morning ferry from the BBC, ITN and

CNN. Nigel went off to the pub and was out of his mind by six o'clock. Philip went up to his bedroom and just lay there.

Aftermath

'I heard the sound of silence'- St Brodag

Philip looked out of his bedroom window and saw the tribe of journalists, cameramen, photographers and sound-recordists waiting on the gravel outside the front door.

Nigel came up and stood beside him. He stank of beer and cigarettes and looked a worse mess than normal.

"They look ready to tear us apart" he said. "Like a pack of wolves".

Philip nodded.

"What shall we do, Philip?" asked Nigel.

"I've got no idea".

"Perhaps they'll go away soon".

"Perhaps".

Mary burst into the room.

"Turn your TV on. Look at this".

Philip turned and pressed a button on the remote control.

"Which channel?"

"GMTV".

Philip hit the '3' button and sighed.

There, on screen, stood George with the inflatable kittiwake that had been used at the previous days celebration. George was carrying a large inflatable axe and was mimicking chopping the bird's head off.

"I can't believe this" said Philip, flopping onto a chair.

"Quick" said Mary, "turn up the volume".

George was being interviewed.

"Your operation was officially sanctioned by the government?" asked the interviewer.

"Aye. I had to put a tender in for the place and everything".

"And no-one told you that the bird was an endangered species?"

"No. They're a bloody pest. My mate Pete is always complaining that they (*bleep*) on his car".

"And how exactly did you kill them?"

George smiled.

"I put my hands round their necks, just like this, and pulled. Lovely job. Did them all in about half an hour. Easy as anything".

The interviewer paused.

"You do realise what you have done, don't you? The St Brodag Kittiwake has now joined the Dodo and the Great Auk as an extinct species".

George shook his head.

"I don't know about that. All I know is that I've got a restaurant to run. I take my inspiration from our new Governor".

Philip groaned.

"Would that be Governor Digby-Fischer?"

"Aye. Champion man. He's behind all this. Gave me the job, did the Governor".

Philip switched the television off.

"It goes from bad to worse" he said.

"That's the last time I'll go for a drink in The Ship" said Nigel with some determination.

"George barred you last week, Nigel, don't you remember?"

"Oh, aye".

Philip sighed again. He had decided on a course of action.

"I need to go out there and make a statement. Short and sweet. Let's get it all over with. I'll need ten minutes on the computer".

Philip walked out of his bedroom to his office. He sat down at the desk and began to type on the keyboard. Mary and Nigel followed him through and hung around, awkwardly, as he typed. Mrs Kinloss turned up with some tea and toast and declared that this kitchen had never seen such goings on before and probably will never do so again.

After a few minutes, Philip pressed a key and the laser printer clicked into life and began to spew out a couple of pages. Philip picked them up and gave one to Mary and Nigel to read.

"Well" said Philip. "What do you think of that?"

Mary looked at Nigel. Nigel looked at Mary. They both looked at Philip.

"They'll eat you up" said Nigel.

"It's not quite right" said Mary.

Philip yanked the piece of paper out of their hands and went back to the computer. After a short while, another speech had been written.

"Too wishy-washy" said Mary.

"Not quite there yet" suggested Nigel.

Back to the computer for the third draft.

"Too aggressive" said Mary.

"Do you have to mention me?" asked Nigel.

The fourth attempt was more successful and both Mary and Nigel agreed that, given the present circumstances, it was probably the best that they were going to be able to come up with.

Philip went back into his bedroom to find his jacket and then came back into his office. He pulled himself upright and tucked his stomach in.

"Let's go" he said and marched out of the office, down the corridor, down the steps and into the entrance hall. There, he paused.

Philip turned to Nigel.

"When I go out the door, lock it behind me. Don't let anyone else in the house".

Nigel nodded and shook his hand.

Mary reached up and kissed him.

"You're so brave" she said, a tear in her eye.

Nigel stood at the door, fingers on the lock.

"Now" said Philip and he started to stride forward.

Nigel threw the door open and shut it firmly again once Philip had left.

Outside, it was total chaos. Everyone started to shout and scream at once. Flash guns went off one after another. Huge, furry microphones were thrust in Philip's general direction. The rush forward carried Philip back at least ten paces.

"I have a statement that....." he started.

"Governor, what about.....can you tell us why......we need to know.......why.....why.....WHY......WHY......WHY??????????"

Philip could see that this was useless. He turned around and jumped onto the front door step. He held his hands out to try and calm the mob. Slowly, the volume began to subside.

"Listen. LISTEN!" he shouted. "I have a brief statement to make concerning the regrettable demise of the St Brodag Kittiwake".

"MURDERER!" shouted a voice form the back.

"Please, please. Hear me out!"

The noise decreased to a level at which Philip believed was tolerable. He looked around at the sea of faces. Most of them were unknown to him, off-islanders following a good story. Some he recognised as the local press. To one side, near the rear of the group, stood Charlie Bright and his sound-man.

Philip took a deep breath then began to read from the piece of paper that he held in his hand.

"Over the years, this island.....".

Suddenly, there was a roar of an engine and the screeching of brakes. A BMW Roadster flew across the gravel, barely missing some of the reporters. All eyes turned to the car. The driver's door opened and out jumped Amanda.

"Philip! Don't do that. Come with me" she shouted.

In an instant, Philip knew what to do. He tucked his speech inside his jacket pocket and ran like the clappers for the car. He pulled open the passenger's door and slid inside.

Amanda slammed the car in reverse and did a neat handbrake turn. Then, she was off down the road.

The members of the press started to run for their own transport and, pretty soon, a convoy of Range Rovers and Toyota Landcruisers were in hot pursuit of their quarry.

However, they didn't know the island like Amanda did and none of them possessed her driving skills. Soon, Amanda had lost them and they were able to slow down to a more reasonable speed.

"I couldn't let you go through that, Philip" confessed Amanda. "Not with everything else that's piling up on your shoulders".

Philip laughed.

"Did you know that you are one of the most amazing people that I have ever met? Do you have no shame?"

"You must remember, Mr Digby-Fischer. I <u>was</u> a medical student!"

Philip looked at her in admiration.

So different from Patricia, he thought. So very different.

Philip looked at her hands, her long fingers with the perfectly manicured nails. He noted her thin wrists that merged into long, thin arms. Her shoulders, her hair, her...

Philip caught himself daydreaming and put a stop to it. He was a married man and she the Prime Minister's daughter.

Sounds like the plot of some crappy airport novel, thought Philip.

A picture of Amanda's back viewed from behind a linen bin flashed into his mind. He noted the bone structure of her shoulder blades, the neat crescent where her back slid down into her....

Think of anything, Philip, he said to himself. Think of snow. Think of mountains. Think of a wall. Keep thinking, keep thinking, keep thinking.....of the smell of her perfume that seemed to fill a room and grow and spread and.....a wall.

It is a big wall made out of bricks. Bricks.....and her smile. What he wouldn't do to see that smile. The wide mouth, the slight creases at either end, the...wall!

"What are you thinking?" asked Amanda.

"Er, what...er, why?"

"You're twitching like you're agitated or something. If you're worried about those goons catching us I can tell you that I lost them. They'll not find you now".

"Yes" lied Philip. "That's what I was thinking of".

The car pulled off the main road a little south of Cragmuir and they headed inland.

"Where are we going?" asked Philip.

"We have a little cottage out here. It used to belong to my grandfather. We use it, now and then, when one of us wants to get away from it all. There's no electricity, no television and you have to draw the water from a well every morning but it'll give you a bit of time to yourself before you go back and face the music".

Philip shuddered.

"It sounds a bit bleak" he said. "At least I've got my mobile phone".

The car screeched to a halt.

"Where is it?" demanded Amanda.

"In my pocket".

"Give it to me!"

"Why?"

"Just do it!"

Philip pulled out the phone and handed it to Amanda. She pressed a button, lowering her window.

"Goodbye, phone" she said and lobbed it into a field.

Philip's mouth dropped open.

"What did you do that for?" demanded Philip.

"This doctor prescribes rest. It's too tempting with a phone. You'll be on it calling everyone within an hour".

Philip couldn't believe it.

"You are mad!"

"I know".

Amanda raised the window and they carried on their way.

They came at last to a small, stone building, sheltered by a group of bent and twisted oak trees. Amanda drove the car around the back of the house and pulled into a lean-to barn. She turned off the engine and turned to Philip.

"Welcome to Gar-my-medda" she said with a grin.

Gar-My-Medda

'Once I saw two peas in a pod' - St Brodag

"Smells like someone died in here". Philip wandered around the downstairs of the cottage with his nose turned up.

"Someone did die here" shouted Amanda from the kitchen.

"Who?"

"My grandfather. He was lying here for about three days before someone found him".

"Yeuk" exclaimed Philip. "Is that the smell?"

"No, you silly bugger" said Amanda walking into the room. "It's just a bit damp. It'll soon get better. What we really need to do is get the fire going".

There wasn't much to the cottage. A main living room and a kitchen downstairs and a couple of bedrooms upstairs.

"No loo?" asked Philip.

"No loo" confirmed Amanda. "There's a potty upstairs. Fill that if you have to and we'll bury it outside".

"Oh".

"Don't tell me you public school types weren't used to going camping".

"We went a lot" said Philip. "In fact, it was on such a camping trip that we found out that Mr Roberts wore women's underwear underneath his normal clothes".

"Really?"

"Yes. Claimed he had a hormonal imbalance that meant he was growing women's breasts".

"Was he?"

"Don't know, I didn't look. We just thought he was a bit of a tart. He didn't last much longer than a term after that".

Philip shook his head.

"Come on, Philip" said Amanda. "Let's go and bring some wood in and get this fire going".

At the rear of the lean-to, they found a store of dry wood. They loaded themselves up and carried the logs indoors. Philip made another two trips while Amanda started the fire.

Click, click. Some distance away a camera with a very long telephoto lens was taking pictures of Philip and Amanda together.

By late afternoon, they had sorted the cottage out as best they could. They had swept the floors, made up the two beds upstairs and brought the provisions in from the car. These involved a couple of sandwiches in triangular plastic boxes, two family sized packets of twiglets, a large tobelerone, a six-pack of bitter, and a couple of bottles of whiskey.

"I thought you were a doctor" said Philip. "Healthy balanced diet and all that".

"It's all bollocks anyway" said Amanda. "You're born, you live, you die. It happens to us all".

"What about that bloke in *Highlander*?"

"What about him?"

"Well he didn't die".

Amanda looked at Philip in puzzlement.

"What the hell are you talking about?"

"Doesn't matter".

"Anyway, I believe that you should eat or drink whatever you want to. Just do it in moderation".

"Says the woman who brought two bottles of whiskey along".

"I make an exception for whiskey" she said. "Come on, Philip, I'm getting thirsty. Get a couple of glasses from the cupboard over there and pour me a drink. A girl could die of thirst in here".

And so began the evening's drinking. The fire roared in the hearth and they had brought enough wood inside to keep it going all night.

Amanda was more than a match for Philip and knocked back the whiskey slowly but steadily throughout the evening.

The conversation got steadily sillier.

"Go on then" said Philip. "If you were a lesbian..."

"Which I'm not".

"Which you're not....not that there's anything wrong with them or anything....but, if you were a.....what was it?"

"A lesbian".

"Yeah, a lesbian, which one of Charlie's Angels would you have fancied?"

Amanda sucked at her teeth.

"Difficult one, that. I mean, Farrar Fawcett Majors became a gay icon".

"Did she?"

"Oh, yeah, I read it once in GQ. So, you have to say that she has an advantage over the other two".

"Other three" corrected Philip. "You're missing Cheryl Ladd who stepped in to fill Farrah's place. Alan Ladd's daughter apparently, you know - Shane"

"You're right. I'd forgotten her. Anyway, Kate Jackson was always firm and sensible. She was cool. And Jaclyn Smith had the best body of the lot. I'd go for Farrah, though".

"Why?"

"Well, if she was shagging the Six Million Dollar Man in real life, then she must be doing something right".

They both dissolved into giggles which eventually subsided and gave way to a thick, heavy silence.

"It's cold" shuddered Amanda.

They were sat at opposite ends of the same sofa, each covered in layers of blankets.

"Come on, then" said Philip, holding his right arm aloft. "Snuggle up".

Amanda shuffled down the sofa and put her head on his shoulder. Philip's arm fell onto her shoulder.

"Can I be blunt with you?" asked Amanda after a short silence.

"I wouldn't expect you to be anything else" said Philip.

"OK" said Amanda slowly. "I need to tell you something".

"Fire away".

"Well" she continued, "it's like this. I don't quite know where to start. I mean....you know, it's difficult sometimes to begin something".

"Evidently" he said with a smile.

"Better out with it, I suppose".

She paused and took a large gulp of whiskey.

"I'm really attracted to you but I don't know why?"

Philip thought for a moment.

"Sounds flattering. What do you mean?"

"I mean. Well, we're so different. We've got different backgrounds. You're a bit older than me. You've got your public school education and attitudes and you're basically so uncool that you're cool, if you know what I mean. You are so stiff and starchy most of the time. Having said that, you're a good laugh, too. Since you've been on the island, you've made so many cock-ups yet you're still going strong. You haven't really given up at all. You're basically a decent bloke, Philip, and there aren't many of those around".

Philip looked deep into the flames.

"How do you feel?" asked Amanda.

"Me? I feel very........married".

They fell silent. The fire spat and crackled in the hearth.

Philip's emotions were raw. He wanted Amanda so much. It would be very easy. Just lean down and kiss her on the neck. That would be a start. She'd respond. He would then unbutton her blouse. It wouldn't stop from then on. It would be so easy. So easy.

Why are you hesitating? he asked himself. Go for it.

I can't.

Why not?

Patricia.

Bollocks to Patricia! She doesn't care about you.

I care for her!

But you don't love her, not anymore.

I don't know.

What do you mean you don't know. This is Amanda. She's here for you. You want her. She wants you. Why are you waiting?

Patricia.

Fuck Patricia!

Eventually, Amanda smiled.

"It's not easy for you, this, is it?"

Philip shook his head.

"I thought you would feel that way, even though I think that you and Patricia are finished. I wanted to seduce you tonight, Philip. An open fire, an empty house, a couple of bottles of whiskey - all washed down with a decent shag".

"I can't..." began Philip.

Amanda put a finger up to his lips.

"Oh, I know. I gave up on the idea as soon as I'd thought of it. Bloody stupid idea. You're far too honourable for that. You'd wouldn't have been able to handle the guilt. Patricia doesn't deserve you".

A log tumbled over in the fire sending brief tongues of flame up the chimney.

You've blown it now, Philip said to himself.

I don't think so, he replied.

Philip started to laugh.

"What? What?" said Amanda sitting up suddenly. "Have I made a fool of myself? What are you laughing at? Philip! Tell me".

"Oh, it's just. I bet Patricia's being humped even as we speak. She's always had a weakness for Toby".

Amanda started to laugh too.

"It's a bit ironic, isn't it Philip? You and me here. Wanting to yet not daring. And Patricia not caring one jot about how you feel".

"That's Patricia. She and I are different".

"Thank goodness". Amanda settled down again on Philip's shoulder.

"She doesn't feel guilt. It's her breeding. The world is centred on Patricia and she can do whatever she likes within that world".

They fell silent.

"Of course" said Philip after a while. "I could just kill her".

"Mmm" said Amanda excitedly. "That sounds tempting. How shall we do it?"

"Ah, so you're my accomplice now, are you?"

"In for a penny, in for a pound. How about poison?"

"Strangulation?"

"Shooting?"

"No. They're just not imaginative enough. What's the worst way you can think of killing someone?"

Amanda thought very carefully.

"Oh, yes" she said suddenly. "You have one of those rooms where the walls move in crushing someone to death. You tie her to one wall and let it advance a millimetre a day prolonging the agony".

"That's sick" said Philip.

"You started it. Go, on. Think of one yourself".

"OK" he said thinking. "I've got one. What do you think about this? You starve a pack of hounds for a few weeks until they're really hungry. I mean, ravenous. Then, you smear fox blood all over Patricia. Then, you let her go in the woods completely naked, giving her a ten minute start. She thinks that she can get away but she can't. Then you let the hounds loose and watch them bring her down. She cries out for help but there is no-one to help her. You hear the growling and snarling as each animal takes their part of her, ripping the flesh from her bones with their sharp teeth. As she lies there she screams, her limbs thrashing and blood exploding into the air. When the hounds have had their fill, you go up to her and have a look at what's left. You see a carcass that just lies there, twitching. She sees you with her one remaining eye and the last thing she sees before eternal damnation is you, bringing a huge mallet down on her head to crush her skull".

He stopped and smiled.

Amanda looked at him in horror.

"I've been doing a lot of thinking recently" he said apologetically.

"You need to see a counsellor" suggested Amanda. "Pour us another drink and try to calm down".

Philip did just that.

"You've got an active imagination" said Amanda.

"I guess I've just been carrying around my problems with Patricia for too long".

"Well, perhaps you need to sort that out. Do something about it".

Philip sighed.

"I can't. I just can't".

"It'll eat you up. You should tell her you want a divorce or something".

"That's easy for you to say".

"It is, Philip. But at least I've been true to myself and not living a lie for years. I'm not saying that you didn't love her once. I'm sure you did. But you don't now, do you?"

"No" he said, his voice a whisper.

"And anyway" said Amanda running her finger down Philip's cheek. "Until you sort things out with her I won't get what I want".

Philip sighed.

"What we both want" he said.

Henry Geruish was not enjoying his late night meeting. With all that he was trying to achieve at the moment, the topic under discussion was an unwelcome distraction.

There was only one other man in the office - a sour faced solicitor called Robert MacLeod.

"You see, my clients are willing to pledge a tremendous amount of money in order to ensure that this acquisition goes through smoothly". The solicitor pulled out an envelope from his case and dropped it onto the table.

Geruish leaned forward. He opened up the envelope with his fingers and pulled out a cheque from inside. The cheque was from a Paris-based bank and was written out to him personally. The value of the cheque was £ 200,000.

"They <u>are</u> keen" admitted Geruish. He fingered the cheque as he considered the offer. MacLeod watched him closely, willing him to accept it.

Eventually, Geruish placed the cheque back into the envelope and slid it back across the desk to MacLeod.

"Very generous, I'll admit. But it will take more than that for me to agree to any deal". Geruish knew he was playing a dangerous game. However, if the lawyer's mysterious clients were willing to offer £ 200,000 on the first hit, they were bound to go higher.

The solicitor put the envelope back into his case and breathed deeply. He fixed Geruish with a stare.

"I find your attitude most disappointing, Mr Geruish. I had hoped that you would be a more reasonable man".

Henry shrugged his shoulders.

"I am afraid not. Now, if you don't mind, I'd rather get home to bed. Goodnight, Mr MacLeod".

The solicitor climbed to his feet.

"Goodnight, Mr Geruish". He turned and left the office.

Geruish stared after him for a moment, listening for the footsteps as MacLeod descended the stairs. Then, he pushed his chair backwards.

"You'd better come in, now" he bellowed.

From a side door, Nigel emerged and walked across to his uncle. The smile had disappeared from Nigel's lips and he looked troubled.

"What news do you have?"

"Nothing to report".

"Do you mean that you haven't yet located Digby-Fischer and my daughter?"

"No, we haven't".

Geruish rose to his feet and stood over Nigel.

"Are you up to this task?"

Nigel muttered something then looked up at his uncle.

"It's not right. It's not proper. Philip's a decent man, we shouldn't be doing this to him".

Geruish leaned closer to his nephew's face.

"Will you be saying that when this is all over? When you are flying around the world in your own jet? When you are spending the winter in Bali or the Seychelles? Will you feel sorry for him then?"

Nigel looked downcast.

"Go on. Get out of my sight and find them. This is a small island. Someone must know where they are".

Nigel made his escape.

Geruish picked up his mobile and stabbed his fingers on the buttons. He lifted the phone to his ear and listened.

"Ah, just the man. How are you doing? Fine, I think. Now, about this new Governor of ours...."

Amanda woke with a start. For a second she didn't know where she was. Then, she heard Philip breathing close at hand. The fire had died down but the embers still glowed a rich orange. She changed her position and looked at his face. A smile came to her lips before she placed her head on his chest and went back to sleep.

As MacLeod left Government House, a car pulled up in front of him. He grabbed the handle of the rear door and pulled it open. Then, he got inside.

All's Well

'Speak the truth and you will never lie' - St Brodag

Philip woke in the morning with a stiff neck and a full bladder. It was cold in the room and he could see his breath. The fire was out and all that remained was a mass of ashes and dust. He was alone.

He stood up, throwing the blankets to one side. He ached in most places and his head was heavy. He moved to the window and looked out on a grey and brown world being washed by a steady drizzle.

Suddenly, he heard a chop-chop noise close at hand. He went outside and found Amanda at the back of the lean-to, small axe in hand, chopping more firewood.

"Morning" said Philip stamping his feet.

"Did you sleep well?" asked Amanda not looking up.

"Fine. I'm a bit stiff now and I need a leak".

Amanda said nothing but grabbed hold of a small log, slicing through it with a smooth arc of the axe.

Philip wandered away and urinated behind a gnarled oak tree. Then, he came back to find Amanda taking some of the firewood indoors. He followed her.

"Breakfast?" she asked pushing a packet of twiglets into his hands.

"Great".

Amanda bent down over the fireplace and swept the ashes away into a bucket. She took these outside and quickly returned carrying the empty bucket. She knelt down and arranged some paper and small twigs on the hearth. She lit a match and the kindling caught fire. She watched it for a couple of minutes, then added some larger twigs. Gradually, she built up the fire until it started to give out some decent heat.

"You must have got your badge at the guides" suggested Philip.

Amanda said nothing but sat down on the sofa at the opposite end from Philip, pulling her legs up and resting her chin on her knees.

This is awkward, thought Philip. I'm not sure what is going on here.

He turned to Amanda who was staring into the flames.

"Everything all right".

"Suppose so" said Amanda rather sulkily.

"It's not, is it" suggested Philip.

Amanda said nothing. She continued to look into the flames.

"Come on, tell me" pleaded Philip. "What's up?"

Amanda turned around to Philip, tears in the corners of her eyes.

"I'm worried".

"Worried?"

"Yes".

"Why?" asked Philip.

Amanda sighed.

"I'm worried that you think I've been stupid, telling you what I did last night".

Philip looked puzzled.

"Why should I think that?"

"Because I must have sounded desperate - needy. I don't do needy. I look after myself. I'm strong and self-contained".

"None of what you said last night has changed that".

"Sure?" asked Amanda not daring to look at him.

"Of course I'm sure. You didn't sound needy or desperate. I mean, you're mad for sure, but I think that's a pretty established fact".

Amanda let out a little laugh despite herself.

"Don't" she said, looking away.

They fell silent for a moment then Amanda said "Hold me" and everything was fine. She turned and rested her head in his lap. He stroked her hair gently.

"What shall we do today?" she asked eventually.

"I need to get back this evening. I've got things to sort out. I'm sure the cameras will have gone by then".

Amanda sighed.

"I like it here - with you".

Philip leaned his head forward and kissed her.

"So do I".

"If it clears up, shall we go for a walk?" suggested Amanda.

"Sure".

They followed a path that reached out into the marshes from just behind the cottage, Philip in front and Amanda behind. It was a very bleak landscape. They hardly saw a single animal or bird during their time there.

They came to a small hillock that rose like an island from the swamp. They climbed the grassy slopes and found, on top of the hillock, a boulder. They sat down and looked around them.

Amanda breathed deeply.

"It's so peaceful here".

"It's quiet" said Philip. "I'm not sure I'd use the word peaceful. It's too empty. Devoid of life. Barren".

Amanda looked at Philip.

"There's something I need to tell you. I was going to mention it last night but I decided not to".

Philip looked at her warily.

"This isn't one of those Jerry Springer moments, is it? You're not going to tell me you're really a man, are you?"

Amanda laughed.

"No. If you'd have been less honourable last night I think that you might have found out".

"Shucks" said Philip.

"No. It's my dad. I think he's up to something. He doesn't let me in on the family secrets, I'm too much of a black sheep for that, but I'm sure he's planning something. And I think that it involves you, too".

"What sort of thing?"

"I'm not sure. All I know is that he's being very secretive about something. He's always at work until very late at night. My mum's very worried".

"He's probably got himself a dollybird".

"No. That's not his style. I know that he vetoed several potential Governors before you arrived".

"He can't. He has no right of veto".

"Not officially, no. But he does have friends of influence. You don't get to where my dad is without knowing which strings to pull".

Philip thought about this for a moment.

"Keep you ears open, Amanda, if you will".

"OK. I'll not do any prying because that wouldn't be right. If I hear anything, I'll pass it on".

The rain began again.

Philip stood up and offered Amanda a hand which she took. He looked at her face, at the raindrops that slid from her hair and fell onto her cheeks. He bent his head down and kissed her. They embraced and held onto each other for a while.

Amanda was the first to break.

"Better get back. I'm getting pissed through here".

They wound their way back to the cottage. Within a few minutes, they had packed everything away and were driving down the track back to the main road.

Amanda dropped Philip off outside the front door and accelerated away across the gravel.

Philip turned and went into the house.

No-one was around. He made his way up to his bedroom and took off his wet clothes. He stood in front of the full length mirror. He turned to the side and held his stomach in. He remembered the tip he heard once - that if you stand in front of a mirror, naked, and jump up and down, you'll be able to see what wobbles and that's the fat you need to get rid of.

Philip tried this and was so disgusted with his jelly-like performance, he stormed off for his shower. The water was warm and comforting, the shower gel fresh and invigorating. He felt a new man.

He dried quickly and checked his bedside clock - three-thirty.

Philip dressed and made his way into the office. On his desk was a pile of post and a note written by Mary.

'Eventually got rid of the reporters. Nigel threatened to turn the dogs on them (I know we don't have any but is sounded good at the time). I think that we'll get some phone calls on Monday but we'll deal with those then. Hope you had a nice time. See you Monday. Mary'

'PS Your wife rang, can you call her on her mobile'

'PPS You received three death-threats. I spoke to the Prime Minister but he wasn't overly concerned'

He picked up a card that lay next to Mary's note. It was from Pete Brody. It said, quite simply, 'Thanks'.

I wonder what Patricia wants, thought Philip.

He reached down to his pocket for his mobile but then remembered it was lying in some far off field.

He picked up the normal phone and dialled her number.

"Hello. Patricia" said a voice.

"Hello, it's Philip".

"Philip" she screeched. "You're quite a personality aren't you. Can't watch the television without your face appearing every now and then. I've even had one or two papers ringing me up. Imagine?"

"Did you say anything to them?"

"Of course not. They were dirty little tabloids. Not my sort of paper at all".

"I don't think Cosmopolitan will be covering this" said Philip.

"That's just the sort of little comment that reminds me what a small-minded person you are, Philip".

"Sorry".

"Mmmm. That's better. Look, it's about time I came over and gave this island of yours a good look over. Make sure you're looking after yourself".

"I'm fine".

"I'll be the judge of that, thank you very much. Anyway, I was thinking. I suppose I ought to do the decent thing and come across there".

"You don't have to..."

"No. There's no stopping me, Philip. I realise that this is my duty. If I can't be by your side day by day, I might as well come on an extended visit. So, if I come across on Tuesday and leave on Saturday morning then there'll be plenty of time for you to show me around your little island. How does that sound?"

Philip was silent.

"Hello. Philip. Are you still there?"

"Yes".

"Well?"

Philip sighed.

"That'll be lovely, Patricia. I'll look forward to it".

"Good. After all, Philip, I am your wife. See you on Tuesday. Cheerio".

"Bye".

Philip put the phone down. He heard a noise from the office next door and went through where he saw Nigel.

"Morning, Philip" said Nigel. "Where did you get to yesterday?"

"Oh, out and about".

"Oh".

"Tell me something, Nigel?"

"Yes?"

"Do you know if there is a pack of hounds on the island?"

"Why?"

"Oh, just in case I ever need one".

"Well, there isn't".

"Good".

Philip disappeared back into his own office leaving Nigel puzzled.

When Amanda got home, her father was out. She went upstairs to her rooms, showered and changed into warm, dry clothes. She popped downstairs to say a quick hello to her Mum then went out to the supermarket to buy some more whiskey.

She rang an old friend from University just to have someone different to talk to. They talked at a very shallow level and Amanda used the occasion to update herself on all the gossip.

When she eventually put the phone down, she felt much better. She went downstairs, was made a hot chocolate by her mum and went back upstairs to watch Match of the Day. By the time she fell asleep after midnight, her father had still not come home.

It was to be another two hours before Henry Geruish would return home and fall exhausted into his bed.

Doing The Job

'Day in, day out - the same, always' - St Brodag

Philip had settled into the various functions of being the Governor. Basically, these comprised of opening something once a week (a school extension, a new shop, a new government initiative), attending various dinners (the St Brodag's Isle Anglophile Association, the Guild of St Brodag Merchants, the Kittiwakers) or chairing various governmental think-tanks (The European Committee, the Island's Initiative, the Information Technology Forum). Each day, he would receive a bag of post from the Foreign Office. Most often they were memorandums detailing departmental business, promotions or new procedures. Occasionally, there were forms to fill in and each month Philip had to complete a performance against budget report. Invariably his expenditure was within the department's guidelines. It was just impossible to spend too much money on the island.

Philip was becoming adept at after dinner speaking, although his list of unused quips and jokes was rapidly diminishing. He was a great hit with the blue rinse brigade who thought he was lovely when he came to speak at charity teas. Amanda found this to be highly amusing.

"Do you realise all your groupies have passed sixty?"

"Don't" said Philip, feeling acutely embarrassed.

Back at the office, Mary kept on top of all correspondence. She was proving to be a real asset. Philip was extremely pleased with the pleasant manner that she tackled any task that she was given. He made a mental note to suggest an increase in her salary at the end of the financial year.

One morning, Mary came through to Philip clutching an invitation.

"What's that you've got there?" asked Philip.

"An invite from Weasel Airlines. They've bought a new plane and want you to be there when it takes its first flight".

"Sounds good" said Philip looking at the letter.

"Hang on" he said suddenly. "They actually want me to go up with them".

Mary looked at him.

"Is that a problem?"

"Well, firstly, I don't like flying and, secondly, for the few months I've been on this island the wind has never dropped below gale force. There is no way I'm going up in the air".

"Oh, go on. It will be fun, I'm sure. They're brilliant pilots. All ex-RAF. There'll be nothing to fear".

Philip sighed.

"Tell them I accept but if the weather's bad, I'll stay on the ground".

The night before Philip was due at the airstrip, Nigel and Amanda joined him for a drink in the Ship.

"You wouldn't get me up there, not with that crew" said Amanda.

"Come off it" said Philip. "They must be expert pilots to work around here. They're all ex-RAF".

Amanda looked at Philip.

"And have you asked yourself why they are all ex-RAF. They were all drummed out for poor discipline".

Philip swallowed.

"Surely not".

"It's true" confirmed Nigel. "This is the only place where they can get a licence. The UK won't let them fly beyond Newcastle airport. They say it's too risky".

"You're pulling my leg" said Philip.

Amanda raised an eyebrow.

"Please tell me you're pulling my leg".

Nigel shook his head slowly from side to side.

"The courts proved, though, that the accident wasn't their fault".

"That's true" agreed Amanda. "Mind you, the Judge did say that he didn't know how their planes managed to stay in the air given the number of safety problems that there were with them".

Philip took a taste of his beer. It wasn't tasting as good as it had been just a few minutes earlier.

Just then, their attention was drawn to a small, greying man who was staggering across the floor from the toilets to the door. As he drew level to where Philip was sitting, he keeled over, knocking Philip's glass out of his hand and dumping the contents across the table.

Philip leapt up.

"Do you know him?" asked Nigel.

"No" said Philip.

"You will" said Nigel. "He's your pilot tomorrow".

"Bugger" said Philip.

The following day dawned bright and fair. The wind had dropped away and was now no more than a stiff breeze. Philip turned up at the airstrip early and wandered around the site looking at the various planes.

A man in a flying jacket approached him.

"Morning" shouted Philip, heartily.

"Sguz morna" said the man.

"Oh sorry" apologised Philip. "Bonjour".

The man grunted. "Sguz morna".

Philip cocked his head to one side.

"Sorry, no" he said apologetically. "Still didn't get it".

"Sguz morna".

"Not quite there. A little slower, perhaps".

The man beckoned Philip closer. Philip took a step towards him. The man opened his mouth and Philip nearly passed out, such was the strength of alcohol on the man's breath.

"I said" started the man slowly and deliberately, "good morning".

"Ah" coughed Philip.

The man walked off and Philip returned to the terminal building.

"So, I am very happy to declare this the latest addition to the Weasel Airlines fleet". With that, Philip let go of the bottle of champagne which swung down onto the plane's fuselage and broke with a satisfying spray of bubbly.

Dick Osthwaite, Weasel Airline's managing Director came up to stand by Philip and a few photographs were taken.

"Marvellous, marvellous" said Dick to the twenty or so individuals who were assembled on the runway. "Thanks, indeed to Governor Digby-Fischer. Now, there's tea and sandwiches in the terminal building. Enjoy yourselves".

Philip turned to join them when Dick placed a hand on his arm.

"Not so fast, Governor. You've forgotten your treat. You'll be the first non-Weasel Airlines person up in that plane. Look, here comes Tony now".

A familiar, ambling shape came towards Philip.

"Sguz morna" said Tony who promptly opened the door on the pilots side of the aircraft and split his head open in doing it. He spun backwards and collapsed on the grass.

"Bugger. It must be those drugs he's taking".

"What are they?" asked Philip.

"Oh, you know. Cocaine, LSD. Doesn't mix with the gin too well".

Philip looked around desperately.

"Well, I suppose that's it" said Philip. "I'm sorry to have to miss out".

Dick smiled at him.

"You don't have to" he said merrily. "I'll take you up".

Philip and Dick escorted Tony back to the Terminal building. Within a few minutes, Dick was ready and the two of them were seated in the cockpit.

"Don't we have to do any safety checks?" asked Philip over the headphones.

Dick smiled and shook his head.

"I like to wing it. It adds to the adventure".

They taxied out over the field and turned at the end of the runway.

"Here goes" shouted Dick and the plane lurched forward.

Philip closed his eyes and didn't open them again until he felt that tightness in his stomach which meant that they had left the ground.

"Bloody marvellous feeling this, isn't it" said Dick.

Philip nodded.

They headed out in an easterly direction first then turned and flew back over the island.

From the air, Philip could see the distinctive starfish shape of the island with its headlands and sweeping bays in between. He could see Ash-Na-Garoo quite plainly from this height. Beyond and out to sea, the *Spirit of St Brodag* could be seen approaching the harbour.

Suddenly, a light started flashing on the control panel.

"What's that?" asked Philip.

"What's what?" asked Dick.

"There. The flashing light!".

Dick took a long and hard stare at it while he rubbed his chin.

"It's either the engine about to stop or the rudder's broken".

"What!" exploded Philip. "Is that serious?"

Dick smiled, hesitantly.

"About as serious as it can get. I'm not exactly sure - I've not read the manual yet. I think that.....oh" he said suddenly clipping his seat-belt back together again. The light stopped flashing. Dick looked sheepishly at Philip who looked out of the window.

Philip looked out over the sea, dull grey below them and dotted with the occasional ship. The engine droned.

"You married?" asked Dick after a while.

"Yes" said Philip. "My wife is coming to the island next week to spend a few days here".

"My wife's just left me" said Dick mournfully. "Said she couldn't stand living with a drunkard. Drunkard! Me!"

Philip looked at Dick and could see his face turning s deep crimson colour.

"I hate that bitch" he screamed. "She put me through hell. It was her that brought on the blackouts, you know".

"Blackouts?" said Philip nervously.

"Oh, yes" said Dick. "I shouldn't really be up here without another qualified pilot - in case I have one of my turns".

Philip began to feel light-headed.

"Can we go down now?" he asked.

"Don't you want to loop-the-loop?" asked Dick.

"I'd rather not" said Philip. "Just get me down in one piece".

"OK but you'll be missing out".

Dick turned the plane around and began the gentle drop back to the airstrip.

Dick coughed.

"Can you smell fuel?" asked Dick.

"No, I don't think so" said Philip.

"I can definitely smell fuel" stated Dick.

The island became larger and larger as they neared the airport.

"Definitely fuel" said Dick. "Can you not smell it?"

"No" said Philip.

The runway loomed up to meet them.

The plane landed with no further problems. Philip thanked Dick and jumped down from the cockpit onto the grass.

Then, side by side, they walked back to the Terminal building.

When they were half way across the grass from the plane to the building, there was an almighty explosion. Philip threw himself to the ground as a wave of heat washed over him and bits of plane came flying past him. He lay there for what seemed ages, his arms stretched over his head to protect him from the flying debris.

When the bits had all dropped to the ground, he raised his head a little and to one side. There was Dick, standing up and looking at the smouldering wreck of the plane.

"I was right" he said. "I could smell fuel".

African Skies

'Idle slumber is the ruin of a good man' - St Brodag

The Fat Man sat in his favourite chair in his Gentleman's Club overlooking Green Park and sipped a well-watered whiskey. On his lap lay a package. He placed his drink down on the leather-inlaid table at his side and began to open the package.

Inside was a further envelope and a small box. In the box was a tape. He also put this on the table. He opened the envelope and pulled out a series of photographs.

They showed Philip and Amanda outside the cottage on St Brodag's Isle.

The Fat Man smiled to himself and put the photographs back into the envelope. He picked up the tape and put it in his inside pocket.

He picked up his copy of the Times. On the front page, though not the main story, stood the headline "NEW GOVERNOR CAUSES EXTINCTION OF RARE SEA BIRD". The Fat Man read on even though he knew the details. He chuckled when it came to the description of the bird's demise. Then, he put the paper down.

After taking another sip of whiskey, he leaned his head back and dreamed of an earlier time.

The hot wind blew across the airstrip, picking up the dust and whirling and twirling it into so many mini tornadoes, that twisted and turned underneath a big, African sky.

A slimmer, younger version of the Fat Man looked out over the rough runway to where a burning wreck lay. That had been his means of escaping the pandemonium that was breaking out all around him. A stray shell had hit the Cessna while it was waiting for his arrival. Whether it had been fired from the Government side or whether it was from the fast approaching rebel troops, the Fat Man neither knew nor cared. He wanted out and that was that.

In the main lounge of the airport were a hundred or so people, mostly residents of this troubled country. They were mostly women with a few old people and some children running around. Someone had a radio that was switched on blaring out *All you need is love* by the Beatles. The irony was not lost on the Fat Man who returned to looking out of the window.

Suddenly, small arms fire broke out at the northern end of the runway. A jeep came racing towards the terminal building. An officer in the Government's uniform jumped down from the vehicle and ran across to the glass doors of the lounge. He pushed his way inside and jumped on a table.

"Everyone, listen. You must leave here. The rebels are getting closer. We cannot hold them off for much longer. You have ten minutes to vacate this place, otherwise, I cannot be held responsible for your safety".

There was a groan of despair from the crowd who quickly upped and left leaving the Fat Man to his own devices.

The officer looked at him.

"I know you, sir" he said, respectfully. "You should go".

"Bollocks I will" said the Fat Man. "This place is my only chance. That lot will be mown down out there, won't they?"

The officer did not reply and looked down at the floor.

"I'm staying here" continued the Fat Man. "You never know, miracles happen".

Just then, six or seven trucks, accompanied by a handful of jeeps, raced past along the runway.

"Those are my soldiers. We have been pushed back. The airport is now in rebel hands".

"Not yet it isn't" said the Fat Man.

The officer smiled.

"Good luck, my friend".

The officer saluted smartly and left, the jeep following the rest of his command. The Fat Man watched him leave.

"Right" said the Fat Man. "Now for some fun".

He pulled out a gun from his jacket pocket and checked it over.

"What I need is a sandwich".

The Fat Man crossed to the small cafe at one end of the lounge, passed around the counter and went into the kitchen behind. It had been abandoned in a hurry. The Fat Man turned off a series of pans that were boiling away. He located the rear door of the kitchen and saw a series of large waste containers outside about ten feet from the main building.

Outside, the rebels made their way warily up the runway. They were a ragbag bunch, trained in the jungle by Soviet and Cuban soldiers who were the main backers of the rebel organisation that threatened to overthrow the democratically elected fledgling Government. The Fat Man had been despatched to offer help and advice. He hadn't been keen and was even less keen now. He should have left a week ago but, for one reason or another, he had been delayed.

The rebels approached the terminal building carefully, not quite knowing what to expect. A squad of about ten then rushed the main lounge, firing wildly into the side of the building, causing great plates of glass to smash and fall to the ground. Within a few seconds, the whole lounge area had been destroyed in a hail of bullets.

The Fat Man witnessed this from the safety of the kitchen. Once the firing had stopped, he hid behind a bench and waited.

The Fat Man struggled to control his breathing. Thankfully, the extraction system hummed gently in the background, masking his wheezing and spluttering. He winced - the space that he was in was a little too small for him. He could hear shouting outside in the lounge. The rest of the rebels had entered the building and started to check the upper storey, firing occasionally as they did.

Then, when all was quiet, the Fat Man heard a buzzing noise - far off at first but then getting gradually closer. A plane.

The Fat Man ventured to scuttle out from behind the bench and made his way to the back door. Sure enough, a small plane was landing on the runway.

The Fat Man breathed deeply. This was his chance.

He stood up and, as he did, a rebel soldier walked in from the lounge. The Fat Man raised his gun and fired, catching the rebel neatly in the forehead. The soldier collapsed backwards through the door. From the lounge came shouts.

The Fat Man threw himself out of the back door and ran to the cover of the refuse bins. He surveyed the situation. Two rebel soldiers with machine guns were strolling out across the tarmac towards the plane. One was only a few feet away from his position. The other was another ten paces in front.

The Fat Man took aim and hit the nearest man in the head. He crumpled to the ground. His partner span around quickly but was hit in the leg. He stumbled over and lay on his side, grabbing at his bloody wound. The Fat Man dashed from his position and shot the stricken man at point blank range.

Then, he turned towards the plane and started to run.

A group of rebel soldiers had by this time found their way out of the lounge and started to fire.

The Fat Man ran.

He remembered all those cross country runs at school. He remembered all those rugby games where he would run until he was nearly ready to drop. He was heavier now but his determination was the same.

Bullets flew over his head and bounced on the tarmac on either side of his feet.

Twenty yard....fifteen.....ten....the door of the aircraft flew open...five yards....then, with a leap, he was inside.

"Buckle up" said the pilot. "It's not over yet".

The plane started to taxi down the runway as the Fat man fastened his seat belt and pulled on the headset.

"We haven't got enough room this way. I'm going to try and bluff them that I'm taking off, hope that they don't follow too closely, then turn and blast the other way. It's a long shot but, hey, I'm feeling lucky".

The Fat Man looked across at the pilot and smiled.

The plane accelerated away from the rebels who seemed to lose heart. They trooped back to the terminal building not expecting to see the plane brake sharply and turn around. When they realised what was happening, they ran forward and opened up with machine gun fire.

As the plane came towards the, the rebel soldiers intensified their fire. As the plane passed the rebels, both pilot and passenger knew that one bullet hitting the fuel tanks would be fatal. One bullet passed through the pilot's side window and exited on the other side of the plane. Both passenger and pilot pushed themselves down in their seats as they flashed past the guns.

Then, it was over. The plane climbed sharply and turned to the West. Up and up they climbed and then they began to level out.

"That was too close" shouted the pilot.

"I thought that your timing was perfect" replied the Fat Man.

They both laughed.

The Fat Man pulled out a flask that he had concealed about his person. He took a swig then handed it to the pilot who did the same. He returned the flask and before he put it away again, the Fat Man took another drink.

The pilot turned to the Fat Man and held out a large hand.

"Hello. I'm Henry Geruish".

One of the club's stewards tapped the Fat Man on the shoulder.

"You have a telephone call, sir"

The Fat Man climbed to his feet and followed the steward out of the lounge.

Cragmuir

'The Lord loves a northerner' - St Brodag

Cragmuir was little more than a collection of houses, pubs and shops gathered tightly together around a little harbour on the northern-eastern coast of the island. Behind the town, Mount Elizabeth rose to dominate an otherwise unforgettable skyline. The people of Cragmuir loved their mountain and told tales of the way that it affected their climate.

"Much sunnier than Port Victoria" they would say. "Not as windy either".

The place was also the centre of Brogadan culture and, once a quarter, the members of the St Brodagan Trust would meet together to speak the guttural Brogadan language or take part in ancient dances. The average age of the Trust Members was seventy-two and so it was expected to have a membership crisis any day now.

These people also preserved the folklore of St Brodag - tales that were built onto the little facts that were known about him. According to legend, St Brodag performed miracles, could understand animals and birds and was even known to ride on the backs of dolphins. He had strange, mystical powers that would protect the island in times of need. He was a brooding presence that pervaded all that happened to the people: a hero; a god.

In reality, all that anyone knew about him was that he came from Lindisfarne and left behind a tiny collection of sayings that were little more than the ramblings of an idiot.

Cragmuir comprised of one main street and everything to do with the town was located on it. For a town of three thousand people, Cragmuir boasted twelve pubs, reflecting, perhaps, not Cragmuir's liking for beer but rather that of the Brogadan populace as a whole. On the island, you went to Port Victoria for a pub crawl but you went to Cragmuir for 'The Session'.

In Victorian days, the Craddles family, who owned the brewery, had tried to develop Cragmuir into a tourist attraction. One of the projects that they had undertaken was Cragmuir Park which once boasted some of the finest fountains in Northern Europe. However, at the turn of the century, the park had been abandoned for lack of interest and the lawns, the mazes, the exotic flower beds and the fountains now lay in ruin, a wilderness that sometimes hinted at its former glory, a playground for children and a retreat for courting couples.

Another project that the Craddles had built was Old Tom's Folly, a tower that stood by the shore. It was supposed to look like a medieval fortress but ended up looking like a municipal toilet, due to the lack of decent building stone on the island.

So Cragmuir was left a very poor distant cousin, twice removed, of Port Victoria, both jealous of its investment and development, yet pitying it for its lack of roots and culture.

Philip drove his own Range Rover to the engagement. It was the Friday before Patricia was due on the island and he was already feeling nervous.

As he approached the school, he waved at the small crowd that gathered at the gates. The crowd hung around for a few seconds then quickly dispersed when it was realised that Philip wasn't going to hand out any money.

The car came to a rest outside the main front door of Cragmuir School. This establishment catered for children up to eleven years of age. After that point, they had to travel to Port Victoria to continue their education. Some didn't bother at all. What good is an education when you can marry your cousin, take over your family's smallholding and wheel and deal in sheep?

Mr Headley was waiting for them. He was known, quite predictably, as 'Deadly' Headley. For a teacher, he was man of little patience, preferring to deal in his own brand of corporal punishment than hand out detentions or speak to parents.

Mr Headley was one of those men who, for vanity's sake, would comb over their hair to conceal their bald patch. This was well and good and looked slightly ridiculous. However, it must be remembered that St Brodag's Isle was a place known for its strong winds and Mr Headley would often be seen with his hair lifting through 90 degrees, his hands frantically scrabbling to keep the matted mess in place.

Today was the official opening of the new computer room at school. This facility was to be shared with the local community as well, so that the people of Cragmuir could enter the world of high technology, which was ironic, really, as they had just about come to terms with the wheel.

Philip jumped out of the car. Mr Headley dashed forward, bowing slightly and shaking his hand.

"Welcome. Welcome Governor to our school. I am Mr Headley but you can call me Gilbert" he said, wringing his hands together in a fawning fashion.

Philip smiled.

"Well, Gilbert, I'm looking forward to seeing your new computer room. I feel that its very important that the children of today understand all the latest technologies, don't you?"

Mr Headley twisted his mouth. Philip took this to be a smile.

"Quite so, quite so. Will you please follow me?"

Philip looked up at a darkening sky.

"Looks like rain" he said.

The headmaster gave him a queer look.

"Aye it does" he said. "Storm coming. This way".

Philip followed after him through the main school doors. In the staff room, Mr Headley introduced Philip to the rest of the teaching staff. Philip spent quite a bit of time chatting to them, trying to find out how they view the latest trends in education. The Education Department on the island had recently introduced a National Curriculum similar to that already established on the mainland and Philip was keen to find out how well it had been received. When they all looked blankly at him, he made a mental note to talk to someone about it.

Mr Headley took Philip through to the technology centre which comprised of a single computer linked to a printer. A woman in her fifties was there, accompanied by a group of small children.

Philip looked round, trying to spot other equipment in the room.

"Is this it?" he asked.

Mr Headley twisted his mouth again.

"Aye, she's a beauty, isn't she?"

Philip hesitated.

"Just the one?"

"How many more do you need?" asked the headmaster. "With this computer, the wonders of the internet will be at our fingers".

Philip looked at him, seeing a strange, far away look in his eye.

"Let's hope everyone doesn't want to have a go at the same time" said Philip.

He unveiled the plaque and said a few appropriate words.

"This way" said Mr Headley when Philip had finished. "A wee drink for you".

Philip was shown into a side classroom where a single cup of tea and a small piece of cake sat on a tray. The rest of the staff stood around awkwardly and watched him.

"No one else joining me?" he asked cheerily as he took a sip of the tea.

He was met by stony silence. The teachers just stared.

Philip felt embarrassed and quickly finished his drink.

"The school is waiting to ask you a few questions" said Mr Headley. "This way".

When Philip and the head teacher were out of earshot of the staff, he ventured to ask Mr Headley what exactly was wrong with his teaching staff.

"I told them that you were the schools' inspector. Always keeps them quiet".

Philip shook his head.   He was taken through to the main hall, were all the pupils were lined up on low benches.

"Will you all say good morning to Mr Digby-Fischer".

"GOOD MORNING MR DIGBY-FISCHER" they droned.

"Good morning, children. It thrills me to be here to officially open your technology centre. It is one of the more pleasurable duties of being a governor that you get to meet so many people".

He looked around at a sea of blank faces.

"I think that getting yourself a good education is the key in this modern world".

Blanker faces.

"Education opens up a whole world of opportunity for you".

Someone coughed.

"So, erm, would anyone like to tell me what they'd like to do when they get older?"

A mass of hands shot upwards.

"I'd like to be a policeman".

"I'd like to be a fireman".

"I'd like to be Governor" shouted one lad.

"Oh" beamed Philip. "And why's that?"

"Cause my Dad says you get paid lots of money for doing bugger all".

Much laughter. Mr Headley scowled at the boy.

"Well....well.." said Philip. "It's not that easy, actually. Anyone else?".

"I'd like to be a chef".

"I'd like to work with horses".

"I'd like to have a monotonous job working on a production line in a boring factory - just like the job my dad says he does".

"Well..."started Philip when a sound like the rattle of a machine gun could be heard. Philip's first thought had been to duck - this, of course, had been the result of his naval training and nothing to do with being scared.

Some of the children started to cry and scream. Mr Headley went to the window, looked out and shouted, trying to calm everyone.

"It's hailstones" he shouted. "That's all. Hailstones".

The whole school leapt to its feet as one and ran to the windows that ran down the length of the hall. Philip followed them. He could see huge, white hailstones bouncing off the playground. The sky was a dark, purple colour, shot through with crimson. Lightening began to flash. There was a dull rumble of thunder.

The children screamed again.

"To your classrooms" shouted Mr Headley. "All of you, back to your classrooms".

The children dispersed to the far corners of the school, shepherded by the teachers, leaving Philip alone with Mr Headley.

The headmaster turned to him.

"I think that you had better go, now, Mr Digby-Fischer".

Philip nodded looking out through the window. He had never seen a sky as dark and foreboding as this one.

"Thank you for coming today. I look forward to meeting you again".

Mr Headley guided Philip out of the hall and down a corridor, back to the entrance. Philip dashed across to his car, splashing water on his trousers as he tried to miss the puddles. He gave Mr Headley a quick, final wave before jumping inside. He switched the engine on and turned the demister fan onto full. He waited there, for a couple of minutes, until the car had been properly cleared of condensation.

Philip rooted among his CD collection. There was only one track that he considered putting on. As the car pulled away from the school, the mad strings and triumphant brass sections boomed out 'The Ride of the Valkyries'.

The hail had stopped and was now replaced with driving rain. Philip looked out over the sea and felt a cold shiver run down his spine as he saw the frothing, foaming mass that crashed against the harbour wall. The swell inside the harbour was causing many of the boats moored there to rock violently.

Philip could feel the wind increasing in strength as the Range Rover made its way down the eastern coast of the island, occasionally causing the vehicle to lurch to the right as a particularly strong gust caught it.

As Philip drove along the road, he noticed that hundreds of little waterfalls were forming between gaps in the hedge that ran alongside the right hand edge. These little waterfalls then gave birth to small streams that would snake across the tarmac and run away down the bank to the left.

Philip switched his windscreen wipers onto top speed as the rain suddenly quickened. He could see little further than twenty feet in front of him and his speed dropped accordingly.

He passed the Geruish's house and that thought about stopping. Yet, the rain urged him onwards and the prospect of getting wet through deterred him from leaving the comfort of the car.

The road took an abrupt turn to the right and headed inland for a while. After a couple of hundred yards, Philip stopped the car quickly. Ahead, a stream normally passed under the road, diving through a narrow archway. Today, the road passed under the stream, a bubbling, fast moving sheet of brown, earthy water, twenty feet across.

Philip assessed the situation. It seemed to him that the water was little more than six inches deep. If that was the case, then it should cause no problems. He put his foot down and moved steadily forward. The water was slightly deeper than he had thought but he managed to get across with little difficulty.

"Try that in a Jaguar" he said out loud.

The rest of the journey passed with no further incidents. He pulled into the driveway of Ash-Na-Garoo and checked his watch. It had taken him an hour and a half to drive down from Cragmuir, a journey that normally took him twenty minutes.

He jumped out of the Range Rover and made a mad dash for the front door. As he ran, he could hear a deep groaning underground as the sea dashed itself against the headland.

The Storm

'The rage of the storm is like the righteous anger of God' - St Brodag

"Thank goodness you've made it back" said Mary on seeing Philip. "They've just closed the coast road from Cragmuir".

Philip nodded.

"I can see why. It was dreadful. Water everywhere".

Nigel walked in from his office.

"You look wet".

"It's because I am wet! I can't believe how damp it is out there".

"They reckon it's going to get worse" said Nigel. "I just heard it on the radio. Near hurricane winds through the night".

Philip whistled.

The telephone rang.

"Hello, Ash-Na-Garoo. Mary speaking. May I help you?"

Mary paused and listened to the speaker.

"OK" she said finally. "Thanks for the information".

Mary put the phone down and sighed.

"That was the police. The road back to Port Victoria is closed. There's a tree down".

Philip looked at them both.

"Look's like you guys are staying the night, then. They won't be sending anyone out to clear the tree now".

Nigel smiled.

"At least you've got enough bedrooms" he said. "Otherwise, Mary and I would have had to share".

"Over my dead body" she said.

Nigel shrugged his shoulders and toddled back to his office.

"I need to get some dry clothes on" said Philip, disappearing back through his own office to his bedroom. He dried his hair as well.

Returning to his desk, Philip decided to ring Amanda at the hospital.

"Hi, Philip" she said when he got through.

"What's it like there?" he asked.

"Fine at the moment. I think we might be getting a few more people coming in to A&E during the night. Have you heard the forecast?"

"Sound a little rough, doesn't it. Have you had a storm like this before?"

"Yes, but not for a long time. Apparently, back in 1876, Port Victoria was nearly destroyed by a storm. They were talking about abandoning the island".

"I hope it doesn't come to that. Look after yourself....please".

Amanda sighed.

"No, I think I'll go for a swim. I'm not stupid".

"Yes" said Philip. "Sorry. I only meant that I worry - when I'm not with you".

"I know" she said. "I'd better go. I've got to tell someone that they're going to die, so I'd better get on with it".

"Sure" said Philip. "Bye".

"See you later" she said.

Philip put the phone down.

On his desk was a large pile of memos, letters and briefings. He spent the next couple of hours going through them, highlighting parts of some documents with a pen, others being screwed up and thrown into the bin.

At about five o'clock, with the fury of the winds outside becoming more intense, the lights went off. Mary gave a little shriek next door.

Philip felt in his drawers for the torch that he knew lay there. He pulled it out and switched it on. Shadows raced up to meet him as he swung the light around the room. He crossed to the office door and went out to see how everything was. Mary was fumbling in her desk. Nigel emerged from his office bearing a huge torch that was the size of a small briefcase.

Mary tried the phones.

"There's nothing here. Dead".

"Right" said Philip. "Let's go down and see Mrs Kinloss".

They made their way slowly down the corridor and down the stairs. Outside, it sounded as though express train after express train were racing past the house. The chandelier swung gently, being moved by the gusts that were able to pass through the tiny cracks in the house.

They found Mrs Kinloss, resourceful as ever, setting up a lighting rig powered by bottled gas.

"It will take more than a storm for this kitchen to stop making meals".

"Right" said Philip. "I propose we do two things, Firstly, we need to get a fire going in the lounge. We'll need plenty of wood so that we can keep it going all night. Secondly, we'd better check some of the houses around here and make sure that everyone is fine. You come with me, Mary, and we'll go and get some blankets together. Then we'll go out in the Range Rover. If you, Mrs Kinloss, and Nigel get the fire going, then when we get back we can sort things out for staying the night".

Mrs Kinloss and Nigel nodded and went to prepare the lounge. Mary and Philip ran upstairs and got plenty of blankets. They piled them up by the back door of the kitchen. Philip hadn't dared open up the front door in case the chandelier came down. He ran outside and was immediately battered by the wind. He got to the car and drove it to the rear of the house. Because the wind was making the rain blow horizontally, they were afforded some shelter by a nearby garage.

Once loaded, they went off into the night to see if any of the locals needed help. Few did, since Brogadans tend to be a hardy bunch and prepare for the worst. They stopped to help an old woman light a fire she was having difficulty with and they dropped off blankets at a house with a young family. Within an hour, they had visited all the houses that they could reach and turned back towards Ash-Na-Garoo.

Brogadans may be many things but they do have keen memories. No one forgot Philip's kind actions that night. The word spread that the Governor cared, that he risked himself on the night of the storm to help others. That meant a lot to them. Philip's stock with the locals started to rise that night.

Back at the house, Mrs Kinloss was busy preparing a meal. Potatoes wrapped in foil lined the edge of the fire and, from time to time, were pushed deeper into the glowing embers. In a pan, she was roasting chestnuts. In a pot hanging from a hook above the flames, she had a stew on the go. She also had another pot that rested on the logs. In it, beer bread was slowly rising.

Nigel had brought as many duvets downstairs as he could find. He piled a series of cushions into the room. Philip brought out a couple of bottles of wine and a bottle of rum. Soon, they were all settled down in front of the fire, telling stories, eating their meal, and trying to ignore the screaming wind outside.

"That was a great meal" said Philip when all the food had gone.

"In this kitchen" said Mrs Kinloss, "we do not pour scorn on the old ways of doing things. Where would primitive man had been if he had not, at a very early stage in his development, decided to organise himself a kitchen based around the concept of a central communal fire?"

Nigel looked at Philip for help. None was forthcoming.

"This wine's gone straight to my head" announced Mary. Philip could see Nigel's eyes light up. He threw a cushion in his direction to disturb him.

"Does anyone have the time?" asked Mrs Kinloss.

"Eight-thirty" replied Philip.

"We should start preparing for bed soon" said Mrs Kinloss. "I'm sure that if the winds die downing by the morning then we'll have plenty to do".

Philip looked around.

"We'll you and Mary should sleep by the fire. Nigel and I will take a few extra duvets and sleep at the back of the room. Give you some space".

"You don't have to" said Mary.

"No" said Philip eyeing Nigel. "I think it would be better if we did".

Each one of them disappeared in turn to the downstairs bathroom. Nigel stoked the fire.

"That should keep us going for a while" he said, rubbing his hands over the heat.

A particularly strong gust of wind hit the house. The windows rattled alarmingly and a low, drawn out groaning sound seemed to rise up from the floor.

"Do you think that the house will hold together?" asked Mary.

Mrs Kinloss grunted.

"Mark my words, young lady" she said sternly. "This house has been here for hundreds of years. The foundations are deep and strong and reach down far into the rock on which it was built. This house will remain when we are all dead and buried".

"I hope the satellite dish is all right" said Nigel. "It's the big fight next week. Don't want to miss that".

The women settled themselves by the fire. Nigel and Philip piled cushions on the floor at the back of the room in two separate heaps and threw blankets and duvets on top. They undressed and climbed inside their respective burrows.

The house seemed to be surrounded by a high-pitched whining noise.

"Philip" whispered Nigel.

"Yes?"

"Drink?"

Nigel produced his hip flask.

"No thanks".

"Go on" pressed Nigel.

Philip sighed and picked the flask up. He unscrewed the lid and took a swig. It was like drinking razor blades.

"What the hell is that?" gasped Philip.

Nigel sniggered.

"It's the local brew. It's a whiskey, of sorts".

"Is it legal?"

"At that strength!" said Nigel incredulously. "No way. This is true Brogadan moonshine".

Philip wiped his mouth on his sleeve.

"Not an experience I would like to repeat, Nigel" said Philip.

Nigel glugged away at the flask.

"You get used to it" he said eventually.

"I don't think I want to" said Philip. "Goodnight".

"Goodnight" said Nigel. They both settled down.

Philip listened to the wind ripping in and battering the house. There was no let up. In fact, it seemed that the noise was intensifying. At times, the house seemed to rock, giving the impression to Philip that the whole thing might decide to topple off the headland and plunge into the surf below. It was not a comforting thought.

"Philip?" whispered Nigel after a few minutes.

"Yes?"

"You enjoy it here, don't you?"

Philip paused.

"Yes".

"Good. It's just that....oh, it doesn't matter. Night".

"Night".

Philip fell into an uneasy sleep.

When they all awoke the following morning, the winds had dropped and a steady drizzle replaced the torrential rain of the previous day. Philip and Nigel took the Range Rover out and managed to by-pass some of the damaged sections of road. They drove into Port Victoria to check the damage and see what they could do to help. They spent the rest of the day ferrying people around the island.

Amanda, as predicted, had endured a busy night. Philip volunteered to drop her off home just after eleven. She fell asleep in the car and he woke her gently. He watched her slip into the house and she gave him a weary wave before she closed the door.

Philip went home and prepared himself for Patricia's visit.

Love And Marriage

'The love of a good woman, I spurn' - St Brodag

Philip arrived at the ferry terminal in plenty of time. Although the weather was damp, the sea was quite smooth and he hoped that Patricia had experienced a pleasant crossing, for no better reason than he didn't want to have to hear her moaning every minute of the next few days.

The Spirit of St Brodag rounded the headland and sailed into the bay with all the tottering grace of an ice skating giraffe. As always, Philip was amazed that the thing stayed upright.

The vessel berthed and the vehicles drove off the ferry one by one.

Philip made his way into the terminal building as Patricia had sailed as a foot passenger. He waited in the lounge watching the doorway through which his wife would come.

The lounge was filled with people waiting to welcome friends and relatives. Two children were running wild around the place screaming their heads off. Their father stood against one wall, too embarrassed to admit they were his.

The first drip of foot passengers came through the doorway, each one warmly welcomed by the man dressed as St. Brodag. The lounge was full of 'hellos' and kisses and hugging and then grew silent, as the people drifted away.

Last of all came Patricia. She had found some poor porter to push her luggage trolley for her.

Philip pushed forward and she deigned to allow him to kiss her on the cheek.

"Who is that dreadful man standing at the doorway?" she asked, motioning with her hand to the St Brodag character.

"Oh, it's a tourism thing. Promoting the island's founder".

Patricia snorted.

"You should get rid of him. He looks like a paedophile".

Philip sighed at her.

"How was the crossing?"

"How do you think?" she said, indignantly. "Four hours with the great unwashed. You couldn't get a decent Cappuccino on that..." she pointed back in the direction of the ferry, "...thing. I complained to the Captain and when I mentioned I was your wife, he let me spend the rest of the journey in his cabin".

"That was nice of him".

Patricia raised an eyebrow.

"Where's the car? I need a bath".

"This way" said Philip and he led Patricia off in the direction of the car park.

When they reached the car, Philip threw the bags into the boot and Patricia climbed into the passenger seat of the Range Rover.

"You should have bought yourself a decent car" she said as she stretched upwards. "A Jaguar or something".

"A Jaguar!" said Philip. "On this island! It wouldn't last two minutes. The roads are far too bumpy for that. Anyway, Jag's are for posers".

"Daddy always used to have Jaguars. Until he retired. Then he had to make do with a Daimler".

"See what I mean" he whispered to himself.

Patricia tutted at him.

"Anyway, what's the point of being Governor if you can't get the roads sorted. Really, Philip, you are such a wimp".

Philip started the engine and they were off. They blasted back to Ash-Na-Garoo and were soon parked on the gravel outside the front door.

Patricia eyed the building with incredulity.

"You live here?" she asked.

"It's quite comfortable inside. Granted, it looks a bloody mess from out here".

"Indeed it does, Philip. Indeed it does".

Philip showed Patricia her bedroom. He had decided that she should sleep in the Guest Room. Patricia readily agreed.

Philip introduced Patricia to Mary ('That's a pretty scent. Is it a local brew?') and then to Nigel ('Ah, the scarecrow look is in again, I see'). Then, he took her downstairs to see Mrs Kinloss.

Mrs Kinloss looked at Patricia with one of her withering stares. Patricia looked at her in her normal haughty manner. They locked horns - and became the best of friends. Mrs Kinloss admired Patricia for the way that she held herself.

"In this kitchen, we approve of people who understand their position in life and who would agree that familiarity breeds contempt".

Patricia approved of the way that Mrs Kinloss ran her kitchen, especially the way that she bossed Philip around.

"He really is useless, Mrs Kinloss. He needs a firm hand or he's lost".

Philip stood there taking it all in.

Patricia soon disappeared to take a bath.

Philip went up to the offices where Mary and Nigel sat, drinking coffee.

"So what do you think of my wife, then?" he asked, enjoying their discomfort.

"She's very..."started Mary.

"Forthright" said Nigel.

"Yes, yes, very forthright my Patricia" agreed Philip. "What else?"

"Nice clothes" ventured Mary.

"Very nice, expensive clothes" agreed Philip.

"Great body" said Nigel.

"For her age, she's very well preserved" said Philip, nodding.

Mary slurped her coffee. Nigel looked down at the floor.

"I actually think she's a rancid old dragon" said Philip.

"She's a cow" agreed Mary.

"How do you put up with her?" asked Nigel.

Philip laughed.

"Don't worry" he said, "she won't be here for very long. She's going back on Saturday morning".

Mary breathed a sigh of relief.

"Nice body, though" murmured Nigel.

"Don't even go there" advised Philip. "She'd eat you up".

Henry called around later on just to say hello. He spent ten minutes being polite before he had to go. As he left, he whispered to Philip.

"You are a very brave man. I have re-assessed my opinion of you.

Later on that afternoon, after Philip had spent some more time in the office, he was walking past the lounge when he overheard Patricia in conversation on the phone.

"Yes, darling. I've managed to escape for a while. This place is really the pits, the back of beyond".

Philip stopped and listened at the door.

"Yes, I know, beastly. But someone's got to do it. How are you, anyway? Feeling OK. Oh, Toby, don't say that. No, Toby, don't".

I was right, thought Philip. It's that bastard Toby.

"Oh, Toby. Oh, Toby. Please. I'm blushing - don't. Don't Toby. Don't. Why not? Because there's some pathetic little sneak listening at the door".

Philip moved on swiftly.

"Where are we eating tonight?" asked Patricia.

"Oh, a place called 'The Wonders of Persia'".

"Sounds beastly".

"It comes highly recommended".

"By whom?" demanded Patricia. "Surely, Egon Ronnay has not darkened the shores of this disgusting piece of rock".

"No. It was Nigel".

"Ah, the scarecrow".

Philip picked up the phone and dialled Amanda. She was between appointments at the hospital.

"She is driving me mad" he screamed. "Why did I let her come here?"

"Because you're pathetic and can't say no to her".

"I didn't need that".

"Sorry".

"It's just that she puts the backs up of everyone she meets. Even Mary".

"What, not little Miss Goody Two Shoes Mary? I'm beginning to like her already. When do I meet her?"

"You don't, Amanda" he said sternly. "I'm keeping the two of you as far away from each other as possible".

"Are you going to mention divorce to her?"

"I'm going to try" he said.

"Which means no, doesn't it?"

Philip sighed.

"I'm serious, Amanda. This time, I'm going to tell her straight".

There was no sound from the other end of the line.

"Amanda! Are you still there?"

"Yes".

"Why did you go quiet?"

"I was suppressing a fit of laughter".

"Very funny".

Just before Patricia went upstairs to change, Philip caught up with her in the lounge. She was reading a copy of the Tatler that she had brought with her and sipping lemon tea.

"Ah, Patricia" said Philip.

"Yes" she said looking up from her magazine.

He crossed the room and at down on a stool near the chair on which she reclined.

"Look, Patricia, can we try and be civil tonight. Let's not fall out".

Patricia looked at him and sighed.

"OK, Philip, just for tonight. It's been quite a day. I'm tired".

"I know" said Philip. "I promise that I won't try and annoy you on purpose".

"And I promise I won't be mean to your friends".

"What about me?" he asked.

"You" she said with a sly smile, "are a different proposition".

Patricia stood up, towering over Philip.

"Don't worry" she said as she walked out of the room. "I intend to be on my best behaviour".

Philip was left alone to worry.

Old Friends

'I welcome the North Wind' - St Brodag

Philip had chosen 'The Wonders of Persia' for their meal together. He had never been there before but Nigel liked it. He said that it had character and sold cheap beer. Philip thought that it was the sort of establishment that Patricia would not normally go to and that's why he chose it.

They managed to park directly outside the restaurant and were, thus, only exposed to the wind for the briefest of moments.

Patricia had dressed immaculately for the evening. Philip had to admit that she had good, if rather pricey, taste. The dress she wore was a dark burgundy cloth and shimmered as she walked. The cut was very flattering, the dress clinging without being trashy. She looked the part: a Governor's wife.

Philip had thrown on one of his light beige suits, a light blue shirt and a maroon striped tie. He felt comfortable which was important. If the opportunity was to arise tonight, he was going to ask Patricia for a divorce.

They pushed their way through the front door into a small lobby area. A man appeared from nowhere, like the Shopkeeper in Mr Benn.

"Ah, good evening and welcome to our humble establishment. I take it that we have the pleasure of welcoming our Governor and his charming wife".

"You do" said Philip. "An eight-thirty booking".

"And this is the first time that you have graced us with your presence. May I take your coats?"

Patricia and Philip slipped off their coats and passed them to the man who spun around quickly and shouted at the top of his voice something unintelligible. A young boy appeared and the man threw the coats in his direction.

"Please. Follow me to our bar area for a relaxing drink, if you will".

Patricia looked at Philip.

"You haven't brought me here for a vindaloo, have you?"

"No" hissed Philip back at her. "It's Middle Eastern, not Indian. It's a whole different concept".

"Well it had better be good" she whispered back.

They followed the man down a corridor and up a broad flight of steps. There, in front of them, lay a smart, New York warehouse-style wine bar with Gershwin playing in the background. They were shown to a table and given menus.

"I hope that this will be suitable. My name is Assam. May I fetch you a little something to drink?"

"Gin and tonic" said Patricia. "Plenty of gin, splash of tonic".

"Good. And for sir....?"

"Oh, a pint of bitter, please".

The man went away.

"Bitter?" sneered Patricia. "You've been on this island too long".

"There's nothing wrong with drinking bitter. Even the women around here drink it".

"Shows a lack of breeding" said Patricia.

"You're such a snob" declared Philip.

"Looks like you need a decent bit of snobbery around here".

Philip looked at her and tutted.

Assam returned with their drinks then whisked away again.

"Do you understand anything on this menu, Philip?"

"Not really" confessed Philip. "It's like that time in Romania".

"Oh, yes" said Patricia, smiling. "When you decided to go to a Chinese restaurant because you thought that you'd be able to understand the menu".

"And I couldn't because it was in Romanian".

"Yes. What did we end up with that night?"

"Chef's special, I think. I didn't realise that they used so many potatoes and beetroots in Chinese cooking".

"Made it easier to hold onto the food with chopsticks, didn't it?"

"And you ruined a dress by dropping beetroot down the front".

"And there wasn't a dry cleaner for miles".

They laughed.

"Do you remember what we did on the tram on the way home?"

"Was that with you?" asked Patricia,

Philip looked downcast.

"Only joking" she said. "I remember every minute of it. I'm sure the conductor does as well".

"Served him right for wearing quiet shoes. Did he charge us?"

"We should have charged him! I swear that he was there for ten minutes before he said anything".

Philip giggled. Patricia smiled at him.

"I've not heard that in a while".

"What?"

"You laughing at something I said. It's nice".

Philip smiled at her. When she was like this, she was excellent company.

The man returned.

"Have you chosen from our humble fare?"

Philip grimaced.

"Could you explain a few of the dishes?"

"Of course, sir. This" he said pointing to one of the options, "is sheep's testicles marinated in red wine and served on a bed of couscous with a small side salad".

"And this?" asked Philip pointing to the next dish.

"Sheep's testicles sliced and pan-fried in butter. Served with rice and a small side salad. The next dish on the menu is..."

"Sheep's testicles?" suggested Patricia.

"....leg of lamb served with a warm avocado salad. There is also steak and chips as an option. May I suggest that you try the mixed starter".

"What does that involve?" asked Patricia.

"Various parts of a sheep cooked in various ways".

"Sounds fine" she said. "I'll have the leg of lamb".

"And I'll have the sheep's testicles cooked in wine".

The man took their menus and disappeared into the kitchen, leaving Philip and Patricia laughing and joking together.

Eventually, they were shown into the main restaurant which was decorated in a modern, relaxed style. There were a few more diners in the restaurant but they were well spaced out.

The mixed starter arrived.

"I think it's still alive" said Philip prodding it with a fork.

"Quick" said Patricia. "Get some oxygen. I think there may still be a chance!"

They tucked in, finding the taste of the food much more palatable than the look of it suggested. They washed the starter down with iced water and a light hock.   "Not bad at all" admitted Patricia placing her knife and fork on the plate.

"Yes" agreed Philip. "I admit that I am pleasantly surprised".

The waiter came and took away the plates.

"So, how is Toby-woby?"

"Fine".

"And your father?"

"Fine, too".

They fell silent.

Philip looked around the restaurant at the other diners. Then he looked back at Patricia and saw that she was looking at him.

"What? Is there something wrong?"

Patricia smiled again.

"I think there is, isn't there Philip?"

"What do you mean?" he asked, not quite understanding her meaning.

"Look, Philip" said Patricia. "We've done a lot over the years. We're had some good times, some bad times and an awful lot of tedium. When it clicks between us, like it's doing tonight, it's super, really super. But most of the time, it just doesn't work between us, does it?"

"No, you're right" said Philip.

"I love you, Philip, and I always will but I think that we both know that it's over between us, don't we?"

Philip looked away.

"Yes, Patricia. It's just not the same anymore".

Patricia took his hand.

"I think that we should divorce. It'll free both of us up".

Even though it was what Philip wanted to hear, to listen to the words was painful. He turned his head back towards her.

"It seems such a shame" he said finally.

"Let's be practical, Philip. Look. Toby and I...well, you know well enough, I guess".

Philip nodded.

"He is speaking to Abigail tonight. He's hoping that she won't object too much. Then, well, we're going to get married".

"Congratulations" said Philip. "Are you sure it's what you want?"

Patricia nodded. "I think so. He's a good man. Very different from you. He actually likes my friends".

Philip smiled.

"Did it show?"

"Always".

"Sorry".

Patricia looked at Philip.

"Well?"

"Well, what?" asked Philip.

"The divorce! Yes or no".

Philip sighed.

"Yes, of course".

Patricia smiled and patted his hand.

"You never know, Philip. One day, you might someone special yourself".

Philip laughed.

"You never know, do you Patricia".

The main course arrived along with a bottle of Moroccan Red.

"This is truly excellent" said Patricia. "What's yours like?"

"Good. Very good".

"Can I have a slice of one of your balls?" asked Patricia.

"How could I resist?" said Philip.

They carried on eating for a while in silence.

"Are you all right, Philip?" asked Patricia after a while.

"Yes, yes, it's just that....well, it's the end. It'll take some time to come to terms with it".

"I know, it does feel a bit peculiar".

She raised her glass.

"Here's to happiness".

"To happiness".

They arrived back at Ash-Na-Garoo shortly after midnight. They sneaked into the kitchen to make coffee, Philip checking to make sure that Mrs Kinloss wasn't doing any midnight baking (in this kitchen, we bake when the urge takes us, no matter what time of the day or night it is). As Patricia was pouring the coffee Philip went off to find some rum to spice them up a little.

They sat in the kitchen for a good twenty minutes or so chatting away before washing up and going upstairs.

The arrangement was for Patricia to sleep in the main guest bedroom, next door to Philip's. They stopped at the top of the stairs.

"It's actually a lovely house" said Patricia.

"Yes, it is" said Philip. "Not bad at all, really".

Patricia turned to Philip.

"Thanks".

"What for?"

"For a lovely evening. For the last twenty years. For agreeing to the divorce. For just being you".

She leaned close to him and kissed him on the cheek. Then, she went into her room.

Philip stood where she had left him, his mind confused.

I should go to bed, he thought to himself.

Yet pity, a great deal of self pity came over him like a wave. She doesn't want me anymore. She doesn't want me anymore. She doesn't want me anymore.

He walked slowly down the corridor and put his hand on Patricia's bedroom door. His heart was beating so fast that he thought it would break free of his chest at any moment. He reached down for the handle. It felt cool to the touch.

Then, he stood back, away from the door.

Go to bed, he told himself. Get out of here.

He turned as if to go, then stopped again. He looked back at the door. He took a step back towards it, then stopped again.

Amanda. You want Amanda, said one voice.

Patricia. You want Patricia, said another.

Philip closed his eyes.

Back to bed, he said, and walked down the corridor to his room.

Once inside, he undressed quickly, found his pyjamas and went into the bathroom to use the toilet and brush his teeth. He looked at himself in the mirror.

"Well done" he said out loud. "That was bloody close".

He rinsed his mouth and spat down the sink. Then he went back into his bedroom and closed the door gently behind him.

There, on his bed, lay Patricia.

"One more time, Philip, for old time's sake".

Philip threw himself onto the bed and kissed Patricia passionately. She dragged off his pyjamas and before long they were locked together.

Patricia climaxed three or four times before Philip came with a whoosh of ecstasy followed by a grim feeling of guilt and betrayal.

As they lay there, Patricia kissing his chest, all he wanted to do was climb under the covers and die. He hated himself and hated her more.

And as she slipped down his body and nibbled and pulled with her mouth until he came again, he thought of Amanda and wanted to die.

Love And Death

'The difference between love and death is a fine line indeed' - St Brodag

Philip woke up in a sweat wracked with guilt. He sat there in bed for a while just panting. Next to him lay Patricia, breathing lightly.

The room was dark and quiet. The wind had died down outside and all was still. He checked the time - two-fifteen.

Philip looked at Patricia again. The delicate nose, the wide, beautiful mouth, the perfect chin. He looked at her. He looked at her and he hated her, almost as much as he hated himself.

It would be so easy, thought Philip. Take the pillow and keep it on her face until she stopped moving.

Philip paused for a moment, then gently picked up his pillow. He moved himself over her, trying his best not to disturb her. Then, he lowered the pillow and covered her face. One, two seconds passed and nothing happened. Then, Patricia started to move her hands and arms slowly at first, then more urgently. She began to scream but the pillow muffled the volume. Her legs and lower body started to thrash about, trying to dislodge him, but Philip began to press harder. Her fingers tried to find a way to push the pillow back but to no avail.

After a couple of minutes, she stopped moving.

Philip kept the pressure on for about five minutes more, just to be sure.

Then, he slowly peeled the pillow back and was surprised to see that it was Amanda's dead and staring face that was looking at him.

"Noooo" he cried.

Then, Philip woke up in a sweat wracked with guilt. He sat there in bed for a while just panting. Next to him lay Patricia.

The room was dark and quiet. The wind had died down outside and all was still. He checked the time - two-fifteen.

Bollocks, he thought, that was a bad dream.

He looked over at Patricia.

Funny, he thought, she doesn't seem to be breathing. He prodded her with his finger. No response.

"Patricia" he said. Nothing. "Patricia" he said in a louder voice. Nothing.

He switched on the lamp that lay on his bed-side table. He pulled the covers off her.

"PATRICIA!" he shouted. "Come on, wake up".

He knelt over her and slapped her on the face. He tried to pull her to her feet but she was a dead weight.

A dead weight! thought Philip.

"I've killed her. Fuck, fuck, fuck. I've killed her".

Philip began to slap his own face to try and wake himself up.

"Come on" he shouted. "This is another nightmare. Wake up!"

It didn't work. He was already awake.

He began to pace.

"What to do, what to do?" he muttered frenetically.

"Phone the police, that's right". He crossed to the phone and picked up the receiver. Then he slammed it down again.

"Prison. Prison" he said. "No police. No police".

He looked at her again.

"Fuck, fuck, fuckity fuck".

Amanda was woken by her mobile phone. She leaned over, picked the phone up and pressed a button.

"Amanda" said a voice.

"Yes, who's that?"

"It's Philip".

"Philip" she said matter-of-factly. "I don't know a Philip who would wake me up in the middle of the night".

There was silence on the other end for a moment.

"She's dead".

"What?"

"I've killed her".

Amanda began to come to her senses.

"Patricia?"

"Yes".

"What did you go and do a thing like that for?"

"I don't know. I dreamt that I'd smothered her and then when I woke up she was there - dead!"

"Have you phoned anyone else?"

"How can I?" said Philip. "I'm a murderer. 'Excuse me, officer, but I think that I've just killed my wife'".

"Are you sure she's dead?"

"Well, if not breathing is one of the symptoms of being dead then she's dead".

Amanda thought.

"I'm coming round".

Philip answered the door to Amanda.

"What the hell have you done, Philip?"

"It wasn't my fault. I didn't mean to kill her. It just happened".

Amanda looked at him.

"Good defence, Philip. I'm sure that will go down well with the jury".

"It's no time to joke, Amanda. I've got a dead woman in the house. In my bed!"

A frown came across Amanda's face.

"In your bed? What's she doing there?" exploded Amanda. "Why is she in your bed? You told me it was over!"

Philip began to say something then thought better of it.

"Look, come upstairs and have a look".

Philip led the way and Amanda followed.

Philip slowly opened the door to the bedroom and the two of them crept in. There, on the bed, lay Patricia looking very deceased.

"Did you do first-aid?" asked Philip.

"I am a doctor, Philip" said Amanda very slowly. "Anyway, first-aid won't do any good if she's dead".

"I wonder if there's a pulse?"

"Do you mean you've not checked?"

"No. I mean, I don't know where the pulse is".

Amanda shook her head then walked across to the bed, Philip sneaking along behind her. She sat next to Patricia and picked up her wrist.

"Can you feel anything?" asked Philip.

"Only your breath on my neck. Back off!"

Amanda tried to find a pulse on the wrist but couldn't. She tried the pulse in the neck as well with no luck.

"Get me a spoon, Philip" she demanded.

"Table or teaspoon" he asked.

"Look, just get a fucking spoon, will you. Tablespoon".

Philip looked hurt.

"No need to shout".

"Yes there is. You slept with your bloody wife tonight" cried Amanda getting to her feet and pointing, accusingly, at Philip.

"I'm married to her!" he shouted back. "It's hardly a capital offence".

"No, it's not. But you said it was over. You lied".

"It _is_ over. She wants a divorce".

"Then, what was this, tonight, eh? The first down payment on the settlement?"

"No. We slept together. I can't explain it but that's how it is".

"But you don't want to sleep with me".

"I do want to sleep with you. I can't".

"You can with her".

"Not anymore, I can't. She's dead!".

"Who's dead?" asked a voice from the bed.

Both Philip and Amanda swung around to see Patricia sitting up looking rather groggy. Philip and Amanda both stared.

Philip turned to Amanda, waving his hands in the air.

"You can't even diagnose death. What sort of doctor are you?"

"The kind of doctor who doesn't tell deceitful lies to someone she respects. And, anyway, you didn't even check for a pulse and she's your wife!".

"I didn't know how to".

"No, but you feel pretty confident at smothering people".

"What are you talking about?" asked Patricia feebly.

"Shut up!" said both Philip and Amanda turning to her.

"Who's she?" asked Patricia.

"She's supposed to be a doctor" said Philip.

Amanda looked at him darkly.

Patricia yawned.

"I don't think I should have mixed my tablets with all that drink tonight. It's knocked me completely out". And with that, she fell backwards into bed, fast asleep.

Philip watched her fall, his mouth falling open.

"That's it" said Amanda and stormed out of the room, rapidly followed by Philip. She ran along the landing and down the stairs and it wasn't until she was crossing the entrance hall that Philip caught her up. He grabbed at her elbow.

"Get off" she shouted.

"Amanda!"

"Get off me" she screamed, shaking herself free.

"Look, I'm sorry".

Amanda stopped and looked at him.

"Sorry? Sorry for what?"

"All this" he said with a wave of his hand.

"What sorry that you slept with Patricia or sorry that I found out?"

"Both" said Philip.

"Both!   You can't have both, Philip. Both is not an option".

"Look" he said, trying to calm the situation. "Patricia's real reason for coming here was to talk to me about getting a divorce. We went out for a meal to talk about it. We drank quite a bit. We came back here and it happened, it just happened".

Amanda started to cry.

"But it didn't happen for me, did it, Philip? It didn't happen for me".

"Amanda!" pleaded Philip.

"Leave me alone. I don't want to see you again".

Amanda ran out of the house. Philip went to the door and saw the BMW accelerating away.

He let the door close and slumped down on the floor with his back against the wall.

"Fuck!"

A Deal In The Dark

'We each must face our own dark night of the soul' - St Brodag

Henry Geruish watched his daughter's car pull away from the house. He wondered, briefly, where she was going at that time in the morning. He was tired and confused. He couldn't sleep. He hadn't had a good night's sleep since he didn't know when.

He looked across at his wife who was irritatingly in a deep slumber. He didn't mind really. She was a good woman.

Henry left the bedroom and walked down to his study. He switched the lamp on and collapsed into his big leather chair. His 'thinking chair' Amanda had christened it many years before. It was where Henry sat when he needed space, when he needed to cut himself off from family life and ponder the big and bad things of this world.

Henry wondered if he had gone too far this time - bitten off more than he could chew.

He looked across at the family portrait that hung on the wall opposite his desk. There he was, a little younger for sure, with May and all the children. He smiled, remembering the awful problems they had getting everyone to sit still for the photographer.

On the desk was a picture of Henry and May taken on their wedding day.

Did we really look like that? he thought.

He sat back in his chair, put his hands behind his head and put his feet on the desk. He looked at the ceiling, noticing the contours for the first time. He thought that he could see a patch where the paint had been applied a bit too thinly, yet this could just have been the awkward casting of a shadow.

There has to be a way forward, he thought. Problems always have solutions, even when you don't particularly like the outcome.

He focussed his mind and began to form a plan.

Henry picked up the phone and dialled a number.

"Hello" said a weary voice.

"Set up the meeting, MacLeod. I want to see your clients tonight".

"This is all a bit sudden, Mr Geruish. I will have to ring them and see if they're available".

"They'll be available if they want to do business. Meet at my warehouse on the quay at, say, four-fifteen?"

"Four-fifteen. OK, I'll tell them. Goodnight".

"Goodnight".

Henry replaced the receiver. He went back upstairs, dressed quickly, and was out of the house without disturbing anyone.

Out at sea, half a mile from the coast of the island, a submarine broke through the surface of the water and came to rest between the waves.

From several hatches, men began to clamber out. Dinghies were inflated and these were lowered into the water. Very soon, two inflatables were being manoeuvred towards the shore, each one carrying a crew of six dark figures. It took them twenty minutes to reach the beach. When they did so, the men rapidly deflated their boats and disappeared into the woods beyond the shore.

Out at sea, the submarine slipped silently away again.

The Geruish Family Warehouse had passed into St Brogadan legend. Many people believed it to be the place where the family fortune was stored.

"Great bars of gold and caskets full of jewels" was the general local understanding of what the building contained.

Others believed that it was a hot bed of international drug-dealing or something just as sinister.

In reality, it was a warehouse and housed nothing more than a few old family heirlooms and a few cases of whiskey.

The black Mercedes turned up at the main gate and was quickly waved through by the security guard. They drove around to the back of the building and parked the car there. Then, two men climbed out and crossed the yard to the rear door. Then, with a final look around them, they entered.

They found inside a brightly lit building, empty, save for a few crates neatly stacked against the walls. At the far end was a desk and at the desk sat Henry Geruish.

When he saw the men, Henry clambered to his feet.

"Good evening, gentlemen" he said as they approached the desk.

"I think that should be, good morning" suggested MacLeod.

"Perhaps" said Henry.

"This is my client, Monsieur Jean-Claude.".

Henry offered a hand which was firmly clenched in return.

"It's nice to meet you, Monsieur".

The Frenchman nodded. He was a tall man, as tall as the Prime Minister himself. He had grey hair and a long, thin nose. His mouth was small and tightly lipped. He wore a thick black coat over his suit and a scarf around his neck.

"Please, take a seat" suggested Geruish with a wave of his hand.

"I prefer to stand".

"As you like".

MacLeod cleared his throat.

"I take it that you have reconsidered our proposal".

"I have".

"And?" asked MacLeod.

"It is still unacceptable".

The Jean-Claude looked at MacLeod, then back at Geruish.

"Why, then, have you called us out of our beds?" asked MacLeod.

"I would like to make a counter-proposal to you".

The Frenchman's eyes narrowed to slits.

"Tell us what you mean" he said.

"Well" said Henry leaning back against the desk. "You consider that we had a deal at one stage. You contend that I went back on that deal".

MacLeod looked at his client who nodded.

"That's about it, Mr Geruish. I believed that we had an agreement. You went behind our backs and now you have set up an arrangement with a third party. Is that not true?"

Henry nodded in return.

"We have entered into negotiations with a third party, for sure. But let me explain that nothing has been finalised yet. Nothing has been signed, just as nothing was signed when we began to consider doing business together. Whoever makes the best deal for this island will get the contract".

The Frenchman sneered.

"And what about you, Mr Geruish".

"Well, my services don't come that cheaply. This island runs as a democracy. We have elected officials and I am just one of them".

MacLeod started to laugh.

"Everyone knows that the power sits with you, Mr Geruish. All the elected officials are members of your family. They'll do what you ask them to".

Henry shrugged.

"That may be so" he said. "However, I would need ten times the amount that you have offered me to agree to the plan".

"Two million pounds?" asked the Frenchman.

"Your arithmetic is excellent, Monsieur. That's about it" said Henry folding his arms in front of him and staring at them from underneath his bushy eyebrows.

MacLeod started to speak but the Frenchman silenced him.

"It is a dangerous game that you are playing, Mr Geruish. Did you not know that the organisation that I represent can be very....ruthless". He grimaced for dramatic affect.

"I'm sure they can be" nodded Geruish. "However, if your organisation wants to set up this deal on this island so desperately then they won't want to do anything that will bring attention to themselves".

"I don't want to have to use force, Mr Geruish. I already have many associates positioned on this island".

"I'm sure you have. It won't go down very well with the British Government at all, will it. There'll be a battalion of paras here before you'll know it".

The Jean-Claude looked at him then chuckled.

"I am sure that it will not come to that. We are both reasonable men. Come, Mr MacLeod. Let us return to our beds. We will give your proposal due consideration".

They turned and left.

Henry flopped down onto one of the chairs and hung his head. He had to delay these people until his own plans had come to fruition. That meant re-jigging the timetable. It was all getting rather messy.

The Frenchman was not a happy man. As they left the warehouse site, he turned to MacLeod.

"That man needs to be taught a lesson" he said carefully.

MacLeod looked at him.

"What kind of lesson?"

"That is my concern. I must talk with my superiors immediately. You, Mr MacLeod, must keep the pressure on Mr Geruish".

The car left the warehouse enclosure and headed off up the promenade.

MacLeod nodded in agreement with Monsieur Jean-Claude.

"I'll ring him later this morning. Try and find out what he is up to".

"Good" said the Frenchman. Now, stop the car".

The car slowed to a halt.

"Get out, Mr MacLeod".

The car stopped and the driver got out and opened the passenger door.

"Why is it every time I meet up with you people you never take me home. You always end up dropping me miles from home".

"The exercise will do you good" said the Frenchman.

"I will have to add it to the final bill. Inconvenience expenses".

"Whatever" said Monsieur Jean-Claude.

The Mercedes drove off leaving MacLeod to his own devices.

Amanda had spent the early morning hours sitting in her car overlooking a beach. She watched the sunrise, bright and golden, then drove back to Port Victoria. She parked the car on the promenade and made her way to a small cafe just behind the ferry terminal that did excellent breakfasts.

As she walked through the door, she saw her father sitting at a table near the back. He had his back to her and was reading yesterday's paper. She steeled herself and walked up to the table, sitting down opposite him.

"You look rough" she said.

"Thanks" he mumbled.

"You having the works?" she asked.

"Yep".

"I'll have the same then".

And both of them sat in their in silence, each one wondering why life was so bad for them at the moment and what the immediate future might hold.

Goodbye And Adieu

'Fare thee well, where'er ye travel' - St Brodag

Breakfast was awkward at Ash-Na-Garoo that morning. Philip came down first, closely followed by Patricia. Mrs Kinloss brought in breakfast which was then eaten in complete silence.

Patricia looked at Philip out of the corner of her eye. He was frowning and deep in thought, chewing on a piece of bacon. She looked back down at her plate, her appetite fading rapidly.

They carried on in silence for a good twenty minutes until Patricia could stand it no longer.

"Philip, about last night...".

"Don't".

"It's just that...."

"I don't want to talk about it".

Mrs Kinloss came in and removed the plates.

Philip half-turned away from Patricia to look out of the window.

"Who was that girl last night?" asked Patricia.

"I said I don't want to talk about it" he said sharply. "A doctor".

"I'm sorry, Philip. I should have told you about the tablets. They calm me down, help me to sleep".

"I thought you were dead".

"Yes, well, sorry".

Silence.

Patricia cleared her throat.

"Did I do anything wrong last night?"

"You didn't. I did".

"Oh".

Philip stood up.

"I need some air" he said leaving the room.

Patricia's eyes followed him as he left. She rubbed her face with her hands and sighed.

Philip took a walk down through the terraced gardens. Eventually, he came to a stone seat that had been carved out of the base of a rocky outcrop. He slumped down onto the seat and looked out at the grey sea below him that foamed and swirled at the bottom of the cliffs.

Philip felt numb. It wasn't the sort of numb that a person feels when they were over tired, it went much deeper than that, right to the centre of his being.

How could I do it? he said to himself. How could I do it? I betrayed Amanda.

In his mind's eye, he went over the ground time and time again. He should have been less friendly in the restaurant. He should have been cold towards Patricia. He should have gone straight to bed, not sat chatting. He should have locked his bedroom door. He should have said 'no' to Patricia. He should have made some excuse to Amanda as to why Patricia was in his bed. He should have not been so rude to Amanda when she was trying to help. He should have been more forceful, prevented her from leaving, begged her to stay. He should have followed her.

It was no use. No matter how he willed it, reality was there. Amanda didn't want to see him again.

He began to grieve for their relationship: for the friendship that was now gone; for the laughs that they were not going to share together; for the feelings that would now not be experienced. He put his head between his legs, as though the despondency of it all would overwhelm him.

He must have been sitting there for a good two hours when he heard footsteps near to him. He looked up and there stood Patricia.

She smiled at him, the smile scarcely hiding the sadness that she was feeling.

"I'm going to go. I've booked a ticket on the afternoon ferry".

"You don't have to".

"Oh, I think I do, Philip" said Patricia sitting down next to him. "I think that I've been here too long already".

"But Patricia...".

"No, no. There's no need to be polite. You are sweet, Philip. You may think that you want me here but, for some reason, me being here is not good for you, is it?"

Philip smiled feebly.

"No. It's not".

The surf rumbled and roared below them. Above them, only the gulls cried.

"Thanks, again, for everything, Philip. I'm sorry that I've been so mean to you. You don't deserve it. You're such a nice man. A very nice man".

Patricia put her arm around him.

"It's the girl isn't it?"

He nodded.

"Very pretty, quite young if I remember. I hope that I haven't spoilt things between you. No matter what, Philip, if she cares about you, if she loves you, you'll be able to sort it out".

They fell silent again.

"How are you getting to the ferry?" asked Philip eventually.

"Oh, the scarecrow's taking me".

Philip smiled.

Patricia stood up and kissed him on the cheek.

"Goodbye, Philip. Good luck. Phone me soon".

And then she was gone.

When Philip returned to the office, Nigel had left to take Patricia to the ferry. Mary was there, busily working away. She looked at Philip when he came in and sensed that all was not well.

"Any post?" asked Philip.

"Nothing special: three invites to social functions, a couple of government papers, a circular from the Foreign office and another death threat".

"No calls?"

"None".

Philip picked up the death threat. It was made by cutting out pieces from magazines and papers.

"YOU WILL DIE LIKE THE KITTIWAKE" it said.

"Have you told the police again, Mary?"

"I have. They're keeping an extra eye on visitors to the island".

"I can't believe that anyone will do anything".

"Neither can I. I know that you were directly responsible for the extinction of the bird but you didn't mean it, did you? I mean, you don't deserve to die, do you?"

Philip shook his head.

"I suppose I don't deserve to die for killing the kittiwake, no. Maybe for some other things that I have done but not for the kittiwake. There are some sad and sick people out there, Mary. Keep an eye out for them".

"Er, thanks, Philip" said Mary.

Philip went into his office and busied himself with the paperwork. He was disturbed a few minutes later by a phone call from Henry Geruish.

"Are you all right?" asked Henry when Philip turned up. "You don't sound so good".

"I don't feel so good. I feel like shit".

"Where's Patricia?"

"Gone" said Philip.

"Oh. For good?"

"I think so".

"I'm sorry" said Geruish genuinely.

Philip nodded.

That night, Philip found his way to the Ship Inn. He found the bar comfortably full. He pushed his way through to the front.

"Pint, please, George".

"Look's like someone pissed in your milk, like, tonight" he said.

"Things aren't working out too well, George".

"You know what you should do, Governor. Take that lass out, Amanda. I think she likes you. A bit of female company will do you the world of good".

Philip sighed.

"You don't know just how wrong you can be, George". A pint landed on the beer mat in front of Philip. He handed over some change, picked up his beer and tried to lose himself in the crowd.

A few minutes later, he saw Nigel making his way towards him, glass in hand, cigarette in mouth.

"Hiya, Philip".

Philip nodded to him.

They stood there, awkwardly for a few minutes. After a while, Nigel offered to buy Philip another drink. Philip tried to refuse but Nigel was having none of it. One further drink led to another and then another.

At eleven o'clock, George called time. The bar emptied. George looked over at Philip and Nigel and motioned to them that they should adjourn to the back room, which they did. After locking up, George joined them, bringing a couple of jugs full of beer. They sat there for a little while longer, getting steadily more and more inebriated.

"Well, Governor" said George. "It's not too bad here, is it?"

"I love it here" slurred Philip. "It's a lovely place full of lovely people".

"Aye" drooled Nigel. "Lovely people".

"No, I really mean it" said Philip. "I mean, look at the people I know. You guys. You guys! What a team we are. Aren't we?"

"Just like Newcastle under Keegan!" said George.

"Or the Arsenal under George Graham" said Nigel.

"Or the England cricket team.....or another good team" ventured Philip.

They all took a good draught of beer.

"It'll soon be Assembly Day." said George. "Bumper day for me, as well. I'll be run off my feet all day".

"Big day" echoed Nigel.

"Will your wife be coming back?"

Nigel looked at Philip who dropped his head.

"No" he said eventually.

"Ah" said George. "You should get that Amanda girl to accompany you, then".

Philip paused.

"She hates me".

George looked puzzled.

"Hates you, why?"

"Because I was faithful".

George looked at him again. Nigel started to titter.

"You what? You're kidding me, aren't you".

"No" said Philip, stifling a laugh. "It's true".

Nigel began to guffaw. George started to shake and Philip, against his better judgement, began to laugh as well.

"Don't please" he pleaded. "It's serious, it really is. I'm heartbroken".

This only caused them to laugh more. Nigel slid off his chair. George kept on banging the table. Even Philip threw his head back and roared.

This carried on for a good five minutes. They would stop for a while, look at each other and start all over again. Nigel spilt his beer before he passed out, rolling on the floor and coming to a rest at the bottom of the wall.

George went over to him and checked to make sure he was all right.

"I've got a blanket upstairs. I'll make sure he's comfortable".

George called a taxi for Philip. He got back to Ash-Na-garoo shortly after one o'clock, climbed the stairs and went to bed.

At one o'clock in the morning, Henry Geruish's mobile phone buzzed into life with a quick burst of Beethoven. He reached across and picked it up.

"Hello, Geruish".

"Expect us to make a move soon" said a voice before ending the phone call.

Geruish leaned backwards and started another fitful night's sleep.

Only The Good Die Young

'I wipe away the tear that falls from your eye' - St Brodag

A week went by. Philip knew nothing but self pity. Self pity and guilt. Self pity, guilt and a deep regret that he and Amanda hadn't made love at the cottage when they had the opportunity to. Philip knew nothing but self pity, guilt, regrets and a pain deep inside that he could not explain. It was a peculiar pain, raw and intense, and every time he thought of Amanda, it throbbed and smarted.

He had tried her mobile phone but it was always switched off and he dared not leave a message. He started to hang around outside the hospital but either she was taking some holiday or her work pattern had changed.

Philip started to write her a letter but he didn't know what to write so he just screwed up the paper and threw it on the floor.

Mary and Nigel were deeply worried. Nigel suggested that they repeat the drinking performance of the other night but Philip couldn't be bothered. He knew that Amanda would no longer come into The Ship for fear of meeting him.

Mary bought him a small hairy gonk to sit on his desk. It had the words 'Thinking of You' written on a ribbon that was sewn to its body. Philip put it next to Patricia's picture.

Henry rang up Nigel one day.

"He hasn't started talking to dead pigeons yet has he?" he asked.

Nigel declined to comment, only suggesting that Philip needed a bit of time to think about things.

Philip came down for breakfast, one morning, and made his way to the Morning Room. He sat down and waited. Mrs Kinloss didn't like him to go in the kitchen in the mornings (or at any time to be truthful).

He looked outside at the clouds racing by.

His pain twisted and turned as his mind wandered back to Amanda.

After five minutes had passed, Philip began to wonder what he had done to upset Mrs Kinloss so much. After ten minutes, he thought that he must be in a lot of trouble for her not to have made an appearance yet. After fifteen minutes, Philip got up and went next door into the kitchen.

He pushed the door open and looked around. The place was deserted.

"Hello" he shouted. No reply.

He moved forward hesitantly, expecting at any moment for a bellowing cry to emerge from some dark recess. Nothing.

He turned on his heels and was about to leave when he heard a door opening at the back of the kitchen. He looked around and there was Mrs Kinloss.

Her hair was out of place, her pinny was creased and dirty and she wore no make up. She looked up and saw Philip.

"Oh, Governor" she said nervously. "I'm so sorry. I didn't realise what time it was. Sit yourself down next door and I'll have your breakfast ready in a wee jiffy".

Philip didn't move.

"Mrs Kinloss? What's happened? Is something wrong?"

"Ah, nothing for you to worry about" she said, filling the kettle under the tap. "Nothing at all".

She placed the kettle on the work top and plugged it in.

Philip watched her. Something was definitely amiss.

"Look, why don't you go back to your rooms. Leave the breakfast for me to do".

Mrs Kinloss, who had her back to him, laughed light-heartedly.

"You, Governor. Make breakfast! I'll not hear of it. I'll not hear of it".

She busied herself by preparing the porridge.

"This kitchen doesn't believe that Governor's should make their own breakfast. That will never do, no, no, no".

She stopped. Philip could see her shoulders gently shaking. She let out an audible sob. Philip moved towards her and put an arm around her. She shrugged it off.

"Now" she sobbed, "where did I leave that bacon?"

Philip took hold of her hands and turned her around to face him.

"You go and sit down in the Morning Room. I'll make us a pot of tea and you can tell me what's going on".

Mrs Kinloss looked up at him, tight-lipped, and nodded. She moved slowly away out of the kitchen and Philip made the tea. He took it through to the Morning Room and found Mrs Kinloss looking out of the window. He popped the tea down on the table and poured two cups.

"Sunny but fresh" she announced from the window. "You'll need to wrap up warm today if you're out and about".

"Come and sit down here" he said. "I've poured the tea".

Rather hesitantly, Mrs Kinloss turned and sat down next to him at the table.

"So come on, then. What's the problem?"

Mrs Kinloss looked at him.

"I shouldn't be burdening you with this, Governor, I really shouldn't. You have enough to worry about in a day".

Philip smiled and took her hand.

"And where will I get my breakfast from if you're not happy".

She smiled and dabbed at her eyes with her handkerchief. She breathed deeply.

"It's my son, Charles".

"The accountant?" asked Philip.

"Yes" she nodded. "The same. He was in an accident yesterday".

She began to cry again.

"I'm sorry, Mrs Kinloss. I didn't know. What sort of accident?"

She blew her cheeks out.

"A plane crash near Bangkok. It crashed during take off. Two hundred people on board and no survive.........no survivors".

Philip clutched her hand tightly.

"I'm so sorry, Mrs Kinloss. I really am. You must be devastated".

She nodded.

"He has a wife and two children too, doesn't he?"

"Yes. They're at home in Edinburgh. I can't believe it. The two boys will be so upset. And Jane, his wife. What can I say to her, Governor? What can I say?"

Philip shrugged his shoulders.

"I don't know. I just don't know. I....I don't know what to say. It's dreadful, really dreadful".

They sat there for a few minutes, Mrs Kinloss wiping her eyes now and then and Philip trying to help, to share her grief.

"Jane and the boys are flying out tonight. The company's paying for them. That was nice, wasn't it".

Philip nodded.

"Look Mrs Kinloss" he said eventually. "I really think that you need to take today off. I'll fix my own meals. You need some time to yourself. Come and talk to me if you need to. I'll be around all day".

"Are you sure?" she asked.

"I'm sure" said Philip with a smile.

Mrs Kinloss smiled and patted his hand.

"You're a good man, Governor. A good man".

"That's my problem" said Philip.

Philip asked Mary to organise a card and flowers. He also sent a note to Mrs Kinloss's daughter-in-law expressing his sorrow.

The next day, at breakfast, Mrs Kinloss appeared as immaculately as ever, though the spark had gone from her eye. She was quiet and apologetic and treated Philip with a gentleness that was new and unusual.

Two days later, Mrs Kinloss came to see Philip in his office.

"They've found Charles" she said excitedly. "His body at least. But that's something, Governor, isn't it. We'll have someone to bury now".

The following few days were filled with rehearsals for Assembly Day itself. Philip was trying his best to learn his lines in Brogadan. To do this, when the weather permitted, he would walk to and fro in the terraced garden, reading out loud the various words. One day, Mrs Kinloss came rushing out to find him.

"Jane's set the day for the funeral. It's a week on Tuesday. I'll be able to stay for Assembly Day then I'll fly across, if that's all right with you".

Philip told her it was fine.

A Celebration

'What is a party but a collection of people enjoying themselves?' - St Brodag

The preparations for Assembly Day seemed to start earlier and earlier every year. Not only was it a solemn ceremony to ratify the authority of the island's parliament. It was also a huge party. Every community did something every year, whether it be Cragmuir's famed beer festival or Port Victoria's fun fair. Nigel, of course, opted for Cragmuir's delights.

Everyone dressed in their finest clothes, often with a piece of blue ribbon stuck on a lapel or collar. Children would seek out favourite aunties or uncles who would give them small coins as an Assembly Treat.

In short, it was the premier day in the island's life and everyone looked forward to it with great expectation.

"You look nice" said Mary as Philip emerged from his office in full regalia.

"No I don't" he insisted. "I look stupid".

"Still" said Mary. "It's only for a few hours".

"My heart's not in it".

"Well at least put a brave face on it. You look miserable".

"I am miserable, Mary. I can't do happy today".

"How about mildly bored?"

Philip pulled a face.

"No, no" said Mary thoughtfully. "I think that I actually prefer miserable".

Philip smiled at her in spite of himself.

"Any calls?"

Mary smiled apologetically. "Sorry, no".

"It's just that I was....expecting....".

"Nothing, I'm afraid. Some good news, though. Your new mobile has arrived". She pulled out a bright purple object with chrome edging and waved it around.

"I don't know whether I should use it or wear it. Who designs these things?".

"Mobile phone designers" said Mary brightly.

Philip frowned at her.

"Any sign of Nigel?"

"Not yet".

"Could you please ring George at the Ship Inn? Nigel's supposed to be here, now!".

"OK".

Philip went back into his office. He was wearing a light suit under his velvet gown. The collar of the gown was edged in ermine and smelled as though it had gone off. Dangling from his neck was a large gold chain from which a silver star hung. To finish off the 'Governor Ensemble' he carried a small mace in his right hand.

Mary popped her head around the door.

"George has got him up. He'll bring him over in a few minutes".

"He'd better be OK".

Nigel was far from OK.

Philip, himself, had woken up feeling the worse for wear from a slight over indulgance in the Ship Inn the night before. To overcome his heavy head, he had gone for an early morning walk, he had drunk two litres of mineral water and a box of orange juice and had taken two paracetamol tablets. This, and a full-sized packet of twiglets had done the trick and by late morning, he was feeling fine.

Nigel was in a state.

Philip took off his robes and helped George take off Nigel's clothes before throwing him into the shower. Philip washed him while George went round to Nigel's house to pick up some fresh clothes. Mary went down to Mrs Kinloss who prepared a tomato juice based pick-me-up.

George soon returned and within half an hour, they had an, almost, respectable looking Nigel.

At twelve o'clock, the Bentley pulled round to the front of the building. Mary and Mrs Kinloss had left a little earlier to get a good seat.

The Bentley was escorted by two policemen on motorbikes. The entourage then drove the wrong way, as it were, around the coast road. This was to ensure that everyone had a chance of officially greeting their new Governor. They passed by Cragmuir then turned and headed down to Port Victoria. At twelve-forty-five, the procession pulled up outside the main parliament building.

Amanda was busy at work. She was helping to cover the Accident and Emergency Department that day. At twelve she was seeing to a small boy with a toy soldier rammed up his nostril. At twelve-fifteen, she was listening to an elderly woman droning on about her medication. At twelve-thirty, she was extracting a piece of hosepipe from a farmer's arse ('I don't know how it got there, honest Miss'. 'Let's see if this restores your memory' she said with a swift pull). At twelve forty-five she thought of Philip then dismissed him from her mind completely.

There was a fanfare as Philip walked up the main steps of the Assembly Building.

DAA-DEE-DAA-DAA

DAA-DEE-DAA-DAA

Philip waved at the crowds who had gathered in the boulevard outside the building. They were cheering and shouting and, basically, enjoying an extra day off work. As Philip turned to look around, he could see the 'Brodag FM' outside broadcast hut in the far corner.

I wonder if that bastard Charlie Bright's in there, he thought.

DAA-DEE-DAA-DAA

DAA-DEE-DAA-DAA

Philip walked steadily through the main doors and Nigel followed unsteadily behind him. They went past two armed policemen who had been given radio-earpieces as a special treat.

"The Governor is passing checkpoint one. I repeat, the Governor is passing checkpoint one".

The other policeman joined in.

"Confirmation of previous message: the Governor has indeed passed checkpoint one. I repeat, the Governor has passed checkpoint one".

Philip was met at the entrance to the Round Chamber by the Holder of the Scrolls, an honorary position held, at this time, by Henry Geruish's younger brother, Eddie. He knocked three times on the door of the chamber.

"Open the door to receive your new Governor".

Silence.

"Open the door to receive your new Governor".

Silence.

"Open the door...."

"LET THE POOR BUGGER IN" shouted a voice from the crowd.

"....To receive your new Governor".

The door slid silently open and Philip and Nigel were beckoned forward.

The Round Chamber was indeed very round. It was undoubtedly a chamber too. It was packed to the rafters with the great and the mighty of the island's populace. In the centre of the chamber was a raised dais upon which stood an ornate wooden throne. At he foot of the dais was a small, simple chair. On the chair sat Henry Geruish.

Philip looked around quickly. He could see Mary and Mrs Kinloss but no Amanda.

Geruish rose as Philip entered the chamber.

"I welcome you, as representative of Her Majesty the Queen, to our chamber".

Philip walked forward then took his place on the throne.

The rest of the ceremony went off as planned. Philip's Brogadan held up for the duration and Nigel managed to hold himself up too.

DAA-DAA-DEE-DAA

DAA-DAA-DEE-DAA

At various pre-ordained times during the ceremony, a fanfare would ring out. At these times, Nigel would throw back his head and pretend that he hadn't been dozing.

"Do you agree to uphold these statutes during the coming year?" demanded Philip of Geruish.

"I do" he declared solemnly.

"And do you agree to uphold the right of Her Majesty's Government to exercise certain legislative rights over this island?"

"I do".

At the end of the ceremony, the people in the chamber stood in time honoured tradition and applauded another year of Assembly.

Philip, who by this time was feeling rather pleased with himself, smiled broadly and gave a little wave.

The Holder of the Scrolls came forward and Philip stood up. The Holder of the Scrolls then led both Henry and Philip to the back of the chamber and out through a small rear door. Nigel trotted behind them trying desperately to keep up. They climbed a series of staircases until they reached a balcony, set high above the main doors of the parliament building.

As they emerged onto the balcony, a whole series of fireworks were let off in celebration, a fore-taste of the main display that was to take place that night on the promenade in Port Victoria.

The crowds cheered wildly. Geruish and Philip waved down at them. Nigel slumped onto the floor at the back of the balcony and put his head between his knees.

"This is a fantastic day" shouted Geruish to Philip.

"It's wonderful, Henry, truly wonderful".

Philip waved and waved until he felt his arms would fall out of their sockets. He had been smiling so much that he thought his mouth had frozen in that position.

Then, it happened.

As Henry and Philip looked down on the crowds below, three masked men carrying guns burst onto the balcony, threw a bag over Philip's head and bundled him away. One of them pointed a gun at Geruish who backed off alongside the Holder of the Scrolls. Nigel was sick (he was to claim later that this was due to nerves). The gunmen disappeared leaving Geruish dazed and shaken.

A minute later, several policemen arrived on the scene.

Geruish looked down at the crowd who were still waving and cheering. He looked across at the two policemen, looking around and panting. He looked at Nigel. He looked at the Holder of the Scrolls, his own brother, who was whimpering behind him.

Then, Henry Geruish bellowed in rage.

"WHAT THE HELL HAS HAPPENED?"

He flew through the doorway and down the stairs. He pushed his way through the Round Chamber and out to the front of the building. He climbed into his car and accelerated away with a roar.

He made straight for the offices of Robert MacLeod.

He stopped outside the offices. He got out of the car. He burst through the main door of the offices. He clambered the stairs. He ripped into MacLeod's office and grabbed hold of MacLeod by his lapels.

"WHERE'S MY FUCKING GOVERNOR?" he shouted into MacLeod's face.

The solicitor said nothing. He began to shake.

"WHAT HAVE YOU ARSEHOLES DOWN WITH HIM?"

MacLeod began to stammer something.

Geruish threw him down. By this time several people were looking in through the door, clerks, secretaries and the like.

"SHOW'S OVER" he shouted, throwing the door shut in their faces.

He walked slowly back to where MacLeod cowered and knelt down.

"Last night, I get a threatening phone call. This afternoon, our Governor is kidnapped during one of the most important ceremonies this island has. Now, I don't give a shit about Philip Digby-Fischer. I do give a shit about things happening on this island that I, personally, do not know about".

Geruish stood up, picked up a phone and threw it at MacLeod.

"Ring your friends" he said,

MacLeod picked up the phone and began to dial.

"Hello? Hello? Yes, Robert MacLeod here. Can I speak to...Oh, you're going to get him, are you? Very well".

MacLeod covered over the mouthpiece.

"He's just gone to get...".

"I've got ears" snapped Geruish.

MacLeod smiled, nervously. He put the earpiece up tight against his ear.

"Hello? Yes. I know. I know. Listen, I have Henry Geruish here. Do you anything about a kidnapping this afternoon? Yes. Yes. Yes. Yes, I know that you are respectable businessmen. Yes I know that. Yes, I know that...."

Geruish grabbed the phone off him.

"Look here. The new Governor of the island has just been kidnapped in broad daylight. But I don't have to tell you that, do I? Because you already know. Because you did it, didn't you?"

The voice on the other end of the phone was that of the Frenchman.

"I assure you that this kidnapping was nothing to do with us".

"Bollocks. Who else would have the audacity to do such a thing? It certainly wasn't the Mother's Union, was it?"

"It had nothing to do with us".

"Crap!"

"Nothing at all, Mr Geruish. You are making me very angry. You really should not do that".

"Look. Make sure he's back before the end of today. I don't know why you bothered. He's a useless turd".

Geruish replaced the receiver and threw the phone at MacLeod. He turned and marched out.

MacLeod rose to his feet and pointed at Geruish.

"You shouldn't have done that. It's against the law".

Geruish stopped in his tracks, turned slowly around and walked, very purposefully, back to where MacLeod now shook.

"I am the law" he hissed. Then he turned and left. MacLeod slid down the wall and crumpled into a ball on the carpet.

Amanda heard about the kidnap half an hour after the event. She was busy stitching a gash on a young girl's leg. She thought about it for a moment, then put it away in room that lay in the darkest and deepest part of her head that was clearly labelled 'Philip'.

Geruish returned to his office. He roared up to his top floor office not bothering to use the lifts. He sat down on his desk with his head in his hands.

I am losing it, he thought. I should have known about that. It should not have come as a surprise. I am no longer in control.

If it wasn't MacLeods' lot then who the hell was it? Geruish couldn't think of anyone that could possibly gain by kidnapping Philip Digby-Fisher. He checked his watch. It was too late to ring the Koreans now. It would have to wait until the morning.

There was a knock on the office door.

"Go away" he bellowed.

There was another knock.

"GO AWAY"

The door opened and in walked one of the security guards.

"Are you deaf?" bellowed the Prime Minister.

"No, sir. You have a visitor"

"I don't want to see anybody".

The guard coughed.

"I think you do, sir. He has a message from the kidnappers of the Governor".

Geruish looked at him.

"Show him in and you stay out of here".

The guard moved to one side and there, making his way hesitantly through the door was a blindman. *Click, click, click.* He move his cane from side to side as he advanced.

"Mr Geruish?" said the blindman". Mr Henry Geruish?"

"That's me" growled Geruish. "What do you want?"

The blindman felt his way forward and stopped when he came to the edge of Geruish's desk.

"I have a message to give to you. It's from the people who took the new Governor".

"And who are they?"

The blindman licked his lips.

"The St Brodagan Liberation Front".

Where's My Rope?

'And the Lord provided me, handsomely, with a rope' - St Brodag

"He can't have just vanished, can he?" said Peter, the Minister for Agriculture.

The Executive Committee of the St Brodag's Isle Government was holding an emergency meeting to discuss the days events. Tempers were fraught.

"Someone must know where he is" said Sandra, Head of Home Affairs.

"It's a bloody disgrace" shouted John, the Head of Finance. "What are your guys doing about it?"

Brian, the Chief of Police, turned to John, his face turning a deep shade of red.

"If you didn't keep on cutting my budget I'd have a few more officers to go around".

"That's typical of you" said John. "Blame some other poor sod. Never look at yourself. You're a disgrace, you and all you officers. A bloody disgrace".

"Why you jumped up bean counter!" yelled Brian. "You should apologise for that. What contribution do you make to this island. Bugger all! That's what. You and your team of small-minded parasites. You've never achieved anything substantial in your life".

John stood up and leaned across the table.

"At least I didn't allow the Governor to be kidnapped. That's a first, isn't it. You've really excelled this time haven't you!"

"You piece of turd, you....."

"Stop" said Henry, quietly but forcefully.

The two men who were now facing up to each other looked at him and sat down.

"Are there no leads?" asked Nigel.

Brian composed himself.

"None at all".

Henry coughed. They all looked at him.

"Sorry" he said.

"We can find no trace, at all, of where they went to when they left the balcony. They simply vanished".

"Bollocks" muttered John.

Brian looked at him and continued.

"If we knew who had taken him, it would be a start".

Henry continued to look down at the papers that lay on the table in front of him.

"Well, we'll have to wait for whoever's kidnapped him to make the first move" suggested Sandra.

There was much nodding and agreement.

"How does affect the plan, Henry?" asked John.

Henry leaned back in his chair and looked at the ceiling.

"The plan is unchanged".

"But what about..." said Nigel.

"The plan is unchanged".

Geruish pushed himself upright and looked at each one of them with his bright eyes staring out from beneath bushy eyebrows.

"This unfortunate event changes absolutely nothing. It may help us".

"But the timing..."started Peter.

"Remains unchanged" said Henry, forcefully.

"But, Henry..."said Sandra.

Henry stood up.

"This meeting of the Executive Committee is over" he announced.

The various executive members looked at each other in puzzlement. Some immediately stood up, others sat there for a while.

Henry picked up his papers and left.

This was taken by the rest of the Committee members as a sign and they soon dispersed.

All except for Nigel who sat there by himself muttering for a while.

"It's going all tits up" he said. Then, he too, picked up his papers and left.

The Fat Man heard the news of Philip's kidnapping over lunch in a small bistro in Notting Hill. He excused himself from the Prime Minister's Press Secretary and nipped outside to make a call.

"Silly arse" he said as he pulled out his mobile.

Patricia heard the news as she was driving through Stow-on-the-Wold. She was listening to the news on Radio 4. After the main events of the day, Philip's kidnapping was reported as a minor item. Patricia pulled over at the side of the main street and made a few phone calls herself.

Mary and Mrs Kinloss had made their way back to Ash-Na-Garoo as soon as possible. Mrs Kinloss made a huge pot of tea while Mary fended the calls.

Nigel turned up later on and waited with Mary for news.

Brian Geruish called his top officers together. They were all sitting in the operations room at Police Headquarters, near the hospital in Port Victoria.

"Our reputation is on the line here, lads" said Brian. "We're getting flack from on high. We need a result".

"What kind of result?" asked one man.

"A four-three win on penalties" whispered someone.

"Look" said Brian crossly. "This is serious. We need to find the Governor. Has anybody got any ideas?" A number of hands shot up.

"Bob!" said Brian.

"We could use one of them infra-red cameras on a helicopter so that we can all watch the pursuit".

Brian sighed.

"We haven't got a camera or a helicopter, for that matter".

"We could always get one" suggested Bob. "My mate down at the docks reckons he can get hold of anything, even drugs".

Brian looked down at the floor.

"Bob. Come and see me later. Has anyone else got any ideas? Sensible ones!"

Complete and utter silence.

"You lot are going to send me to an early grave if I let you" sighed Brian.

Amanda approached the bar at the Ship Inn. The place was deserted. George came out of the back room and nodded at her.

"Pint?"

"Tomato juice, I'm driving".

George picked up a bottle and flicked the cap off.

"Well, who would've thought that the Governor would be kidnapped".

"The kidnappers?"

"Oh, aye, them, obviously. Aye. But who else?"

Amanda frowned.

"I don't really want to talk about it, George".

"Oh, aye" he said with a sudden burst of insight.

Amanda looked around at the empty tables and chairs.

"Busy, isn't it?"

"Naw" said George, "been shite all day. Put's people off their beer, a kidnapping".

"I bet".

"Shame, really. I'd done a bit of a buffet". He gestured to the room behind.

Amanda looked around him and saw a dozen or so tables piled high with sausage rolls, meat pies, sandwiches and crisps.

"I even got some of them Twiglet things in that the Governor likes. Couple of catering packs to be honest. Cost me a fortune".

"I'm sorry" she said. "It's plain bad luck for you".

"It's the Governor I feel sorry for. They may be torturing him as we speak".

Amanda looked at him.

"You don't think that they'd be doing that, do you?"

"Who knows?" he said shaking his head sadly. "I saw this programme once. I think it was on Channel Four. They used to strap these people up and put cattle prods on their balls, you know, the electric type".

"They wouldn't....."

"Aye. You never can tell. Sleep deprivation, water treatment, beatings. Bunch of bastards that lot. Even as we speak, he's probably being raped by some big bloke with a crush on men with double-barrelled names and an old school tie".

Amanda swallowed her drink and left.

"Was it something I said?"

Amanda shot out of the Ship Inn.

Where the hell was Philip? She surprised herself at her concern.

Then, she put two and two together. If anyone knew where Philip was, it was her dad. She got in her car and drove around to Government House.

Confessions

'Half a truth is half a lie' - St Brodag

Amanda pulled in just in front of the main entrance to Government House. She looked through the sunroof and could plainly see the lights still on in her father's office. She got out of the car, locking it behind her, and walked across the street and up the steps to the main door. It was locked.

She rang the bell and, presently, a security guard arrived. On seeing that it was Amanda, he pressed a button and the door opened.

"Evening, Ma'am" he said, saluting smartly.

Amanda ignored him and walked through.

"A little civility wouldn't go amiss now and then" said the guard to himself.

Amanda carried on to the suite of lifts at the back of the imposing entrance hall. She took the first lift that opened its doors and ascended to the top floor. The lift doors opened and she exited. She took a right turn and came, at last, to a set of double doors in front of which sat another security guard. On seeing Amanda, he rose to his feet and pushed the doors open.

Amanda breezed through finding herself in a small lobby from which a broad staircase rose. She quickly climbed the stairs and came to the small corridor that led to the Prime Minster's office.

The door to Henry's office was open and, for some reason, Amanda stopped outside. There was no reason to do so. Normally, she would have just knocked and entered but this time, she didn't.

Amanda could hear two voices inside, obviously arguing. One was her father's, deep and growling. The other voice was familiar but it took a while for her to recognise it. It was Nigel.

She listened carefully.

"You can't just leave him out there without trying to find him" shouted Nigel.

"Calm yourself down, Nigel" said Geruish. "This has saved us a lot of hard work".

"What do you mean?"

"Well, we won't have to work particularly hard now to discredit him further".

"But why?"

"You know why. We need him off the island so we can enter stage three of the plan".

"Is there really no other way?"

Amanda could detect a change in her father's voice.

"Look, Nigel, you agreed to be part of this. I didn't force you".

"That's before I met Philip".

"Oh, yes, and I forgot: 'He's a decent man'.

"Well, he is" insisted Nigel.

"The world is full of decent men, Nigel. Decent men who achieve nothing. I'd rather be indecent and make my mark - and so would you. If Philip had been someone different, someone, shall we say, who was cunning and manipulative, would he just sit back and let us do everything that we have done to him? Would he? I think not. We needed someone that we could show to the world was a pig's arse, not stupid in himself, but innocent enough for us to manipulate. If we had found the new Governor to be a truly political beast, then our plans would have been scuppered long ago ".

"But we should still try and find him. He may be hurt".

Henry laughed.

"I doubt it. It's more likely that he's being bored to death".

"You know who took him, then?" asked Nigel.

"Of course I do. I'm not Prime Minister for nothing".

"You should have told the Executive Committee. You've kept them....us in the dark".

"It was necessary. I don't want to give them any extra publicity".

"Who?"

Geruish sighed.

"Why should I tell you?"

"Because I'm in this up to my neck as much as anyone" said Nigel.

There was a small pause.

"OK, Nigel. Since you have asked me I shall tell you. He is currently a hostage of the St Brodag's Liberation Front".

Nigel frowned.

"That bunch of prats. I didn't think that they would have been capable of doing such a thing".

"They sent a message to me - I declined to pay any attention to it as you might imagine - wanted me to give up my day job as it were. No, I feel very confident that no harm will come to our Mr Digby-Fischer".

Amanda could not believe what she was hearing. Her father, well, she'd had her suspicions for a while, but Nigel, Philip's right hand man, plotting against him. She had heard enough. She carefully backed down the corridor and left the same way that she had come in.

Nigel spent a further few minutes with Henry before he was dismissed. His mind was in confusion, which, for Nigel, wasn't too difficult a job. He skipped down the steps outside Government House and came to an immediate stop. He looked up the road and then down the road.

Where did I leave my car? He asked himself. Round the corner, he remembered.

He found his battered Mondeo down a side street. He reached into his pocket and found his keys. He pulled them out and unlocked the car door.

Then, he heard a sound behind him. He spun around and as he did, a shadow rapidly approached him. He felt a sharp pain in his groin and felt all the air rush out of his lungs. He slumped to the floor and saw the shadow leaning over him. The shadow took his keys.

"Don't, please don't" pleaded Nigel as Amanda swung his Mondeo wildly around a corner.

"Well tell me what you're up to".

"The wall, the fucking wall!" he screamed, putting his hands in front of his face.

Amanda dropped a couple of gears, gently squeezed the brake, then accelerated out from around the bend. Nigel dropped his hands.

"You're tapped, you are".

"Others have said so" .

"Let me out, please".

"Not until you tell me what's going on with you, my dad and Philip".

Nigel went quiet.

"I can't tell you" he said after a moment.

"Shame" said Amanda, jamming the car into third and bouncing over a small hill. "I wonder what top speed is in this heap of junk". She pushed her foot down.

Nigel was nearly wetting himself. He was scared.

"You see, Nigel. It's my time of the month. I'm a moody cow at best, I realise that, but tonight, I'm feeling particularly bad. You had better start telling me soon because I am at the edge of my driving skills, now, in this car. I might lose it at any moment. Have you ever been in a car crash, Nigel? They don't find much left, not at ninety-six miles an hour on these sort of roads. Have you got any decent music?" she asked bending down to look.

"DON'T DO THAT" screeched Nigel. "KEEP YOUR EYES ON THE ROAD".

He fumbled for a tape, hoping he'd picked one of his Chris De Burgh tapes.

"THE ACE OF SPADES, THE ACE OF SPADES" screamed Lemmy from the speakers.

Fuck, thought Nigel. Motorhead.

"Hey, great selection Nigel" beamed Amanda, twisting the car around another bend.

"I am going to die" said Nigel calmly.

"You don't have to" she called across to him. "Tell me".

Nigel shook his head from side to side and exhaled sharply.

"I'm going to regret this. OK, I'll tell you" said Nigel.

The car screamed to a halt. Nigel was thrown wildly forward then pushed back deep into his seat.

He turned to Amanda.

"What the hell was that....."

"Talk" she insisted.

"OK" he said breathing deeply and composing himself. "What's the North Sea famous for?"

"Water" said Amanda.

"No, not water. What's under the North Sea?"

"Oil".

"Yes".

"And what does this have to do with St Brodag's?" she asked. "All the sea around here has been surveyed. They haven't found a thing".

Nigel smiled.

"Not in the sea, they haven't. All the surveys in the world wouldn't find oil out there" he said, gesturing with his hand in the direction of the sea.

"So what does this have to do with oil?"

"It's here" he said. "Under the island".

"But that's impossible" said Amanda.

"No its not. By a freak of nature, the rocks underneath here are peculiarly formed and folded. There's a huge trapped oil field that's deep rather than wide, like a tube of smarties in the earth".

Amanda's mind was working quickly.

"But if there's oil down there, it presumably would belong to...well, I don't know".

"Well, I can tell you, Amanda, that Britain would get all the benefit. Look at Scotland. That should have been one of the richest places in the world in the eighties. Have you never thought where all that money went?".

Amanda shook her head.

"Straight into the Treasury coffers. Imagine what trouble Thatcher would have been in if she hadn't had the revenues from oil. No, Scotland, whether they like it or not, kept Thatcher in power".

"Bugger" said Amanda.

"Exactly. If we find oil now, the same thing will happen. It's not fair. It's our oil. We should keep the money".

"So how" asked Amanda thoughtfully, "how can we stop that from happening?"

Nigel chuckled.

"Independence".

"Independence!"

"Independence. There are three countries queuing up to recognise St Brodag's Isle as an independent country: China; Russia and France".

"France?"

"Something to do with the beef crisis. It was also a French company that helped us to develop the site, though there's now the option of a Korean concern taking an interest. The French started it, though".

"Bastards".

Amanda thought for a moment.

"But what has this got to do with Philip?" she asked.

"Well. We can hardly declare independence with a British Governor on the island. The plan is to discredit Philip and then, once he's removed, to declare independence while he's off the island. That way there's no direct communication from here to London. It'll muddy the waters for a few hours, if not a few days, and give us time to have the new regime established".

"It sounds a crackpot plan. And you've been working to mess up Philip's plans since he's been here?"

Nigel nodded.

"And you're in agreement with this plan?" she asked.

"I was. Right up until the first week when Philip arrived".

"So what's changed?" pressed Amanda.

Nigel grimaced.

"It's Philip! I know he's a bit 'old school tie' and all that but I've grown to like him. This will ruin his career. I'm worried that it might ruin his life".

Amanda snorted.

"I can't believe this! What the hell is my dad up to? It'll never work. There's no way that the UK government are going to let us declare independence".

Nigel shrugged.

"Your dad seems to think they will. Reckons that he knows some top people at the Foreign Office who'll make sure that it happens. As long as they're kept in the dark about the oil, that is. If they find out about that, there's no way they'll let us go".

"It's the most preposterous thing I've ever heard" said Amanda. "And don't tell me, you're in line to receive a substantial cut of the money".

"All the executive committee are. We've formed a holding company - 'SBP' - 'St Brodag's Petroleum'".

"I can't believe this" said Amanda angrily. "This isn't for the good of the island. It's for the good of the few. Those people my father has deemed suitable. This is rubbish, absolute rubbish"

"Nevertheless, Amanda, that's the plan".

She turned to look at him.

"When Philip is released you must tell him all this".

"I can't" said Nigel.

"You bloody well will. If you don't, I will, and then you'll be deep in the shit on both fronts. If you tell Philip, then he might be able to do something about it".

Nigel sighed. He started to twitch. He was finding this most uncomfortable. He looked out of the window and sat there for five minutes trying to weigh up his options. Amanda watched him carefully, trying to weigh up what exactly was going through his mind.

Eventually, Nigel sighed again. He reached into his pocket and pulled out his hip flask, taking a long swig.

"OK. I...I suppose so. I'll do it. You do realise if I tell Philip I'm going to be saying goodbye to millions of pounds".

"If you don't" threatened Amanda, "you'll be saying goodbye to your balls".

Nigel swallowed long and hard.

"OK I'll tell him".

"Good".

Just then, the lights of a car appeared behind them. The car slowed down and parked behind them.

"Who's this?" asked Amanda.

"Don't know" said Nigel.

Through the steamed up windows, they saw the outline of a man approach the driver's side of the car. The man knocked on the window. Amanda wound the window down.

A torch was shone into the car.

"Is there anything the matter, madam?" asked the voice, obviously belonging to a police officer.

Amanda looked at Nigel and then at the steamed up car.

"It's OK, officer" she said. "We're cousins".

The policeman took a second look.

"Oh, Miss Geruish! I'm sorry, I didn't recognise you in this car. Sorry. Sorry. Good evening".

The policeman walked back to his vehicle.

Amanda smiled.

"Right, you know what you have to do. Now let's get this rusting pile of shit back home".

Nigel coughed.

"Can I drive?"

"Can you bollocks!" said Amanda putting her foot down and screeching away.

Henry Geruish locked his office and made his way out of the building. He said goodnight to the first security guard who saluted smartly. He descended in the lifts and jumped out at the ground floor. He marched across the entrance hall and shouted a cheery goodnight to the guard at the main door.

"Nice to see Miss Amanda here tonight, sir. Lovely girl, that",

Geruish stopped in his tracks.

"Pardon?"

"Miss Amanda. Here. Tonight".

Henry shook his head.

"You must be mistaken. She wasn't here tonight".

"She was. Mind, she was in a bad mood. You can always tell if Miss Amanda's in a bad mood".

"When was she here?"

"About an hour ago. Left just before Mr Nigel did".

Henry frowned.

"Can you please check with the guard upstairs? Just to see if she went past him".

The guard walked across to his small desk and picked up the phone. He had a conversation with the other guard.

"Well, Bob upstairs confirms it. She passed his desk earlier on. Again, he confirms she passed him about five minutes before Mr Nigel came down".

"Well, well" said Henry thoughtfully. "How strange".

His mind was racing thinking back to what he and Nigel had been discussing earlier.

"Can you please make sure that I am informed of all arrivals in the building at such a late hour. She must have forgotten something and gone back home. I'll see her later anyway. Goodnight, now".

"Good night, sir".

A Shot In The Dark

'And I was grasped by the hands of angels!' - St Brodag

Philip didn't at first realise exactly what was happening to him. One second he was waving to the crowds, the next it was complete darkness and the sounds around him became curiously muffled. He thought, at first, that he had fainted - or died. He half expected a bright light to appear and for him to be moving towards it. However, no such phenomena occurred and he soon came to realise that he was awake and with a thick bag on his head and that he was being tied around the feet and around the waist, securing his arms tightly to his sides.

He could hear shouts all around him. He was tilted and then lifted off his feet and bumped and bundled away.

The shouting continued for, maybe a minute, then it stopped. He strained to hear hushed voices.

"It's OK, we got him" said one voice.

"Good work. In here".

Philip could sense that he was on the move again. He heard a low rumbling behind him and echoing footsteps which he presumed were ahead of him. Philip tried to work out how he was being carried. He seemed to be hanging over the shoulder of someone big and bulky.

Philip did not feel any fear, only resignation and annoyance, as though this was the sort of thing that happened to him regularly.

Nothing has gone right for me since arriving here, he thought despondently. Why should today have been any different? Just because I'd got the words right at the ceremony, I started to feel cocky. Well, it just shows what happens. You weren't born to be confident, Philip. It's not in your genes.

The person carrying Philip stopped. There were more hushed voices that Philip couldn't quite hear.

There was the sound of rattling and hissing.

Then, they moved forward again.

Suddenly, Philip detected that they had emerged into the sunlight. The echoiness of earlier had gone and the gloom in front of his eyes became a little less gloomy.

"In here with him" shouted a voice and Philip was flung onto a hard surface.

"Ow" he shouted but nobody heard him.

Philip heard people clambering all about him and he suffered the odd kick. Then, an engine started close by and Philip deduced he was on or in some kind of vehicle. He could feel the vehicle begin to move.

"That was easy" said a man's voice.

"Too easy" said a deeper voice with a thick Brogadan accent..

Philip strained to catch every word. He nicknamed the first voice Lion because of its rich tone. The second voice he named Wolf.

"No point worrying now" said a third, female, voice (Lamb).

"I'm sure we'll be all right" said Lion.

Someone snorted. Philip was sure that it was Wolf.

They drove on in silence for what Philip calculated to be ten minutes. He had started to count and had reached 594 by the time he felt the vehicle beginning to slow down. Then, it stopped.

"Right" said Lion. "Let's get him out".

"Can I have a hand this time?" asked Wolf.

Philip felt someone grabbing hold of his feet and someone else picking him up by his shoulders. He was taken forward.

His head hit something hard and unyielding. Philip could feel it throbbing.

"Watch out, you big oaf" called Lion.

"Watch out yourself" cried the Wolf. "You were going too fast".

There was much grunting and swearing before Philip felt himself being lowered again onto a hard, cold floor. A door was slammed shut and he was left to his own devices.

He lay there and began to consider his present position, which was, of course, trussed like a chicken and lying face down. 'I'll miss *Newsnight*, tonight' was his first strange thought rapidly followed by another large dose of the self pity that he had been developing lately. 'Why is it always me?' he asked himself.

For what seemed an eternity (though it was very much shorter than that) Philip lay there thinking more and more bizarre thoughts.

'I must look like a tea-bag' he claimed at one point. 'A big, black tea-bag full of tea. Except, of course, that tea-bags aren't black - ever. They tend to go for off-white'.

On and on rattled Philip's brain. He conjured up dual personalities in his head: Mr Rational and Mr Irrational. They argued constantly.

Mr Rational: You'll be all right. They'll find you soon.

Mr Irrational: You're going to die.

Mr Rational: They won't harm you.

Mr Irrational: You're going to die.

Finding no solace in their musings, he imagined a gunman who burst into his brain and blasted them away. The gunman worried Philip who tried to bring an air of reality back to his head by remembering the English Test teams averages from that summer's series. Having sufficiently frightened himself, he slipped into a semi-coma and waited.

Then, the door opened and he heard voices - he had been left for no more than five minutes.

He felt hands untying him. Then the sack was lifted off him. He sat there, blinking in the bright lights.

"How are you feeling?" asked a concerned voice - the Lion.

"What do you care?" responded Philip rather sulkily.

"We don't" said the Wolf gruffly.

"What are you talking about? Why have you brought me here?" Philip could make out a couple of shadows. He shaded his eyes with his hand.

"Would you like a drink? Tea? Coffee?" asked the Lion.

"Coffee, please. Black - one and a half sugars".

The shadow that was the Lion motioned to the Wolf who disappeared.

"I don't believe that you have anything to fear from us, Mr Digby-Fischer. I believe that we can enter a mutually beneficial alliance".

Philip clambered to his feet. He looked again and saw a man with blond hair dressed all in black. Just then, the door opened and a large, hairy man entered the room. He, too, was dressed in black.

"You're either professional mourners or mime artists" declared Philip. He now could see quite clearly. He was in a room about ten feet square. The walls were whitewashed but otherwise bare. There were a couple of wooden seats in the room and a bench along one wall.

"We are neither" said the Lion.

Philip walked over to the bench and sat down. The Wolf handed him his coffee, which Philip put down beside him on the bench.

"Who are you, then?" asked Philip.

"I shall tell you first" said the Lion "that we are not friends of Henry Geruish".

The Wolf snorted angrily.

"We are" continued the Lion, "committed to St Brodag's Isle. We believe that Henry is taking the island down the road to ruin. We are known as the 'St Brodag's Liberation Front'. It is our aim to bring down this government".

"And kidnapping me helps your cause?"

The Wolf laughed. "No. We want to make you an offer. We want you to help us".

"You need a good PR man" said Philip with a laugh. "Kidnapping innocent people isn't necessarily the best way to get support. And what's with this 'St Brodag's Liberation Front? Very 1970's".

The Wolf stood up.

"This man is useless to us. He's an idiot. Let's go".

"I'm not an idiot" stated Philip.

"Well here's your chance to prove it" said the Lion. "Are you willing to hear us out?"

Philip waved at the walls.

"Have I any choice?"

The Lion smiled. "No" he said.

"So what do you want to tell me?" asked Philip.

"Firstly, Mr Digby-Fischer. Take a good look at my colleague here. Do you recognise him?"

Philip stood up and looked at the Wolf. Big man, very hairy, deep voice.

"Bloody hell" said Philip suddenly. "You're the spitting image of Henry Geruish!"

The Wolf sighed and sat down on a chair.

"There is good reason for that. I am Henry's twin brother. My name is Gabriel Geruish".

"Good grief" exclaimed Philip.

"I know" said Gabriel, sadly. "It's a bloody awful name".

"Tell me your name isn't Mandy" demanded Philip turning to the Lion.

"No. I'm Tim Johnstone. I'm a geologist. I used to work directly for Henry Geruish on a special project funded, in part, by the French Government".

Philip sat down again.

"I am Henry's elder brother" continued Gabriel, "born fifty-five minutes before him. In Brogadan law, the elder son inherits everything. Henry has stolen my birth-right".

"Hasn't this all gone a bit 'Jules Verne'?" said Philip. "You'll be dragging out the Man in the Iron Mask next and the Three Musketeers".

"It would take a man of Verne's calibre to come up with this story" said Gabriel. "You see, in our late teens and early twenties, both Henry and I decided to travel the world a bit. He went off to Africa and did a bit of flying while I went off to India. Well, I timed it so that I was there at the same time as the Beatles. Great bunch of lads. Got on especially well with that George Harrison. Very spiritual. Anyway, I stayed there for a bit and got caught up in the whole hippie thing".

At this point, Gabriel stared off into space.

"Gabriel! Gabriel!" whispered Tim.

"Yes, oh, right, yes" he said coming back to his senses. "Went off to become a mercenary in Vietnam. I was nineteen. Sure put an end to all that love and peace crap. I was the only non-American to be on that last helicopter that took off from the top of the American Embassy".

This man's talking bollocks, thought Philip.

"Got dropped off in the Philippines. Worked for that Marcos chap for a while. Head of Security. Unfortunately, I got on the wrong side of him and spent three years in jail. All I had to listen to was a tape of the collected works of Gilbert and Sullivan. It was the only thing that kept me going. Anyway, I escaped and off I went again. Started a business shark fishing in Australia. Soon got bored of that. Then, I just drifted for a while before becoming involved with a bunch of Muslim fanatics in Afghanistan. Great times, really great times. Lovely fellows those Mujahadin. After a while, though, I started to think about this place - my home. I rang Henry up from a telephone box outside Kabul. Very friendly. Then, I drive all the way to Rotterdam. Cross to Hull and, all of a sudden, I find out that I'm not allowed back on the island. Apparently, Henry had been going around telling everyone I was dead and inheriting my fortune from my parents when they died".

"Tragic" said Tim, shaking his head.

"Of course, if I had been around, I would have become Prime Minister. It's Brogadan law that only the eldest surviving son can turn to politics. It's something to do with ensuring that there were always some men left on the farms in the old days. So, I have teamed up here with Tim to sort things out and bring Henry to task. The Liberation Front had been going for a few years before we joined it. It wasn't really going anywhere. They just used to print leaflets and have meetings. We soon changed all that. We're into real action now".

"Where do you fit into all this?" asked Philip, turning to Tim.

"Well, I did a survey here three years ago for the Government. However, I was to report back to Henry Geruish personally. I wrote a long and intricate report. It contained all the background information too. I submitted this to Geruish. When I got back home, my office had been ransacked. Every single piece of information relating to this survey was gone - disks, files, papers - everything".

"And you reckon that Geruish was behind that?" asked Philip.

"Undoubtedly. I tried to speak to him directly about it but all I got was threatening phone calls and the like. They even took my computer, the whole thing. No one wanted to know about the robbery. If I could get hold of even a tenth of that information, we could stop Geruish in his tracks. If that report got into the right hands in the British government, his scam would be over".

"So what did this report contain?" asked Philip.

Tim smiled.

"It described a way of making money. Lots of money".

"How?"

"Oil. You see under this island, by a freak of nature, is a massive oil field. There's no where quite like it in the world. By concealing this from the UK Government, Geruish is hoping to make a lot of money for himself and a few close associates. They have already set up a small facility".

"Where's that?"

"In the marshes in the centre of the island. They have an underground pipe that runs from there to a point below the headland near your official residence. There's a pump housed in a wood just around the corner from you".

Philip smiled in realisation.

"And old Ted keeps the pump running".

"Exactly" said Gabriel. "I was at school with him. Completely nuts".

Tim nodded.

"The plan is for tankers to pull into the bay at night and load up by means of a flexible pipeline. It's very ingenious. Very clever".

"So what do you need me for?" asked Philip eventually.

Tim looked him in the eye.

"We need that report" said Tim.

"And also some publicity" added Gabriel.

"That's secondary" said Tim. "But we also want to show you the facility that has been set up so that you can see with your own eyes". Tim looked at him. "We need you, Philip, and you need us. Henry is no friend to you. He's trying to undermine your position here. I'm not entirely sure why but you can bet it's got something to do with oil".

Philip sighed.

"OK. I'll come and have a look. Let me see the evidence and then I'll be able to make up my own mind".

"Good that's settled, then. We'll introduce you to the others".

Tim and Gabriel climbed to their feet.

"Oh, before we go can you tell me one thing? How did you get me out of the building today?"

Tim sat down again.

"The centre of Port Victoria is built on a big chunk of rock. Over the years many secret passages have been made. Initially, they were for smuggling purposes in order to hide things from the Royal Navy when they put into port. Later on they were used for more diverse uses. There's even a nuclear fall out bunker down there. Basically, the passages have all been forgotten about.

"So not even Geruish knows that they exist" said Philip.

"Exactly" said Tim.

A Stroll In The Swamp

'A nasty, nasty place' - St Brodag

Philip was introduced to the rest of the St Brodag's Liberation Front. There were about sixteen in total. Some he recognised, some he didn't.

"Henry Geruish has just been on the radio" called out a dark haired man at the back of the assembly, "denying that he has received any communication from the kidnappers".

"We'll get no publicity from this" said Gabriel.

"That wasn't the main aim" said Tim. "We wanted someone with some power to see what they are up to".

They all ate a quick meal together, then Philip was given dark, warm clothing and a pair of boots.

The three men stole out of their hideaway just before midnight - Tim in front, Philip in the middle and Gabriel tramping steadily at the back, whistling *Three Little Maids from School* to himself. It was cold. They passed swiftly along a rough track for a few minutes, then jumped over a fence and into the light woodland beyond.

For what seemed an age, all that Philip could see was the soft, broad beam of Tim's torch in front of him. They had found a path that continued on deeper and deeper into the wood. The trees became thicker, crowding in on either side. Close by, an owl hooted causing Philip to jump. Gabriel laid a steadying hand on his shoulder.

For an hour they marched into the wood. Philip's mind was full of the events of the last twenty-four hours: the ceremony; the kidnap; the long discussion with the SBLF.

One day, he resolved, I'll make sense of all this.

At last they came to the end of the wood. Tim turned off his torch and beckoned the other two forward.

"Ahead are the marshes" he whispered.

Philip looked out. The stench of damp, rotting vegetation hit his nose.

"Lovely" he said sarcastically.

"There's a path that runs through here to that small rise over there",. Tim pointed and Philip followed the direction of his finger. As he did, the moon came out from behind a cloud and shone down on the lifeless pools ahead. Beyond the marsh, Philip could see a more solid feature - the rise that Tim was talking about.

"Beyond that rise is a dense wood. In the wood, is the facility that we want to show you".

Philip nodded.

"OK. But won't the site be guarded?" asked Philip.

Gabriel chuckled behind them.

"Most definitely. But what are they going to say when they see me, eh? If we can avoid detection, we will. But if not, then deception is our hope".

"Great" said Philip, gloomily.

"Just one thing" said Tim.

"What's that?" asked Philip.

"Be careful".

They moved out from the cover of the trees and descended a steep, muddy bank. At the bottom, they stopped for a while to find the path.

"Here it is" said Tim pushing forward.

Off they went, into the lifeless desolation. They disturbed no creatures for there were none to disturb.

At one point, Philip's foot slipped off a stone and pushed down into the oozing slime.

"Bugger" he whispered.

"Quiet" hissed Tim.

They carried on across the marsh. It must have taken them half an hour to negotiate the narrow, tricky trail before they were able to put their boots on firmer, more solid ground. The slope before them was about twenty feet high. Tim slowly crawled up the bank, inching his way towards the top. He raised his head and looked around. He then beckoned the others forward with a wave of his hand.

Philip found this all a bit boy-scoutish,. He didn't mind, really. He used to enjoy going to the scouts.

Philip peered over the top of the slope. There was an open space of about thirty feet in front of them. Then, the trees started.

Gabriel dashed across the space first, followed by Philip. This time, Tim brought up the rear.

Gabriel pushed forward. It took them another ten minutes of pushing through the undergrowth before they saw lights up ahead and heard a dull, rhythmic noise. They edged forward until they could see clearly what lay ahead.

The trees in the centre of the wood had been cleared and in their place were large bits of machinery that moved slowly up and down. Philip remembered that the machines were called 'nodding mules' or something similar. They could only mean one thing: oil. A flame burnt brightly from a tall, narrow chimney.

Philip gave a low whistle. He shuffled across to Tim.

"How long has this been here?" he asked.

"About a year now. They started selling the oil to a French company 'Petroleum de France'. It's an outfit with support right up to the top in the French Government - like *elf* but a bit smaller. They were buying the oil at two-thirds of the OPEC rate, then selling it on. It's only a small operation but very profitable. However, Geruish has double-crossed them and he has now signed some sort of deal with a Korean outfit. It's relatively new so I don't know the ins and outs of the arrangement but if I know the French, they won't be happy. Remember the Rainbow Warrior in New Zealand? They don't care about other countries' rights when it affects them. Henry Geruish is playing a very dangerous game. He doesn't know what he's up against".

Philip swallowed. The taste of oil on his tongue was becoming unpleasant.

"This shouldn't be happening" said Gabriel looking around at the site. "This money should be used to help all the people of this island, not just Henry's cronies".

Tim looked across at Philip.

"Have we convinced you that this is no joke, that sheer personal gain is driving Henry Geruish and the Executive Committee to declare independence from the UK, that we must stop him?"

Philip nodded.

"I'm appalled at the audacity of it all".

"Good" said Gabriel. "Then, it was worth kidnapping you. I won't have to kill you now".

Philip looked at him and to his relief, Gabriel was smiling.

The site was deserted except for a small portable cabin across on the other side of the site. A light was on inside.

"Time to go" said Tim.

As they prepared to slink away, the door of the cabin opened and a man in a hard hat strolled out. Tim waved to Gabriel and Philip to lie down again.

The man in the hard hat was carrying a clipboard. He walked around the site, taking measurements from various read-outs and dials and writing them down on sheets of paper attached to the clipboard. He did this for about ten minutes, then stopped and looked around.

The man stopped and looked over at the bushes where the three men lay on the ground. He started to walk towards them. Philip tried hard to breathe more quietly than he was doing. The man stopped inches from where the three men were hiding. He let down his zip and started to urinate, humming a Robbie Williams song to himself. Tim, Gabriel and Philip buried their faces in the earth. Philip felt small splashes hit against his coat. Then, with a sigh and a quick shake, the ordeal was over. The man went back to the hut.

The three men stood up and walked back through the trees. They came to the open space and ran across quickly, throwing themselves down the bank. They retraced their steps back through the marshes and assaulted the muddy bank on the far side. They then set off back through the woods.

Philip, by this time, was as tired as he had ever felt in his life. He stumbled often and on one occasion, walked straight into a tree. On and on, they marched, with Philip going slower and slower.

At last they came back to the fence. Gabriel helped to haul Philip over it and soon, they were back in the hideaway.

Tim looked at Philip.

"You know what to do. We're counting on you".

Philip nodded.

"You can report back what you've seen but it will have no credibility. You've got to have something concrete. You need to locate the report I wrote. Geruish took everything from me. That report will give you evidence to present to your superiors. Then, you'll be in a position to challenge Henry Geruish".

"I need my bed" he yawned.

Tim showed him upstairs to a small room in which a bed had been made up.

"Goodnight" said Philip falling face down onto the bed and not bothering to take his boots off.

"Don't forget" said Tim as he left Philip. "Find the report".

In the morning, Philip woke and wondered why no Brogadan cottages had bothered to install central heating. He was cold and stiff and tired.

He wandered downstairs but could find no trace of the others. All their gear had been removed. He wandered from room to room until he came to the kitchen. A few biscuits were left on a table next to a letter with Philip's name on it.

"Must be for me" he said out loud.

Philip opened the envelope and read the short note inside.

> *Philip,*
>
> *We have had to leave quickly this morning to avoid detection. You know what you saw last night. If Henry Geruish's plans work out, then it will mean disaster for this island.*
>
> <u>*WE NEED THAT REPORT*</u>
>
> *You must help us - you're our only hope.*
>
> *SBLF*

One minute I'm an arse, thought Philip, the next I'm the saviour of the whole bloody universe. He pocketed the letter and walked out of the hideaway. He took the rough track back to the main road. There, he waited for a good half an hour before a van appeared.

"Ash-Na-Garoo, please" he said to the driver.

Soon, he was being deposited on the gravel outside the front door. The van drove off leaving Philip alone for a while. He looked out to sea. It was grey and miserable. He turned away and went into the house.

When Mary saw him, she nearly jumped out of her skin. Then, she ran forward and hugged him.

"Nigel" she shouted over her shoulder. "It's Philip. He's alive".

Philip showered and began to feel human again. Mrs Kinloss had prepared a small snack for him (In this kitchen, we do not approve of eating between meals except in the case of a kidnap victim). She had made a nice pot of tea and tuna sandwiches, Philip was sure that she had put an extra dollop of mayonnaise on for him.

The phone rang. It was Henry Geruish.

"You OK, Philip?"

"Yes" .

"I'm so relieved nothing bad happened to you. You don't know how worried we've been. Speak to you soon, bye".

Philip lay back on his bed, loving the soft feel of the duvet around him.

There was a knock on his bedroom door. Someone was in his office.

"Wait a minute" he shouted as he quickly threw on his dressing gown. He opened the door. It was Nigel.

"Philip...I've got....well.....something to tell you".

Philip grimaced.

"What? Can't it wait".

"I'm afraid not, Philip. I've brought a friend as well".

He stood back and the round face of Charlie Bright appeared.

Later that evening, Amanda received a call on her mobile from Nigel.

"Philip's back" he said.

"I know. Did you tell him?"

There was a pause.

"Yes. I told him what I had been up to and Charlie Bright admitted to him that your dad had been behind the questions that he had asked him on the radio".

"How did he take it?"

"OK, I think...". There was another pause. "Why don't you ring him yourself, Amanda?"

"Why would I want to do that?"

"Because....because....I don't know. I'll speak to you later. Bye".

Amanda looked at her phone. She dialled Philip's number then quickly pressed the cancel button. Her pulse was racing as she threw down the phone.

"Bloody men" she cried.

Archieves

'Keep well the words that have been written here' - St Brodag

Philip and Nigel had formulated a plan. Philip had told Nigel of the need to get hold of Tim Johnstone's report. Nigel had said that if the survey existed, then it was to be found in the archive room at Government House.

"It's such a big place you could lose anything in there. Far more secure than any old safe".

They brought Mary into their confidence and decided that they would try and find the report that very evening.

"Dress in black" urged Philip. "It'll be harder for anyone to see us".

They decided to meet back at Ash-Na-Garoo at ten o'clock.

When Philip saw Mary for the first time, he considered that she wasn't taking this too seriously. She was wearing a tight leather cat suit that showed off her figure to the full. Small zips seemed to locate flaps of leather around her nipples and crotch area. A small chain dangled from the reinforced collar. On her feet, she wore leather boots with sharp, stiletto heels.

Mary saw him looking at her.

"What?" she asked. "What?"

Philip grimaced.

"The...the suit!"

"It's all I've got in black" she said defensively.

"I bet your boyfriend likes it" said Nigel.

"No, he doesn't. He's allergic to leather. Brings him out in spots".

"Where?" giggled Nigel.

Philip sighed.

"That's enough, Nigel" he said sternly. He turned back to Mary.

"You don't squeak when you walk do you?"

Nigel snorted and had to leave the room.

"No, " said Mary. "I've rubbed myself all over in talcum powder. It'll be fine".

Philip gulped.

"Right. I've got everything. Let's go".

They piled into the Range Rover and Philip drove the car away from the residence towards Port Victoria. They parked at the side of Government House, near a small door. Nigel got out first and produced an enormous bunch of keys. He looked back at Philip and winked.

"It'll be one of these" he mouthed.

Five minutes later her turned around and smiled apologetically.

"Nearly there".

A further five minutes went by. Then, Philip saw the door push open.

"Here we go" he said as he and Mary left the safety of the car and followed Nigel into the darkness beyond.

"Let's wait here for a minute until our eyes get used to the dark" suggested Philip. The others agreed. Then, after a short while, Philip switched on his pencil thin torch and they moved off. They came immediately to a flight of stairs that they slowly ascended. At the top of the stairs was a door. Philip pushed this slowly open. It creaked and groaned as it did so. He could see nothing beyond - all was dark. As all three of them emerged into the corridor, Philip whispered to Nigel.

"You'd better take over".

"It's this way" said Nigel before blindly walking into a cul-de-sac.

"This way" he said with renewed confidence and setting off in the opposite direction.

It was strange atmosphere to be in. The air-conditioning made a gentle hum and the water fountains gurgled to themselves. Against this were waged the gentle footsteps that their soft shoes made upon the vinyl floor and their breathing which was rasping and harsh.

They found their way to the bottom of one of the main stair wells. They climbed steadily up the flights of stairs until they reached floor five. Here, they pushed their way through a fire door and made their way down another darkened corridor.

"Ow" yelped Mary.

"What's up" asked Philip.

"It's my chain. It's caught on something".

Philip went back to her and felt from her throat to where the chain was caught. It was nestled between a photocopier and a guillotine. Philip freed her an then unbuckled the chain from her suit.

"You won't need this" he said, dropping the chain into a nearby bin.

" T h a n k s "   h i s s e d   M a r y .

They carried on their way and eventually Nigel stopped in front of a door.

"I think this is it" he whispered.

Philip breathed deeply. He placed his gloved hand on the door handle and pushed it open. He put his head around the door and shone his torch into the room.

"What can you see?" asked Nigel.

"I can see rows and rows of cubicles and there's this strange gurgling noise".

"Is it the archive room?" asked Nigel.

Philip brought his head out of the room.

"It's the ladies toilet" he said.

"Bugger" said Nigel.

"Oh, can you let me through" said Mary. "I'm dying for a wee". Mary pushed past leaving Nigel and Philip alone in the corridor.

"How do you think...?" started Nigel.

"Zips" said Philip in reply. "Where's this bloody archive?"

"Well" said Nigel. "If this is the ladies toilet...."

"Which it is".

"Which it is" continued Nigel, "then it must be the next door on the right".

"Good. All we need is Mary"

They waited for ages. Philip was getting impatient.

"What the hell's she doing in there?" asked Philip.

"One of the mysteries of life, that. What do women do in toilets?"

"Go and get her" said Philip.

"Bollocks I will" said Nigel. "I'm not going in the ladies".

Philip grunted at him, then pushed the door open and went inside.

He walked slowly past the sinks and the huge mirrors and started down the corridor of cubicles. He stopped when he heard a voice.

Funny, thought Philip.

He continued to creep forward. He found himself level with a cubicle door from behind which the voice was emanating. Philip raised his hand and pushed the door open.

"Arrrgh" screamed Mary.

"Arrrgh" screamed Philip. "What the hell are you doing?"

"Phoning my mum" said Mary, brandishing her mobile. "She gets lonely".

Philip breathed out.

"Come on. Hurry up".

"I've finished" said Mary.

Outside, Nigel was relieved to see them.

"Thought you two had been killed, the noise you were making".

"And you didn't think to check up on us?" asked Philip.

"I've told you before it's the ladies. I don't go in there".

"So, you would've just left us?"

"Oh, aye" said Nigel with a smile. "Every time".

They moved onwards and found the door that Nigel was convinced would be the archive room. Philip shone his torch onto the door. It said, in plain letters, 'Archive Room'.

"I think this is it" said Nigel.

Philip looked at him and shook his head.

Philip opened the door and they all went in.

It was a massive room with a mezzanine floor running along three sides. It was full of racks and on each rack were thousands and thousands of files.

"Needle in a haystack" said Nigel.

"It's going to be a long night" said Mary.

"We'd better find the index" said Philip.

They looked around and Mary soon found a computer terminal.

"This will be it" she said.

The others crowded around.

"What's the password?" asked Mary.

"If it's like all the other systems" said Nigel, "just hit the 'return' key. They don't go much for security around here".

Mary did as Nigel had suggested.

"OK" she said. "We're into the main document index. What now?"

"Try searching for 'oil' to begin with" suggested Philip.

Mary typed the word in.

"It's coming up with machine oil for moving parts, oil-based paints and, this looks promising, oil surveys".

Mary read out the reference code and Nigel went scuttling off to find it. He brought back two box-files.

"Let's look through this" he said.

They spread the papers out on the table and set to work.

Philip checked through page after page of survey information. However, everything he checked through was concerned with surveys off the coast of the island. There was nothing there relating to Tim's survey of the island itself.

"Have you two got anything yet?" he asked. Both Mary and Nigel shook their heads.

"I don't think that it's here" said Philip. "Not in these files anyway".

"Perhaps they're stored somewhere else" suggested Mary.

Nigel shook his head.

"They'll be here. They'll just be stored under a different name or reference code".

"We'll never find it, then" said Mary.

Philip leaned back in his seat.

"This project, Nigel. Was there a special word or phrase associated with it - a keyword that the information might be stored under?"

Nigel ran his hands through his hair.

"Try 'olive'".

"Olive?" said Philip.

"Olive" said Nigel. "As in olive oil".

"OK" said Philip.

The three of them crowded around the computer again.

"Olive" said Mary as she typed it on the keyboard.

A message flashed up requesting security clearance.

"Right" said Nigel. "Don't worry. Carry on. Press 'return'"

Mary did so and a series of references flashed up on the screen.

"Right. What have we here? Olives- import duty, olive oil embargo 1978-79, olive oil tax rates and......olive oil (Geruish)"

"That's it" said Nigel triumphantly. "That's the one".

He ran off down the isles and brought back a box file. He placed it on the table and opened it. It was empty.

"Nothing there!" said Philip.

Suddenly, the lights were switched on and a voice boomed from above.

"Well what do we have here then?"

"Shit" said Philip.

The Mousetrap

'I found a mouse and named him Michael' - *St Brodag*

Philip looked up to see Henry Geruish on the mezzanine floor above them, flanked by two security guards. Geruish had a broad grin on his face.

"You really have surpassed yourself, this time. Breaking and entering. What ever will you do next?"

"The game's up, Geruish. I know what you are up to".

"Good" he said. "It'll save me having to explain it all to you".

"I've told him everything I know" said Nigel, nervously.

"That would not have taken very long, then, would it, Nigel?"

Nigel looked down.

"What shall I do with you? You could have been shot, you know, for trespassing".

Geruish began to climb down the stairs, the security men falling in behind him.

"And what do you think will happen to you when I tell the Foreign office of your plans?" retorted Philip.

Geruish smiled.

"Absolutely nothing. Firstly, you have no actual proof, secondly, you have little or no credibility left with anyone and thirdly, well, they know quite a bit all ready".

"You're lying" hissed Philip.

"Am I?" said Geruish. "Try me. I know your boss. We hung around together in Africa when I was out there. Yes, we're very good friends".

"Don't be fooled" said Nigel. "He's lying".

"Oh, shut up, Nigel" said Geruish with a snarl. You were only allowed to get involved in this because I am soft when it comes to members of my own family. Especially those closest to me, no matter how dense they are. Tell me, Nigel. What did your mother say happened to your father?"

Nigel frowned.

"Said he was a sailor. Wooed her, shagged her, then buggered off".

"That is not entirely true, Nigel. She lied to you, Nigel, to protect your feelings. I am you father!" he said menacingly.

"That's impossible" cried Nigel.

"Search your feelings, Nigel, you know..."

"That it's a pack of lies" interrupted Nigel. "I've wondered for years if you'd try a trick like this on me. So I got Amanda to run some tests. Sent them over to some lab in England. We're not related at all".

Geruish stared at him strangely for a moment.

"But the....the bitch" he bellowed. "She's tapped me for a fortune all these years".

Philip laughed.

"The hustler hustled. How unfortunate!"

Geruish rounded on him.

"Not as unfortunate as the Governor who's made such a cock-up of governing the island that it can only be days now before you are sacked".

"Is this your friends in high places?"

"Oh, yes" said Geruish. "You'd be surprised at who and what I know".

"You'll never get away with it. I'll have my report into the Foreign office by the morning".

"And I'll have a copy of this videotape on the desk of every editor in Western Europe". Geruish held up a tape.

Philip could feel the colour draining out of his face.

"What is that?" he asked.

Geruish laughed.

"It's a compilation we've been making over the last few months. It chronicles all your mistakes during your time on the island. The day when the RSPB came, you venting your fury in a radio studio. It's all quite graphic, I'm afraid. It will also have the pictures from tonight's little escapade with you breaking into Government property". He laughed. "Oh, and I almost forgot, it also carries pictures of you and your wife together in bed".

"Well we are married" said Philip defensively.

"Quite so" agreed Geruish. "However, I wonder if Amanda would be so understanding".

"You bastard. You'd even hurt your own daughter's feelings".

"Really, Philip, you do have an inflated opinion of yourself. She really doesn't care about you at all. Quite forgotten all about you. But, of course, there will definitely be no reconciliation if she sees this". He waved the video tape again.

Philip frowned.

"Well, how did you get hold of a tape of Patricia and I in bed?"

There was a cough from behind him.

"That'll be my fault, then..."

Philip turned around to see Mary climbing to her feet.

"You don't think that I would have entrusted looking after you to Nigel by himself, do you?" said Geruish.

"You mean you didn't think I was up to it?" said Nigel indignantly.

"Of course not" snapped Geruish.

"But I was doing all right. I sorted out the radio interview for you. I could have had Philip's career in tatters much earlier if I had wanted to".

"Nigel!" said Philip.

"It's OK, Philip" said Nigel. "I'm on your side, now".

"I am so relieved" said Philip. "Mary, I'm ashamed of you".

"Don't be" said Mary strutting over to stand by Henry. "I was very impressed by you. You were so.......hot!"

Philip blushed.

"So where does this leave us?" he asked.

"Me with all the cards, Philip, and you with a very empty hand". He put his arm around Mary who looked up at him and smiled.

"Think about your position, Philip. You might want to tender your resignation".

"You bastard" yelled Nigel.

Geruish looked at them both with disdain.

"Throw them out" he said to the two security guards.

As the two security guards bundled Nigel and Philip out of the building, Philip thought back on the mistakes he had made. As he and Nigel went flying through the air, he wondered what he could do about it. As Nigel and he landed in an untidy pile on the ground, he realised that the situation was hopeless.

To put it quite simply, Geruish had won.

"It's no good" said Philip. "I can't do anymore. I can't stop Geruish from going ahead".

Philip were sitting in Philip's office in the small hours of the morning.

"There must be something we can do" said Nigel. "We can't just give up".

"Well look at it. I can't contact the British Government because Geruish has my boss eating out of his pocket and nobody else will believe me. I can't go to the press because my credibility has been completely eroded. I can't do anything on the island because everyone's related to Geruish. I'm stuck. It's quite simple. He's won".

Nigel stood up and began to pace.

"Look, Nigel, without that report, we've got nothing. Nothing at all. We had a chance, a slim one, I'll grant you, if we could have got hold of it. It's probably destroyed now".

"But what about taking pictures of the facility that you saw".

Philip shrugged.

"No one will believe us. He's right. I've no standing left. I've no power. I'm running on empty and it's a long way to the next petrol station".

Nigel stopped pacing.

"So what are you going to do?"

Philip sighed.

"I'm going to do what Henry wants. I'm going to resign".

"But that's playing into his hands. That's what he wants".

"I can't help that, Nigel. It's what I've got to do. I'll make the call in the morning".

"Is there no other way?" asked Nigel.

"No" said Philip. "There isn't".

Resignation

'My principles will never fall' - St Brodag

"So, in a nutshell, that's it. I want to tender my resignation".

There was silence on the other end of the phone.

"With immediate effect!" added Philip.

No reply.

"I'll start packing today".

There was a grunt on the line.

"I think you should seriously consider what you're telling me" said the Fat Man. "I don't believe you've given this enough thought".

"Look" said Philip. "You know that I've had a bad time since coming here. My marriage has broken up, my relationship with the Government here has gone down the pan and I've a catalogue of disasters behind me. If I was a dog, you would have put me down by now".

"I'm sure that you are exaggerating your problems, Philip" he said. "Perhaps you need a little time off. I need you there on the island".

Philip snorted.

"Oh, yes. There's one further thing. You forgot to tell me that you and Geruish go way back. Big mates, apparently".

The Fat man was caught off balance by that remark.

"Well, Philip" he said slowly. "It is true that we worked together in Africa in the late sixties and early seventies".

"Don't try and pull the wool over my eyes. I know what's been going on. You know all about Geruish's plans for the island, don't you. I suppose you're getting a cut of the profits too".

The Fat Man sounded confused.

"I really don't know what you are talking about, Philip. What plans? What profits?"

"I don't want to be part of those tainted schemes. That's why I want out".

"Listen to me, Philip" said the Fat Man. "I have no idea what you are going on about".

Philip laughed.

"I bet you don't. Well. I've said all I need to. I've got a ferry booked for the day after tomorrow. Thanks for everything. Goodbye".

Philip slammed the receiver down and placed his forehead on the desk in front of him.

"How the hell did I find myself in this position?" he said out loud.

He sat like that for ten minutes until he heard a noise next door. He clambered slowly to his feet and walked across to the door, opening it slowly.

Mary was there collecting her personal belongings.

"Morning, Mary" said Philip.

Mary didn't say a thing. She just kept on throwing her belongings into her bag.

"You know, I don't blame you, Mary" said Philip gently. "You don't understand yet. You'll know it was wrong when you're older. Henry Geruish can be quite intimidating when he wants to".

Mary continued to look away as she worked.

"It was nice working with you" said Philip beginning to turn away.

Mary let out a loud sob and turned to Philip. She ran across to him and put her arms around him. She buried her face in his jumper.

"I'm sorry, Philip. Very sorry. I wish that I hadn't done it but I have and now you're having to go".

Philip patted her on the back.

"It's OK, it's really OK. Don't worry. Here. Take this tissue. I don't blame you. I really don't".

She held onto him for a few minutes. The other door to the office opened and in strolled Nigel. He saw the two of them and started to back out. Philip waved him into the room. On hearing Nigel enter, Mary leaned away from Philip and wiped her eyes again. She picked up her bag.

"I'll say goodbye then" she said and then was gone.

"What was all that about?" asked Nigel.

"I'm not sure" said Philip. "Either she's genuinely repentant or she's trying some sort of ruse. I won't fall for it again".

Nigel coughed.

"Are you still going?"

"Yes. I've told my boss".

Nigel grimaced.

"So that's it then".

"I'm afraid so. I've booked a ferry for the day after tomorrow".

"Well, be in the Ship tomorrow night, then".

"OK"

Later that day, Philip left a message with Henry Geruish's secretary to tell him that Philip was leaving.

Amanda sat in her office going through some records. Paperwork was not her thing but in recent weeks she had thrown herself into her work. It wasn't to forget Philip, no, no, no. It was just that she had got behind in a few things and had to bring then up to date.

There was a knock at the door.

"Come in" she shouted.

The door opened and in walked Nigel.

"Nigel! What a pleasant surprise. That boil on your bum come back".

"He's leaving" he said solemnly.

"Who?" said Amanda after a short pause.

"You know who. Philip. He's going. Your Dad has forced him out".

Amanda leaned over and put some papers into her briefcase.

"And why are you telling me?" she said disinterestedly.

Nigel slammed his hand down on the desk.

"You know why, Amanda. He's going. He's not coming back. You won't see him again".

"Good. He can go and pretend to cheat on his wife elsewhere".

"Stop it, Amanda" he said forcefully. "If you let him go, you'll regret it for the rest of your life. This is your chance, Amanda. You and Philip. Together".

Amanda looked at him. Her right hand began to shake so she hid it under the desk.

"That little escapade is over, Nigel".

"Bollocks and you know it. Don't forget, Amanda, that I've known you for all my life. You've been my big cousin. You were different with Philip. You let your defences down for once. It's the real thing. You love him".

"And look where that's got me" said Amanda getting agitated.

Nigel sighed.

"I know, I know" he said. "But that's love. You've got to chance things. I think that you and Philip could make a real go of it".

Amanda looked down at her papers.

"No chance. Is that all?"

Nigel looked around.

"Look. We're having a do in the Ship Inn tomorrow night. Be there, will you. Please!"

"Bye Nigel" said Amanda not looking up.

Nigel spun around and left.

Amanda looked up and checked to see that he had gone. She got up and crossed to the door. She turned the latch to lock it. Then she slid down the wall and curled up into a ball and started to cry.

Philip was sat on his favourite bench in the garden looking out to sea. Mrs Kinloss approached him and at down beside him.

"So, you're off then".

"Yes".

"You're going a bit quicker than I had reckoned on".

Philip smiled.

"It's quicker than I thought as well".

"I just thought that I'd thank you for everything. You know, Charles".

"That's all right, Mrs Kinloss. Thanks for everything that you have done as well. You're the best cook I've come across".

"I'll put that down to your lack of experience, then. I'll see you before you go?"

"Of course".
She squeezed his hand and left him.

The Last Waltz

'Dance, then, whoever you may be...' - St Brodag

Philip spent the next day packing most of his belongings into crates. He was taking a few cases with him in the car; the rest would follow on in a few days time.

He had agreed with Patricia that he would take over the London flat for the next few weeks until he had a chance of sorting himself out. He had made a few calls already to contacts that might be able to guide him towards a new job and a new career. He found it rather sad walking through Ash-Na-Garoo and knowing that it was to be his home for just a few hours longer.

The pain of leaving re-awakened the pain that he felt for Amanda. This had lain dormant for a few days. Having to deal with Mrs Kinloss over the death of her son put it a little into context. Yet still the pain was there, gnawing away inside.

Philip wandered around the house moving silently from room to room remarking to himself how much he hadn't noticed before - a painting here, a statuette there, a particular view from a window, an exotic fragrance from a certain plant.

He made his way up to his bedroom and looked long and hard at the bed, remembering it as the scene of his disgrace. He checked the time: six-thirty. Nigel would be calling for him in an hour.

Philip went into the bedroom and undressed. He switched on the shower and stood, for the penultimate time, under its warming spray. He squeezed out a little liquid soap and lathered himself all over. He did the same with some shampoo and washed his hair. He turned off the water and stepped out of the cubicle.

He crossed the bathroom floor to the sink and wiped the mirror with his towel. He sprayed a little foam onto his fingers and worked it into his face. Then he took his razor and carefully began to shave. He remembered when he was younger and had caught his face with a twin-bladed razor leaving a lovely set of parallel cuts trailing down his cheek. He could still see the mark if he looked at himself closely.

He splashed on some aftershave, repeating the actions of countless times before. He rolled on his deodorant and then brushed his teeth. He rinsed with mouthwash and left the bathroom.

Philip looked in his drawers and pulled out a pair of boxer shorts and some socks. He selected a bright green shirt and a pair of beige trousers. He dried his hair and then dressed. He selected a brown jacket and a pair of brown shoes. Then, he went downstairs to wait for Nigel.

"This vehicle is disgusting," said Philip as he cleared the passenger seat of old chip papers.

"Never mind. After tomorrow it will be no concern of yours".

The Mondeo spluttered away from the house and down the lane towards the road.

"Can you believe you're going?" asked Nigel.

Philip shook his head.

"It's a very peculiar feeling. I don't really want to go".

"You still don't have to".

"Oh" said Philip. "I think I do".

Nigel parked the Mondeo outside the Ship Inn and they crossed the pavement to the front door. Nigel stood back and beckoned Philip forward.

As he put his nose through the door, there was an almighty cheer from inside. The bar was packed. A huge banner hung from the roof. It read 'Goodbye, Philip'.

"What is this?" asked Philip.

"Just a few friends" said Nigel with a grin.

George beckoned him forward.

"Over you come, Governor. We've laid on one of our special spreads tonight. Hope it will suit you".

Philip smiled at him.

"It'll do just fine, thank you".

"We've got your favourite band through in the back room tonight, Rowdy Scythe. They'll be doing a turn later".

George placed a pint in Philip's hand.

"Best Craddles that" he said. "Something you'll miss back in England".

Philip took a sip.

"You're right, George. It's a great pint".

Philip looked around at the assembled mass. He knew all of them by sight and most of them by name. They were all people that he had dealt with during his time on the island. He was touched that they had all turned out.

Philip continued to scan the faces, looking for one person in particular. Nigel watched him closely.

"I asked her to come, Philip" said Nigel. "She knows you're leaving".

Philip nodded.

"Thanks, Nigel. Thanks for everything".

Nigel placed his hand on Philip's arm.

"I've enjoyed working with you".

"Good".

"Now let's get pissed" said Nigel downing his pint.

"Another two, please" said Philip to George.

Rowdy Scythe started their set at half eight.

"I'm Ron" said the keyboard player.

"I'm Sheila" said the accordionist.

"And I'm Randy" said the violinist.

"And together" continued Ron on the keyboards, "we're Rowdy Scythe".

The place roared its approval.

"This is a special celebration tonight. Our Governor, Philip Digby-Fischer, leaves us tomorrow. Cheers, Philip. All the best".

The crowd exploded into applause again.

"You might know this one" said Ron. He played the opening bars to *Stairway to Heaven.*

"There's a lady who's sure, all that glitters is gold.....".

"This is new" said Nigel. "They've not done this one before".

Ron played the keyboard quietly, slowly building the song. The accordion groaned into life and eventually the violin started to scream.

"Ooooooooooo and it makes me wonder" sang Ron.

"Ooooooooooo and it makes me wonder" echoed the crowd lighting little candles.

Ron hit a button that started the synthetic drums and the song rose in a crescendo. Sheila's fingers ran up and down the accordion, a string on Randy's violin broke and Ron kept the melody going underneath screeching vocals.

Suddenly, the music stopped.

There was silence.

"And she's buy-i-i-ing a stair-air-way to heaven. Oh oh oh oh oooooh oh".

Ron's voice faded and as it did, the back room of the Ship Inn seemed about to crash down around them all, such was the cheering and the applause.

Ron smiled at them while Randy changed a string.

"Did you like that?" bellowed Ron.

"YES" came the reply.

"Right, great. Do you remember this one?"

And Rowdy Scythe leapt into a rendition of *I Should be so Lucky.*

Philip dipped out at this point and made his way back to the main bar. He had just ordered himself another beer when he heard the door open behind him. He turned and saw Amanda.

Philip's heart not only jumped but seemed to perform a triathlon as he looked at her. She gave him a half smile and then crossed the floor to where he stood.

"Hello" she said.

"Hello" said Philip. "Glad you could make it".

"I can't stay long" she said. "One drink, I'm afraid".

Philip nodded.

"What would you like?"

"Bitter, please".

"Pint?"

"Yes".

Philip passed the order on to George.

"I should be so lucky, lucky, lucky, lucky" sang Ron in the background. "I should be so lucky in love".

"Have you been keeping well?" asked Philip.

Amanda shrugged.

"So, so. And you?"

"OK".

They fell into silence.

I love you, said Philip in his head.

"Sorry?" asked Amanda.

"Didn't say anything" said Philip.

"Could have sworn you did".

"Oh"

Amanda stared around at the other people in the bar.

"This is a bit awkward, isn't it?" said Philip eventually.

Amanda nodded.

"You know why I'm leaving, don't you" suggested Philip.

Amanda shrugged.

"Something to do with my Dad".

"Yes. Nigel told you all about it. He's forced me out".

Amanda looked at him.

"I'm sorry Philip" she said. "I'm sorry that it hasn't worked out for you".

"So am I" he admitted.

In the back room, the music stopped.

"And now" announced Ron. "For all you rockers out there, Rocking all over the world".

Philip smiled.

"They're playing our song" he said.

Amanda looked at him. She looked at him and gently shook her head.

"They're not, Philip, are they? They're just not".

She put her beer down.

"Bye". She turned and left.

Philip watched her go. His mind started to race. What should he do? Should he let her go or try and stop her? Was this the end?

He stood up, then sat down again. He felt a hand on his shoulder.

"Go" said Nigel.

Philip bolted out of the door and looked down the street. He saw Amanda approaching her car.

"AMANDA!" he screamed.

She stopped.

"AMANDA!" he screamed again.

She turned around.

"AMANDA!" he screamed as he ran towards her. He stood in front of her, waiting for some response.

"You're making a prat of yourself, Philip. Everyone's looking at you".

"I don't care".

Amanda sighed.

"Look. I'm not convinced you know what you want at the moment".

"I want you" he said.

"Do you, Philip? I am not sure that you do".

It started to rain.

"I do, Amanda".

Amanda gave him a sad smile.

"Look at you. You're going to get drenched".

Amanda reached up with her hands and drew Philip's face down to hers. She looked into his eyes.

"When you're sure, find me".

She kissed him then turned, climbed into her car and drove away.

Philip stood there getting wetter and wetter.

Then he turned and went back to the pub.

"You all right" asked Nigel as Philip came back into the bar.

"I think so" said Philip.

"You look wet".

"That's because I am".

"Oh".

In the back room, Rowdy Scythe were playing *Anarchy in the UK*. George could be seen pogo-ing up and down.

"I want to be an anarchist" screeched Randy, who had taken over lead vocals from Ron.

Nigel looked at Philip.

Philip looked at Nigel.

"Let's dance" said Philip.

And the two of them joined the madness.

Elsewhere, the Frenchman was deep in conversation with his superiors.

"I believe that Geruish will sign the deal with the Koreans" said Monsieur Jean-Claude.

"That must not happen" said a voice on the other end of the phone.

Jean-Claude smiled.

"Then, I request authorisation for Plan B".

The other man sighed.

"Authorisation is granted".

The Frenchman put the phone down and laughed.

The Bags Are Packed

'Light winds for easy travel' - St Brodag

Philip threw his last bag into the back of the Range Rover. He looked back at the house with sadness, wishing that he could have spent more time there.

Earlier that morning, Nigel had come around and said goodbye. Philip could tell that the younger man had found it difficult and so the parting had been short.

"Not very good at saying goodbye" admitted Nigel. "It's something to do with having lived here all my life".

"You should get away some time" suggested Philip.

"No" said Nigel. "I belong here".

Philip had said goodbye to Mrs Kinloss and had promised to write. Jane and the children were due on the island within the next few days so she was going to have her hands full.

Philip took a few steps towards the garden and looked down at the terraces below him.

"Goodbye garden" he said. "Goodbye house".

He turned and clambered into the car. Without looking back again, he drove out of the drive and was soon travelling along the promenade at Port Victoria, heading for the ferry terminal.

After saying goodbye to Philip, Nigel had driven into town and parked near to Government House. He was going to try and sort things out with Henry Geruish, who hadn't spoken to him since the night in the Archive Room.

"So, Nigel, to what do I owe this pleasure?"

"Philip's gone".

Nigel was standing in front of Geruish's desk in his office at the top of Government House.

"Really. Well that's all very well and good. Best of luck to him. Very soon, we will be very rich men".

Nigel looked at him.

"Me too?"

Geruish smiled at him.

"Nigel" he said patiently, "you are family, of a sort. I wouldn't cut you out of the deal. Granted, your share will be much diminished, considering that you tried to scupper the whole thing".

Nigel looked down at his feet.

"Sorry about that".

"Sorry? What do you have to be sorry about, Nigel? You were too trusting and a little naive but you've learnt from it, haven't you".

Nigel was downcast. He nodded.

"Good".

"Which deal are we going with?" asked Nigel.

Geruish grunted.

"The Korean optional".

"Isn't that a little dangerous? What about the French?"

"What about the French?" retorted Geruish. "We signed nothing with them. There's nothing on paper".

"But they financed the facility".

"That's their problem" said Geruish.

Philip sat patiently in line waiting to be waved onto the boat. There were about another thirty cars waiting to board as well as a dozen or so large trucks.

He switched on the CD player. The strains of Nimrod by Elgar began to roll out of the speakers. Philip closed his eyes.

Amanda finished her incontinence clinic and washed her hands thoroughly. She was going to have lunch with her father at which she had decided to give him the biggest bollocking that he would have had for years. She checked her watch. It was ten to twelve.

Philip was woken from his slumbers by a loud banging noise. He sat bolt upright and looked around him. A gap-toothed man in lime green waterproofs and bright red ear defenders was banging on the window.

"DRIVE ON" he shouted.

Philip started the engine and moved off. Every ten feet or so he found similarly dressed men waving him forward with gusto.

Philip smiled as the boat swallowed him up in its noisy innards.

"So what's the next step?" asked Nigel.

Geruish smiled.

"Well, I have just finished writing a note to the British Government detailing our declaration of independence".

"That soon" said Nigel.

"Why wait? I'll send this to them by e-mail and fax and await a reply. Of course, before the British Government responds, we will have been officially recognised as a sovereign state by China, Russia and probably also by France, though our relations with them have become a little tense lately".

"And that'll be that, then".

"And that will be that. I'll sign the deal with the Koreans this afternoon and by this time tomorrow we will all be richer".

Philip sat down on a seat in the forward lounge overlooking the bows of the ship. A steward appeared and Philip ordered coffee and a pecan flavoured pastry. He had brought two books with him and a copy of the previous day's paper that he had picked up at the Ferry Terminal Building. He was beginning to relax.

"Your daughter is on her way up now" announced the security guard over the phone.

"Thank you" said Geruish who promptly replaced the receiver. "You can both witness a historic moment in the life of this island".

Presently, Amanda came rushing in.

"You done?" she asked.

"Not quite. I'd like you to be here as I declare independence".

Amanda frowned at him.

"You're definitely going to do it?"

"Yes. Why not? We'll be millionaires by tomorrow".

"Does the rest of the Executive Council know that you're going to do this today?" she asked.

Geruish shrugged his shoulders.

"Who cares? They're not important".

"Your arrogance knows no bounds, does it?" she said.

"Probably not". Geruish's hands hovered near the keyboard of his computer. He paused. "I feel that we should have some champagne or something" he remarked.

"Get on with it" said Amanda impatiently. She had moved to the window and could see, quite plainly, the *Spirit of St Brodag* at rest in the harbour.

Geruish made a movement towards the keyboard when Nigel spoke to him.

"One thing I would like to know is whatever happened to that report? You know, the one detailing the results of the survey".

Geruish sighed and looked at them both.

"I suppose it's not going to matter now". He bent down and picked up his briefcase and popped it on the desk in front of him. He felt around the back and pressed a hidden button. The briefcase had a false bottom in it. Geruish pulled the file out and put it on the desk top.

"This hasn't left my side in the last six months. I've gone to bed with it, been on holiday with it, I've even taken it to a funeral. It's been as safe as houses in their. Ingenious little device, that compartment. Very clever".

Nigel couldn't keep his eyes off the file.

"Now. Where was I?" asked Geruish. "Ah, yes".

His hands approached the keyboard but as his fingers neared the keys, the lights in the office went out and it became dark.

"What the f..." he said.

"It's probably a power cut" said Amanda.

Geruish stared at the screen.

"Oh, well. The backup power should kick in on the computer circuit".

Geruish watched the screen and saw it fade to black.

"Oh bollocks. It's gone".

Nigel moved closer to him.

"Didn't we leave the back-up system out of the budget last year?" said Nigel.

"Well who's idea was that?" exclaimed Geruish.

"Yours" said Nigel.

"Oh".

Nigel backed towards the door.

"There's a walkie-talkie on the security desk downstairs. I'll go and radio the power station and see what's up". Nigel turned towards the door then turned back to Amanda. "Could you come with me a second, Amanda. I need someone to hold the torch".

"OK. If I must" she said and followed him out of the room.

They walked quickly down the short corridor and down the flight of steps. At the security position, Nigel grabbed Amanda's arm and kept her walking, waving at the security guard as they passed.

"What are you doing?" demanded Amanda.

"I've got that report under my jacket. If we hurry, we can get it to Philip before the ferry goes".

They walked faster and faster, eventually breaking out into a run.

They reached the top of the stairs through a fire door and threw themselves down the steps.

"Remind...me...to...get...fit" gasped Nigel.

They emerged out of the emergency door at the bottom.

"Where's your car?" asked Nigel.

"I left it at the hospital".

"Bollocks, it'll have to be the Mondeo".

They ran around the side of the building and across the street to where Nigel's car was parked. Government House was beginning to empty.

"Give me the keys" demanded Amanda.

"No way, I'm not..."

"This is not the time to argue. Give me the keys".

"I'll regret this" said Nigel passing his bunch of keys over.

No sooner had Nigel's backside hit the car seat, then Amanda was sending the car into a screechingly tight turn and heading towards the sea front. At one point, she tried to brake but found that an empty coke can had slipped under the pedal. She just managed to steer around the car in front and accelerate quickly past the oncoming traffic. She was then able to kick the can out of the way.

"Clean you car out, Nigel" she cried.

He nodded and, as a token gesture, put a few wrappers into the glove box.

"The ferry's not gone yet" shouted Nigel as they zoomed out onto the promenade causing a couple of other vehicles to swerve.

"It's nearly ready though" cried Amanda. "Look at the funnel".

Dark clouds of smoke were pouring from the bright orange funnel on top of the boat.

Amanda roared the car into the Ferry Terminal. A couple of the green-coated assistants tried to wave them down. They had to dive out of the way to avoid becoming bumper fodder. At the customs point, two of the special policemen also tried to stop them. They pulled down a barrier across the road but Amanda just put her foot down and smashed through it. They twisted and turned through a series of bends and were out onto the quayside.

The ferry was pulling away.

They jumped out and started to wave their arms but to no avail.

"Fuck" said Nigel.

"Fuck" said Amanda.

They watched the gap between land and the boat widen. Twenty feet. Thirty feet. Forty feet. Fifty feet. The water at the back of the boat was being viciously churned up by the rotation of the propellers.

They turned back to the car.

Behind the Mondeo, on the quayside, was a familiar vehicle. A dark blue Range Rover. Philip jumped out of the car and ran up to Amanda.

"I've found you" he said.

"So you have" she replied with a beaming grin.

Philip kissed Amanda, this time with some urgency and force, and not without a little passion. Amanda hooked her arms around his neck and Philips hands reached around her waist.

"I thought you'd gone" said Amanda eventually when they both needed air.

"I thought I'd never see you again".

They stood there just looking at each other and smiling.

Nigel coughed, awkwardly.

"I don't mean to spoil the moment but we were just trying to save the island".

"What?" said Philip turning to him.

"The report. Tim Johnstone's report. Nigel's got it" said Amanda excitedly.

"Really! Let's have a look" said Philip.

Nigel gave the file to Philip who flicked through it quickly.

Philip blew out his cheeks.

"We've got it! If Henry tries to declare independence now, the British government will fight it all the way. If it was just for this piece of rock, they wouldn't have cared but oil is a different matter".

"He's about to send an e-mail to London" said Amanda. "We should try and stop him. He'll get himself into even deeper water if it goes ahead now".

"Right" said Philip. "Nigel. Take the file and go back to Ash-na-Garoo. When the power comes back on, make copies and send a fax of it to the Foreign office".

"OK" said Nigel and ran back to the Mondeo.

"Come on, Amanda. Let's see if we can save your father from making an idiot of himself".

Philip ran back towards the car. He looked around. Amanda had not moved.

She beckoned him to her with a wave of her fingers. He retraced his steps. Amanda stood on her toes and kissed him again.

"We really must go" said Philip.

Amanda nodded.

They ran over to the car and climbed inside. Then, they drove back to Government House.

A Change Of Plan

*'The best laid plans of mice and men turn out, invariably
, to be a disaster' - St Brodag*

As Amanda and Philip drove back to Government House, they were increasingly aware of the crowds of people on the streets. Every office and every shop must have closed due to the power cut. At one point, it felt as though they wouldn't be able to pass through as the mass of people became so dense. They wound the windows down and shouted and Philip sounded the horn. Eventually, the crowds moved to one side and the Range Rover continued up the boulevard.

Philip parked the Range Rover across the street from Government House and he and Amanda ran to the front door, quickly climbing the steps on their way. Inside the entrance hall, they were amazed to see it empty - not a single security guard was present. The security desk seemed to have been abandoned in a hurry. The guard's cup of tea was still steaming.

They stopped in their tracks and looked around.

"There's something not right here" whispered Philip. "I don't like it".

"What shall we do?" asked Amanda.

Philip nodded back towards the door. They left quickly.

Outside, they joined the press of people.

"I wish I knew what your dad is up to" said Philip as they walked around the corner of the building.

Amanda grabbed his arm and pulled him back.

"There" she said pointing down a side-street.

Philip looked. A van was pulled up outside one of the emergency exits. Four men were leaving the building. One of them was Henry Geruish and he didn't look too happy to be doing it.

"What the hell has he got himself mixed up in?" asked Amanda.

Philip shook his head.

The rear doors to the van were pulled shut. Then, the van did a neat three point turn and started to advance towards where Philip and Amanda were watching. The two of them ducked back around the corner and watched the van pass them by. It, too, struggled through the mass of people. Philip and Amanda started to follow the van on foot.

The van came to a place where the crowd was scarcer and started to accelerate away. Philip began to chase the vehicle. He crashed into an old lady, sending her bags crashing to the pavement. He picked himself up, shouted a quick 'sorry' then continued on his way.

The van kept a good twenty yards in front of him.

Suddenly, he could see it no further. He spun around, furious with himself that he had lost the van. He looked close by him and, on seeing a nearby waste bin, climbed on top of it to try and locate the van.

There it was, parked just outside the Assembly Building.

"It's there" he shouted to Amanda.

Amanda didn't reply.

Amanda wasn't there.

"Amanda! Amanda!" he shouted. A few faces looked up at him. None of them belonged to her.

"Amanda!" he shouted again,. A note of desperation entering his voice.

It was no good. He couldn't see her. Philip jumped down from the waste bin. As he landed, he could sense someone approaching him.

"Amanda?" he said.

A big hand rested on his shoulder.

"Not likely" said George. "Look" he said pulling up his shirt, "no tits".

Philip looked at him in amazement.

"What the hell are you doing?" he asked.

"I've been sent to find you" said George.

"Who by?"

"A couple of mutual friends" he said tapping his nose.

"I need to find Amanda" said Philip looking around.

"But you need to come now" said George. "It's urgent".

"But Amanda..."

George put his arm around Philip's shoulder.

"Amanda'll look after herself" he said reassuringly.

Philip struggled away.

"Look, Governor" said George. "My friends will help you to sort this mess out. But you need to come now".

Philip looked around, trying to spot her. Then, he sighed.

"Come on, let's hurry".

The Round Chamber was in complete darkness. Henry Geruish was being led across it's floor by two of the Frenchman's agents. The Frenchman, himself, strode quietly behind them. At the rear of the chamber was a door. The party went through into a room beyond. Inside, a small generator had been set up and a series of lamps were being powered.

Four more of the Frenchman's men were inside.

"I'm sorry about this, Mr Geruish" said the Frenchman. "We need a secure place to talk. We have some negotiating to do and I'd rather we weren't overheard".

"What do you want from me?" asked Geruish.

The Frenchman laughed.

"Just your signature. That's all".

Amanda had lost contact with Philip when he had dashed off. She had tried to follow but the milling people had got in the way.

She found herself in the shadow of the Assembly Building. She looked around but could see no sign of Philip.

The bastard, she thought. Imagine running off and leaving me.

She continued to walk onwards and, suddenly, she saw the van appearing over the top of the crowd in front of her. She edged her way forward until she was up against the rear door. She stood up on the bumper and looked inside. It was empty.

She made her way around the side of the van and looked in through the driver's window. No one in there either. She turned around and noticed that one of the fire exit doors to the building wasn't shut properly. She looked around again to make sure that no one was watching her. She put her fingers in the crack between the door and the door post. It was only just open.

"Shit" she cried as her fingers slipped and she banged them against the wall.

The next time, she was luckier and the door opened. She went inside and shut the door behind her.

Amanda found herself inside a small concrete corridor. She waited for a few seconds to get used to the dark, then she began to grope her way forward. The corridor was no more than thirty feet in length. At the end, she found another door. She pulled on it and it opened smoothly. She slipped through the gap and into a larger and darker space beyond.

Amanda crouched down. She was thinking hard, trying to work out where she now was.

This has got to be the outer corridor, she said. If I cross this, I should find a door to take me into the Round Chamber.

She stretched out her hands, stood up and began to walk forwards. Eventually, her hands met the wall on the other side of the corridor. She began to walk along it and soon found a door. She felt down for the handle. She turned it slowly and pulled it backwards. She took a step forward.

A dull glow could be seen ahead of her.

What's that? she asked herself.

She took step forward then heard a nearby click.

"Do not move".

She froze.

"Put your hands on your head".

Bollocks, she thought.

Philip and George arrived at the Ship Inn having run most of the way. They walked through the main bar and strode into the back room beyond. There stood Tim Johnstone and Gabriel Geruish sipping whiskies.

"What's going on Tim?" asked Philip.

"Not exactly sure" he said reaching forward to shake hands. "I think old Henry's played a hand that has lost him the game. He double-crossed the French and I don't believe they liked it".

"Why would they go so far as to kidnap him?" asked Philip.

"They probably want him to sign the deal. We know that he was going to go with the Koreans instead. The French didn't like that as an idea".

"Bastards" said Gabriel.

"They probably want that report of mine" continued Tim. "That's political dynamite. If only I knew where it was".

Philip smiled.

"I've got it".

"You've got it!" said Tim springing forward.

"Well" said Philip. "Technically, I have. Nigel has it. He's on his way to Ash-Na-Garoo with instructions to fax it to the British Government as soon as the power comes back on".

Tim rubbed his forehead with his hand.

"Do you know how much danger Nigel is in? If the Frenchman finds out that's where the report has gone, well, I wouldn't like to think what could happen".

Philip smiled, hesitantly.

"I'm sure Nigel will be all right".

Amanda was shown into the room where her father was being held. Henry had been tied to a chair and the Frenchman was standing over him.

"Ah, Miss Geruish, I believe" said the Frenchman when he saw her. " How convenient. Maybe you can help refresh your father's mind".

The Frenchman slapped Henry.

"Where's the report?" he shouted.

"I don't have it" shouted Henry.

"Leave him alone" screamed Amanda racing forward. Two of the agents grabbed hold of her and pushed her back onto a chair. They started to tie her up.

"Quite a family reunion" said the Frenchman with a chuckle.

He strode across the room to where Amanda was now sitting. He put a hand under her chin and forced her to look at him.

"Perhaps you will talk if we include your daughter in the discussions, Mr Geruish".

"Don't you dare touch her" said Geruish, threateningly.

"Then tell me where the report is" shouted the Frenchman.

The lights flickered and came on.

Amanda laughed.

"Your plan has failed, you French turd" she cried. "Even now, over in Ash-Na-Garoo, the report is being faxed to the British Government".

The lights flickered again and went off.

"Fuck" said Amanda.

"Thank you for the information" said the Frenchman with a smile. He signalled to two of his men who left the room immediately.

"All we need to do is wait and see".

The Frenchman settled down on another chair.

Nigel had driven like the clappers back to Ash-Na-Garoo. The Mondeo had screamed and droned it's way along the road.

Nigel felt important.

This whole adventure depends upon me, he said to himself. Me, Nigel Geruish - the Island's Saviour.

He pulled off the main road and up the drive to the Governor's Residence. He stopped the car outside the house and went inside. He made his way down the dark passages to the kitchen where he found Mrs Kinloss.

"He's back. He's back" shouted Nigel.

"Who?"

"Philip" he said. "We've got the report that means that Henry Geruish can't declare independence". He waved the report around his head.

"Philip doesn't need to go" he emphasised.

Mrs Kinloss gave him one of her looks.

"You're mad" she declared.

Just then, the lights came on.

"I'd better go and fax this now, then" he said.

"Don't you want a cup of tea, now that the power's back on".

Nigel thought for a moment.

"Aye, go on".

Mrs Kinloss filled the kettle and plugged it in. Then the lights went off again.

Nigel looked at the report in his hands.

"Bugger".

The black Mercedes left Port Victoria and was soon on its way to Ash-Na-Garoo. Apart from the driver, there were three other men in the car, each carrying a semi-automatic machine gun.

The car left the road, pulled into the drive and came to a stop behind a battered Mondeo. The four men got out of the car. Two headed straight for the front door while the other two headed off around the back of the building.

One of the agents took a path that led him to the rear kitchen door. He looked inside but could see nothing. He tried the door. It was open. He pushed it back, then scampered inside, his gun waving madly in case of danger.

The kitchen was quiet. He took a step forward. Then another. Then another. Then, he heard a cough behind him. He spun quickly around. There was Nigel.

"Hands in the air" shouted the man.

Nigel did just that.

"Keep them up" shouted the agent as he took a step back towards him.

BANG.

The man didn't hear the huge, cast iron frying pan come whistling through the air and hit him on his head. All he felt was a heavy blow and all he saw was darkness descending. He crumpled and fell to the ground. Behind him stood Mrs Kinloss, the frying pan still quivering in her hand.

"Quick, let's get him into the store room" said Nigel. Together, they dragged him out of the kitchen and into the place where Mrs Kinloss stored the food. As Nigel kept watch, Mrs Kinloss trussed the agent like he was a huge, Christmas turkey.

"Oh, for a bit of stuffing" she said.

"That's one of them done" said Nigel. "Three to go".

The Saving Of The Day

'A miracle can happen in the twinkling of an eye' - St Brodag

"So what do you hope to achieve by all this?" asked Amanda. "You surely don't think that you'll get away with it, do you?"

The Frenchman looked over at her.

"Why should we not get away with it? It is your father here who has brought all this on himself. His pure, naked greed had brought this little island to the brink of disaster. Only I can save you, now".

"That's big of you" said Amanda. "And how do you possibly come to that conclusion?"

The Frenchman clambered to his feet and began to pace.

"The British don't care about this place. It is of no use to them. You are an embarrassment to them. Why should they have to bother about a bunch of alcoholics clinging to a rock in the middle of the North Sea?"

"You're forgetting the oil" said Amanda.

"Ah, yes, the oil. But please remember that the British know nothing of that. Thanks to your father, they have been kept entirely in the dark. If the island declares independence, well, why should anybody mind? A parliament for Scotland, an assembly for Wales. Devolution is the in thing in politics, Miss Geruish. This forsaken little island will not trouble the high and the mighty if it decides to plough its own furrow".

"And you provide the plough".

The Frenchman smiled.

"Quite so, quite so. You see" he continued, "your father commissioned the geological survey. To his credit, he always had an inkling that something was under this island. Didn't you, Mr Geruish?"

Henry nodded.

"So, he kept the knowledge to himself, knowing full well if he declared what was in the survey, then all the revenues from the sale of the oil would go back to Britain. So he approached *Petroleum de France* to do some exploratory drilling with the implied agreement that the company, and, therefore by default, the French Government would reap the rewards. Provision would, of course, be made to pay the rulers of this island handsomely for their services, making millionaires out of many of them".

"Dad!" said Amanda crossly. "Why?"

Henry shrugged his shoulders.

"I like money" he said.

The Frenchman grew serious.

"And that is your problem, Mr Geruish. You like money too much. You are greedy. When the Koreans came along with a better deal for you, personally, you started to back track on the agreements with PDF. All that investment that they had made here was going to be lost".

"And so that's where you step in, is it?" asked Amanda. "Throw your weight around a little. Intimidate. Bully?"

The Frenchman sighed.

"I am a businessman, Miss Geruish. I like to see all my deals completed, in time and on budget".

"And this one has been drifting away from you, hasn't it".

"We have had to make a few adjustments to our schedules" admitted the Frenchman.

Amanda thought for a moment.

"So, the island has to become independent before you can do any of this, doesn't it? You are the driving force behind the push for independence".

The Frenchman waved his hands in the air.

"An equal partner, that is all. It suits your father's ego as well as our business interests. The first President of St Brodag's Isle. Very impressive, eh, Mr Geruish?"

Henry just looked down at his feet.

"So, what's the next step. I mean, you can't hold us here at gunpoint for ever, can you?"

"No. Once we have the power back on, several things will happen. Firstly, Mr Geruish will send his e-mail to London, telling them that the island will now be a sovereign nation in its own right. Secondly, Mr Geruish will sign an agreement with *Petroleum de France* giving them sole access to the island's oil field. Thirdly, the island regime will be recognised by several world powers, thus giving moral support to the scheme. Given all the fuss about Kosovo recently, the British are hardly going to send in the tanks".

Amanda thought.

"But you're dependent on finding the survey, aren't you?" said Amanda.

"Yes" chuckled the Frenchman. "But after your tip, I feel that I will have that report in my hands any moment now".

Amanda looked across at her father who wouldn't meet her eyes.

Luc came from Dijon. He had lived an idyllic childhood on the family farm. When he grew up, he wanted to serve his country. After military service, he joined the army full time. He had served with Nato and also with the UN. He had been in Bosnia in the early part of the war there and was a tough, battle-hardened individual.

He crept though the house, checking the upstairs rooms. He moved through a suite of offices and on through a bedroom with a four poster bed. He checked the bathroom beyond. Nothing.

Suddenly, he heard a dull thump downstairs. He left the bedroom and came out onto the landing. He looked over the banister into the hall below him.

Nothing moved. Above him, the huge chandelier caught the light an upper window.

Luc descended the wide staircase. He crossed the hall and made his way carefully down a dark passageway. He edged slowly forward, not daring to breathe. He found a door and opened it. He looked inside.

There, in the morning room, enjoying a round of tea and toast was Nigel.

"Hello" he said warmly. "Would you like to join me?"

"Stand away from the table" said Luc firmly pointing his gun at Nigel. "Keep your hands where I can see them".

Nigel obeyed. Luc stepped forward.

"Put your hands behind your head and lean forward onto the floor".

Nigel did just that.

Luc felt in his pocket for some rope. He pulled out a length and tied Nigel's hands together.

"Now sit back against the wall". Again, Nigel did as he was told.

Luc dropped his gun to his side and sat down.

"How many of you are there?"

Click.

"Two" said Mrs Kinloss brandishing a gun.

"Merde" said Luc.

Someone was knocking urgently at the rear door of the Ship Inn. George went to open it. In dashed a small man who was vaguely familiar to Philip.

"They've got the Prime Minister's daughter" he gasped.

"Amanda!" said Philip.

The man nodded.

"We've got to go" said Philip. "We've got to save her".

Tim looked at him.

"And how do you intend to do that? Walk in the front door and take them all on yourself. You wouldn't get far".

Philip threw his hands in the air.

"Well, what do you propose we do?"

Gabriel smiled at him.

"Wait. Just for a bit longer".

"I can't wait. It's Amanda. I....".

There was another knock at the door.

This time, Tim went to open it. In came the members of the Liberation Front. All of them carried weapons of some sort. One or two had handguns.

"Time to do some liberating" said Gabriel.

Philip looked at them dumbfounded.

"What exactly are you up to?" he asked.

"Follow us" said Tim.

He led the way down into the inn's cellars. At the rear of a stack of beer barrels was a small door. Tim took out an ancient key and popped it into the lock. The key turned easily and the door opened. A dark passage lay beyond.

"Sometimes, a little knowledge comes in useful" said Tim with a smile. "Come on, Gabriel. You lead the way".

Gabriel crouched down and moved forward into the blackness. Switching a torch on as he went. Gabriel began to sing to himself. Philip didn't recognise it but reckoned that it must be something from Gilbert and Sullivan. Gabriel never sang anything else.

Soon, all the members of the Liberation Front had disappeared into the passage, leaving Tim, George and Philip behind.

"Are you coming?" asked Philip of George.

"No way" said George. "It's the rats".

"Don't tell me you're frightened of a few rats" said Philip with a chuckle.

"Frightened -no" said George. "Bloody petrified- yes. I'll see yous later".

Tim switched on his torch and led the way forward.

Nigel and Mrs Kinloss admired their morning's work. All four of the agents were sitting in the store room looking decidedly foolish. One of them started to struggle. Mrs Kinloss went over to him, put her foot on his chest and placed the barrel of the gun she was holding against his nose.

"Feeling lucky" she demanded.

The man stopped struggling.

Nigel was seeing Mrs Kinloss in a new light and made a mental note to himself to be always kind and courteous from now on.

"How long can it take to get the power back on?" said an exasperated Frenchman.

"Took three days, the last time" said Amanda.

"This place doesn't deserve electricity" said the Frenchman, flopping back down onto his seat.

Suddenly, the lights flicked on. The air conditioning started up with a groan.

"We're back in business" announced the Frenchman standing. "It'll just take a few moments for Pierre, here, to set up the laptop. Would you like to see the contract you're going to sign, Mr Geruish?"

"Not really" said Henry. "Are there any major changes?"

"Not to the contract" said the Frenchman with a smile. "Only to your own personal perks".

"You bastard" said Geruish.

"The laptop's up and running" shouted Pierre.

"Now, let's prepare to declare your birth as a fledgling nation".

Suddenly, a deep voice could be heard in the main hall.

When I was a lad I served a term

As office boy in an attorney's firm

The Frenchman waved two of his men forward to check out the noise. They opened the door and peered out. They looked back at the Frenchman and shook their heads. He waved them forward.

....Polished up the handle on the big front door
I polished up that handle so carefully

The two men made their way out into the main hall.

Then, three things happened at once. Firstly, Tim and one of the other members of the St Brodagan Liberation Front appeared from behind the door and closed it quickly, bolting it.

Then, Philip emerged from a panel in the wall behind the Frenchman and pointed a gun at his head.

"Drop the gun. All of you, drop your weapons".

The two remaining agents looked at their leader who nodded. They dropped their guns. Tim rushed forward and collected them. Then Philip untied both Henry and Amanda.

"Now then" said Philip. "Let's all sit down and talk about this".

There was a loud knock on the door. Tim skipped across and pulled back the bolt. In walked Gabriel.

"Gabriel" hissed Henry.

"Hello, Henry" said Gabriel.

"Gabriel, my friend" shouted Monsieur Jean-Claude.

"Jean-Claude!" cried Gabriel in surprise. "What are you doing here?"

"Trying to get everyone killed" said Amanda climbing to her feet.

"You two know each other?" asked Philip as Gabriel and the Frenchman embraced.

"Go back a long way, me and Jean-Claude. We were in jail together in the Philippines and went on to work in Afghanistan. Haven't seen you in , what, twelve years?"

"Twelve years indeed, my friend" said the Frenchman laughing heartily. "How is that leg of yours".

"Fine, fine now. It's all thanks to you, though. Thought I was a gonna when that Russian came over to me with his bayonet held high. Do you folks know what happened next? Quick as a flash, Jean-Claude here jumps up, grabs the Russian around the neck and slits his throat. You've never seen so much blood. There's the young Russian chap, twitching and gurgling. Great days".

"This is all very pleasant" said Philip. "But we've just saved the island".

"No you haven't" said Henry. "I had set up a back up system for the e-mail at home, just in case I got distracted today. It's going to be sent at six o'clock and May's out getting her hair done. It's five forty-five now. We can't stop it.".

"Fifteen minutes! Oh yes we can" shouted Amanda. "Philip, come with me".

A Race Against Time

'A moment is longer when shared' - St Brodag

The two of them dashed out of the room and ran across the Round Chamber. They flew down the stairs and ran up the street to where Philip's Range Rover was parked.

"You'd better drive" shouted Philip, handing the keys to Amanda.

They jumped inside the car and blasted away.

"Today is a funny day" said Philip.

Amanda nodded.

"Why did you change your mind and stay?" asked Amanda flashing through a red light.

"I just did" said Philip.

"Why?"

"It doesn't matter".

Amanda threw a look in his direction.

"Yes it does, why did you come back".

The car left the built up area of Port Victoria and was now streaking through the countryside.

"Because I was worried about you".

Amanda applied the brakes. She turned to him.

"Worried about me! Is that all?"

The car came to rest by a field. A sheep put its head through the fence, wondering what was going on.

"Well, no. You know. I'm.....I'm rather fond of you".

"Fond of me!" cried Amanda. "Fond is for puppies and old maiden aunts. You can be fond of an old jumper".

"What are you doing?" asked Philip, panicking. "We haven't got time. Please start the car".

"Fond is for a favourite book or a poem. Fond is not enough, Philip!"

"What? Come on, we can talk about this later. Let's get on".

Amanda looked at him.

"Why were you worried about me?"

"Because....you're a friend".

"Is that all?"

"Because .....because....because you're a really great friend"

Amanda looked at him again.

Philip sighed.

"Because I love you".

Amanda smiled.

.   "Because I'm crazy about you. Because I can't get you out of my mind at all.
Whatever I'm doing, you're there. Whatever I'm thinking, I keep thinking about
you. Because I miss you in the mornings when I get up. Because I miss you at
night when I turn the lights off and I'm there alone. Because I've not felt this
way about anyone ever before!"

Amanda frowned slightly.

"For real?" she asked.

"For real" exploded Philip. "Now, start the car and let's get to your father's
house - quickly".

Amanda put her foot down.

"Do you want children?" she asked.

Philip frowned.

"What? What......er, yes, I suppose so"

Amanda smiled to herself.

"Never thought I did until ten seconds ago. I like Elliot as a name, don't you.
For a boy, I mean. Bloody awful name for a girl".

"Can you just drive, please" begged Philip.

Amanda had a big grin on her lips as they rounded bend after bend.

"Where shall we live?" she asked. "I mean, we can't stay here, now, can we?
You haven't got a job anywhere. And I think that I'd like to move away".

"Not London" said Philip. "Definitely not London".

"Or the Outer Hebrides" piped up Amanda.

"What about the Isle of Man?" said Philip.

They looked at each other.

"No!" they said in unison.

They approached Geruish's house and Amanda brought the car to a halt on
the drive. They both jumped out and Amanda pulled out her keys. She unlocked
the door and led the way into her father's study.

"How do you stop this thing?" asked Amanda.

Philip looked around and did the only thing he could. He pulled out the
plug and the computer died.

Amanda crashed onto the chair. Philip slumped to the ground.

"Did it!" said Amanda.

Philip just lay there panting.

"I wonder if your dad will ever thank us".

"Doubt it" said Amanda. "I think that we've just cost him ten million
pounds".

Philip started to laugh. Amanda joined in. Philip dragged himself over to the
chair that Amanda was sitting on and, before either of them knew it, their hands
were all over each other.

Philip unbuttoned her blouse and ran his fingers down her neck.

Amanda fiddled with the buttons at his flies.

"I...always...preferred.....zips" she panted.

Just then, they heard a door slam.

"Hello. Anyone in?"

It was Amanda's Mum.

They re-buttoned and straightened themselves down just in time.

They drove back into Port Victoria, planning their future together. They stopped outside the Parliament building. Amanda jumped out first followed by Philip. They held hands and crossed the road together.

In the middle of the road, Philip stopped and turned to her. He looked deep into her eyes.

"I love you, Amanda Geruish".

"I love you, too, Philip Digby-Fischer".

They kissed. Then Philip took a step forward.

A shot rang out and Philip fell backwards. Stunned, Amanda looked down at him, watching the blood beginning to spill onto the tarmac.

"Got him" shouted a triumphant David Brannigan, ex of the RSPB, from behind a dustbin.

Several people came racing across. Two security guards ran down the steps and wrestled the gun from Brannigan's grasp.

Amanda knelt down beside him.

"Philip?" she whispered. "Philip?"

Bullets And Blood

'Never give up hope, no matter how hopeless it is' - St Brodag

The Air Ambulance settled on the lawns outside the hospital in Port Victoria. Two paramedics jumped out and dashed inside. Seconds later, they emerged with a trolley and Philip securely tied to the stretcher that lay on top of it. He was wearing a mask that fed oxygen into his lungs and he was attached to a drip. Amanda was by his side, holding his hand.

The paramedics manoeuvred Philip into the helicopter and Amanda climbed in after him. The rotors began to spin faster and faster as the door slid shut. Then, the ambulance lifted off the ground and soon they were racing over the North Sea towards Newcastle.

Amanda looked through the window at her island home receding into the distance, a patch of green in a grey ocean.

Half way through the journey, Amanda saw a series of army helicopters on their way to the island. It seemed that the British Government were going to do something at last.

Within forty minutes, they touched down outside the Infirmary in Newcastle and Philip was bundled away into the operating theatre.

Amanda hung around outside, drinking coffee and eating Kit-Kats.

As Philip was being worked on by the surgeon, he dreamt.

He thought back to his earliest memories: a birthday party when he was four. His mother and father both being there for him. He remembered the prep-school he attended as a day pupil and saw a thousand faces that he once knew. A sudden coldness came over him and his mind turned to boarding school. He recollected the all consuming dark and the squelching noises of an adolescent youth. Then, the chill became deeper and froze him. His headmaster was telling him that both his parents had died and that he was now, officially, alone in the world.

Philip found himself on a roller coaster, rushing up and down, up and down and round, as tight as can be.

The ride stopped and he was on a ship. A big ship. The biggest ship ever. And Patricia was there and Amanda too. The ship floated on a calm sea until, in the distance, he heard the sound of rushing water. The sea narrowed to a river and the river was leaping over a cliff edge down to a foaming mass below.

He floated out into a wide open space. A giant sea bird seemed to be chasing him. He ran and ran but the bird flew faster. Then it picked him up and he went soaring into the air. The bird flew for many days and eventually dropped Philip into a cave.

This time, the air was damp and cool. He wandered on and on. The cave narrowed to a tunnel and it became pitch black. He stumbled forward. He saw a light and walked towards it.

"Philip. Philip" said a warm, golden voice.

"I wonder what heaven will be like" said Philip as he neared the brightness.

He opened his eyes and saw the Fat Man.

"Shit, I've ended up in hell" he said.

The Fat Man looked down at Philip as he lay in the hospital bed. He checked his watch. He needed to make a phone call shortly.

Philip's eyelids flickered, then opened. The Fat Man leaned over him.

"Philip. Philip" he said.

"Shitzzerlanderhell" said Philip.

The Fat Man smiled at him.

"Well, you've pulled through. Good show".

He stood up and left the room.

Seconds later, Amanda burst in and rushed to his side.

"Philip, you're awake. Good. How are you?"

Philip chuckled.

"I've been better" he whispered through dry lips.

Apparently, Philip had been extremely lucky. The bullet had come to rest near his spine. The surgeon had managed to remove it before it could do any damage.

A few days later, when Philip was fit enough to sit up in bed, the Fat man came to visit him.

"I really thought that you were on Geruish's side" admitted Philip.

"That was Geruish's biggest mistake. We go back a long way, old Henry and me. We had a lot of good times back in Africa. In those days, we would hit a town and really paint it red. However, he thought that I regarded my friendship with him above my duty to my country. He was wrong. I may be old and cynical but I haven't forgotten what it's all about".

"I suppose that if he hadn't felt so confident that you would smooth things over for him back at the Foreign Office, he would never have tried his scam".

"I think you're right".

Philip looked down for a moment.

"So where do I fit into all of this? Why appoint me to the job? Did you know about Geruish's plans at the time?"

The Fat Man sat back in his chair and smiled.

"I selected you to do this job, Philip, primarily because you know little of European politics. Your experience was elsewhere. That was an asset. I gave Geruish a false picture and told him you were next to useless. That fitted in with his plans and so he didn't object to your appointment like he had done to a number of others. I had plenty of agents on the island looking out for you. Please pass on my regards to Mrs Kinloss next time you see her".

Philip raised an eyebrow.

"I knew that you wouldn't join in with his plans" continued the Fat Man. "You're too honest and decent to do that. So, when you told me that you were resigning and accused me of being in with Henry, I knew that the end was near".

"And if you had received Geruish's declaration of independence...?"

"Well, he would have been facing a long stretch in jail for deception and fraud. As it stands, you saved his bacon and he should thank you for that. Granted, he'll lose the job of Prime Minister. Gabriel will get that. No, it's a peaceful retirement for Henry, I'm sure".

"What about the French?"

"What about them?" said the Fat Man.

"Well, first of all they set up the oil wells illegally. Secondly, they were plotting to make the island independent of UK control. And, let's not forget, they ran around Port Victoria pointing a lot of guns at people".

The Fat Man sighed.

"It's all part of the game, Philip. We'd do the same to them, given half the chance".

"And that's it?"

"That's it, Philip. No more to be said".

Philip fell silent.

The Fat Man checked his watch.

"Time to go. I've sorted out your pension for you. Details will be in the post. It should see you right. Hope to see you in London soon".

Philip nodded.

"Bye, then" said the Fat Man.

"Bye" said Philip.

"Oh" said the Fat Man turning in the doorway. "Thanks. You did really well".

He left.

Philip watched him leave. Then, he half turned and looked out of the window.

A few days later, Philip went for his first walk, just down the ward and back. His shoulder felt on fire, though the pain killers helped take the edge off the pain. Amanda was by his side at all times, looking out for him, helping him.

When he was able to, Amanda took him for walks around the hospital grounds. They would play cards endlessly, cribbage and dutch rummy being the favourites. Amanda invariably won. She was very competitive and Philip was sure that she made some of the rules up.

Patricia sent him a card and some flowers. The card said 'Try to make your life a little less exciting in future'.

The time in Newcastle was important for them both. They talked endlessly. They talked about their childhoods, growing up, adolescence, their first eager fumblings in the dark. They talked about their hopes and their aspirations. They talked about what they wanted and what they felt. They talked about their love for one another and began to plan a life together.

After a couple of weeks, Philip was transferred back to the island's hospital.

All's Well That Ends Well

'Many partings are a necklace of tears' - St Brodag

Two months later, Philip drove away, once again, from Ash-Na-Garoo. This time, although he was still sad to see the back of the old place, he knew that he had a brighter future to look forward to. At the end of the lane, he turned right instead of left and took the coast road to Henry Geruish's house.

He passed the cove where the grey seal colony lay, basking in the sun. He wound the window down and breathed the salty air for one last time. He put a CD on and Vivaldi's 'Four Seasons' filled the air.

Amanda was waiting for him at Henry's house. Philip got out of the car and opened the rear doors. Amanda put her bags on the back seat. She turned back to face Philip and kissed him. They both jumped back into the car and Philip drove away towards Port Victoria.

"I can't believe we're going" said Amanda.

Philip put his hand on hers.

"It'll be fine".

"Drive slowly" she said.

Philip nodded.

They passed by Cragmuir in stately fashion and were soon on the edge of Port Victoria.

They came to the hospital and Amanda made Philip stop outside. Then, after a few seconds contemplation, she asked him to drive on.

They drove down the main boulevard passing both the Assembly Building and Government House. They hit the promenade and drove towards the Ferry Terminal. The *Spirit of St Brodag* could be seen in all her grandeur.

When they reached the gate, they were diverted a different way from normal and asked to park in a shed. Philip and Amanda got out of the car and an attendant directed them through a side door.

They both stopped and stared.

The whole quayside between the Terminal Building and the *Spirit of St Brodag* was filled with people. When they saw Philip and Amanda, they gave a huge cheer. A banner that read 'GOOD LUCK' hung down from a crane that stood at the side of the harbour. A band struck up in the background.

Nigel came walking towards them.

"Just a few friends" he said with a wink, beckoning them forward. "Don't mind the car, I've arranged for it to be put onboard".

The crowd continued to cheer as they walked down a passageway that had been roped off before them.

"Good Luck" the people cried. "Come back soon. So Long. Bye".

They held out hands and as Philip and Amanda walked towards the ship, they would grip the hands as they went by. So many faces, so many friends.

At the end of the walkway stood Henry Geruish and May. Amanda hugged them both. Henry stretched out a hand to Philip.

"No hard feelings?" he said.

Philip looked at him, then smiled.

"No hard feelings".

"Good" said Henry relaxing. "And if you hurt her I'll kill you".

Philip gave a half smile, looked at the great big bear-man, then moved away.

Flutes of champagne were thrust into their hands. Amanda wiped at her eyes. Philip gulped awkwardly, not quite knowing what to do.

Nigel came forward, fighting back the tears.

"I'll come and visit" he said.

"No you won't" said Philip. "You get a nose bleed just looking at an atlas. We'll see you when we're back on the island".

"It won't be long, will it?" he asked.

Philip smiled.

"I hope not".

They shook hands.

Philip and Amanda said their remaining personal goodbyes then turned to leave. Tim and Gabriel were there. George was wandering around with a plate of sandwiches trying his best to get people to sample his latest concoctions.

Behind them, Nigel jumped onto a small platform and grabbed hold of a microphone.

"Goodbye, Amanda. Goodbye, Philip. It's been great. Now to play you on your way, here's the combined talents of Rowdy Scythe, the Port Victoria Working Men's Brass Band and the St Brodag's Community Gospel Choir".

The members of Rowdy Scythe took to the stage,

"I'm Ron" said Ron.

"I'm Sheila" said Sheila.

"And I'm Randy" said Randy.

"And together" continued Ron on the keyboards, "we're Rowdy Scythe".

The crowd cheered.

"And they're the Port Victoria Working Men's Brass Band" announced Sheila pointing to the band.

Even bigger applause.

"And" shouted Randy, "they're the St Brodag's Community Gospel Choir".

This was met with a thunderous reception.

"Let's see if you know this one".

Ron played a few notes then Sheila began to sing.

"Who knows what tomorrow'll bring....".

Amanda looked at Philip.

"Let's go"

They ran, hand in hand, up the covered gangway and onto the ship. They emerged onto the deck and looked at the crowd down below them.

"The road" sang Ron, "is long. There are mountains in our way".

Philip frowned and looked at Amanda.

"Hasn't this been done before somewhere?" he asked.

Amanda stopped waving and kissed him.

"But we've done it better" she said with a smile.

"Love lift us up where we belong" sang Ron, Sheila and the choir. "To a mountain high, where the eagles fly".

The ship's horn blew, drowning out the music. A thick plume of black smoke poured out of the funnel.

"We're off" shouted Philip.

Nigel lifted his glass in farewell, then disappeared into the crowd.

As the ship lurched away from the quay, thousands of rose petals were thrown into the air by some of the ship's crew on a higher deck. The petals fell down like a red snow storm. Amanda caught a few in her hair. Philip put his arm around her.

"I love yaarghh" he said as a petal found its way into his mouth.

They both laughed as Amanda removed the offending object.

"I love yaargh too" she said.

Back on the quayside, the musical ensemble changed key and changed song. A throbbing beat could be heard and the brass band came into its own.

DEE-DAH-DE-DA-DAH

"Your love" sand Ron, "keeps on lifting me - higher and higher".

Jackie Wilson lives!

"Your love keeps lifting me. Your love keeps lifting me" sang the choir.

"Higher and higher" sang Ron.

Amanda and Philip held hands and continued to wave.

"Your love keeps lifting me. Your love keeps lifting me".

As the *Spirit of St Brodag* left the safety of the harbour, hundreds of fireworks were let off into the afternoon air.

"This is just magical" said Amanda. "Completely magical".

Philip agreed.

"It's like nothing I've ever seen before".

Several boats bobbed beyond the harbour, their occupants looking up at the ferry and waving as they passed. Amanda and Philip waved back. Captain Ahmed was there on board *Margie's Dream*. He gave them a thumbs up sign as they sailed past him. Philip remembered that it wasn't so long ago that he had first come to the island.

They hung around on deck for a while, savouring the occasion. Soon, they could not pick out individuals on the quay side. Then, the whole Ferry Terminal merged into the background. Then, Port Victoria became nothing more than a dark mark at the base of the island. Then, the island disappeared completely. They stood there for a while, hardly believing that they were leaving.

Amanda sighed.

"That's it gone".

"Any regrets?" asked Philip.

Amanda burrowed her face into his chest then looked up at him.

"None at all".

Suddenly, a large sea-bird alighted on the railing near to them. It stood there looking as though it was watching them.

"Shoo, gull" said Philip with a wave of his hand.

Amanda stared at the bird.

"Philip" she said slowly.

"Yes".

"That's a kittiwake".

"What type?"

She gulped.

"A St Brodag's Kittiwake!"

Philip looked at her, then back to the bird.

"Are you sure?"

"Definitely".

Philip laughed.

"Well. Blow me. George must have missed some".

Amanda looked out across the waves.

"There's another one there, as well. And another. And another. Seems like you didn't kill them off after all".

Philip rubbed his shoulder.

The kittiwake squawked at them, then flew off. Philip and Amanda watched it for a while until it disappeared from view.

They stood there for a moment or two longer staring out over the waves.

"Let's go in" said Philip eventually.

"Where shall we sit?" asked Amanda.

Philip reached into his pocket and pulled out a key.

"What's that?" asked Amanda with a frown.

"A cabin key" said Philip with a smile.

"Oh" said Amanda taken aback.

Philip continued to smile at her and then she knew what he meant.

"Oh" she said with a grin.

They left the deck hand in hand and spent the rest of the journey living for the moment.

And that was the end of that.